FIRE OF THE GODS

"Behold the Fire of the Gods!" his voice cried out in dramatic pitch. "A fragrance of beauty and form." His voice lowered. "A striking scent for one woman alone."

He removed the top and held the bottle out for Lizzie to inhale. Her nostrils quivered as they discovered the fumes. Her cheeks flushed.

Then he took a wooden match and struck it against the table. The fire flared and hissed. Haddi extended the fire into the mouth of the bottle. A few seconds passed before anything happened. Then a pinkish-red smoke began rising from within the bottle. The smoke grew heavier as it drifted up to the folds of the fabric above.

Soon, everything was hidden within the pink cloud. Lizzie called out: "Leo?" I reached for her outstretched hand before it completely disappeared into the mist. . . .

See No Evil

Evil

❧

Jay Finkelstein

A Dell Book

Published by
Dell Publishing
a division of
Bantam Doubleday Dell Publishing Group, Inc.
1540 Broadway
New York, New York 10036

ISBN 0-440-22293-1

Printed in the United States of America

Published simultaneously in Canada

October 1996

10 9 8 7 6 5 4 3 2 1

RAD

To my parents, Lenore and Maurice Finkelstein.
Who've taught through example, the value of laughter.

Many people have contributed to the life of *See No Evil* and I would like to thank a few of them here.

I am most grateful to Nahum Sharfman and Eli Lazar for supporting my efforts with generosity and understanding, and to Sandi Borger (a real doll) and Jacob Hoye for appreciating the tale and bringing it to a wider audience.

I would also like to thank all of those who read the manuscript and offered either feedback or the appropriately placed chuckle. Unfortunately, so much time has passed since I said: "Here, read this," that I can no longer remember everyone to whom it was said. Thus, the following list is by no means complete and includes only those people who suffered longest and most severely under my continued barrage: David and Shelly Brinn, Elliot Cohen, Debra Hakimian, Ziv Lewis, Iris Rodan, Michal Shin, Hillel Wax, and Sharon Yerushalmi.

For sharing their artistic talent I am grateful to Jeanne Goodman, Gaby Hamburg, Alon Hameiri, and Ben Hillman.

I am also grateful to Lainee Cohen, Rebecca Epstein, and Alice Finkelstein for their encouragement and logistical support.

Also thanks to Richard Green, Joanne Jackson, and Jimmy Vines for working to widen the audience even more.

Finally, my biggest thanks of all goes out to you dear reader, for daring to turn the page.

Enjoy.
jf
nyc 1996

Email: jayf@bway.net
Home Page: http://www.bway.net/~jayf

Contents

1

The Cairo Conspiracy

THE CAIRO CONSPIRACY

Dr. Haddi came into my life as did nearly everyone else I met in Cairo, through the great conspiracy. At first I thought it was by chance. After all, who could have known we'd sleep through our wake-up call and miss the tour to the Pyramids and make up for our error by losing ourselves in Tahrir Square?

The answer, I learned, was: don't ask. Someone invariably knew. Though it took time, I eventually became aware that there was no such thing as a random event in Cairo. Coincidences piled on coincidences until it became impossible to distinguish between the expected and the chance event.

In short, looking back, it is blatantly obvious that everything was planned in advance and carried out with precision. All of it: Muhammad, the diary, the girls, . . . even the trial.

AMMAN, JORDAN

Strangely enough, my first *known* encounter with the conspiracy took place in Amman, Jordan. Lizzie and I were relaxing over drinks in the lounge of our hotel. Another lull had fallen over the conversation. Lulls, I thought to myself, first in our love, now in our conversation. Or was it the other way around? No matter. Any way you look at it, lull is an ugly word. Lizzie must have been thinking the same thing when she turned to me and said in her high-pitched, London-accented tone, "Honestly, Leo, how much longer must we suffer this desert kingdom?"

"Where would you have us suffer?"

"I'm serious. I think we need a change."

"Isn't that why we came to Jordan?"

"Don't be so cynical. As I recall, we came on this holiday to see if we could save our relationship. We chose Jordan because you wouldn't agree to any of the conventional tourist spots. Now I've given this place five days, Leo. *Five* days of nothing but sand and sand—out the window, on the floor, in the food. One thing has become clear to me during this period, Leo. One thing, and that's that 'Jordan' and 'crisis' are both six-letter words."

That's what I loved about Lizzie: you could depend on her to relate the unrelated. Maybe that's why, I thought, she's fighting so hard for this relationship.

"Five days," she continued, "is enough." Then she took a deep breath. "I believe there's hope for us, Leo, I do. But not if we stay here. Now I'm willing to compromise. I'll stay in some godforsaken, off-the-beaten-path hole with you, so long as it *intersects* with civilization at some nearby junction."

I considered her suggestion with a sip of my drink and a spin of the little red paper umbrella within it. She was right about the desert, all right. It *was* vast, empty, and dry—a condition that only reminded me of our sex. "Where would you have us go?" I asked.

"If you really want to know, I was thinking of Egypt."

"Egypt? Really? But aren't 'Egypt' and 'waste' both five-letter words? And more to the point, wouldn't we just be trading one desert for another?"

"Oh, what do you Americans know of the Middle East? To you it's just bombs and deserts, isn't it? Just think: the lush green of the Nile Valley . . . the Pyramids of Giza . . . the bustle of Cairo. It sounds terribly romantic to me."

"Romantic, you say? Well, I suppose we could use a change of scenery."

"Supa! I knew you'd see it my way." And with that she produced two one-way tickets to Cairo for that afternoon. "And don't despair, 'happy' is also a five-letter word."

WELCOME TO EGYPT

The central foyer of the Cairo International Airport was filled with porter types hustling to make a buck. Yet in spite of the fact that we were two of just seven total passengers on our flight, we could not seem to attract a porter to help with our bags. We finally managed to elicit the aid of one very battered-looking guy. Our first feeling when he approached in his laceless sneakers and three-day beard was that he wouldn't be up to the job. Yet he quickly proved that his modest size and build belied an impressive strength which enabled him to carry Lizzie's trunks and bags, as well as my pack, with a graceful expertise thought only reserved for French waiters. More amazing still was his obsessive need to make conversation with us.

"Welcome," he said. "Welcome, welcome, welcome. Welcome to Egypt. Happy, happy, happy."

"Yes, thank you," I answered. "We're very happy to be here. You have a beautiful airport."

He shot me a toothless grin from beneath the trunks. "Happy, happy, happy. Happy welcome to my country."

"Thank you. We are happy to receive your friendly welcome. Thank you, thank you, thank you. Don't strain yourself speaking. Let's move slowly towards the cabs over here."

"Thank you, welcome, thank you, welcome, thank you, welcome."

The conversation continued like this until we arrived at a row of cabs parked by the exit. Our man loaded the bags with help from the driver, then began moving off after pocketing the tip.

"Thank you. *Allah Akbar,* God is great. Thank you, thank you, welcome."

"Thank you," we called back before entering the cab. "Thank you!"

"You know," I said, turning to Lizzie, "I think I'm going to like Egypt."

"Welcome," said the driver from the front. "Where you go?"

BORN TO BE WILD

I was about to answer with the name of a hotel I'd picked from my travel guide, when Lizzie spoke up.

"Amman Hotel, please," she said.

Our driver responded by swinging the vehicle into a screeching U-turn, a maneuver which brought my body hard against the door to my left, and Lizzie's body hard against mine. This pose remained frozen for many a moment until our driver saw fit to floor the gas pedal in the direction of the evening sun.

I looked for a traffic light as we straightened our bodies, in the hope that it might slow our headlong plunge. But working lights, I soon learned, were almost as rare as drivers who obeyed their signals.

Outside the window a sea of damaged cars engaged in a grotesque ballet of scrap in motion. Vehicles dodged in and out of unmarked lanes, while honking horns and flaying hands filled the dusty Cairene air. Thus it continued, this movement in *allegro fortissimo,* for nearly an hour, until it reached a second screeching climax punctuated by the sound of metal crashing against metal.

"Amman Hotel," cried the conductor as he backed off the fender of the car in front of us. "Welcome."

AMMAN, EGYPT

Amman Hotel. More than five hundred hotels in Cairo, she picks the Amman. Was it just coincidence that we'd lunched that day in Amman, Jordan? I thought so.

Actually, it wasn't bad for a three star. The price was reasonable—just slightly more than the cab ride, and the lobby was clean and elegant in an Egyptian sort of way. Most unusual of all was the fact that the price included a one-day tour to the Pyramids of Giza and the Cairo Museum.

We decided to sign on for the next morning's tour even though the seven A.M. departure time seemed a trifle (Lizzie's word) early. Perhaps we did it because everyone was so polite and hospitable, or because the complete environment was so uniquely charming. In any event, it seemed a rather pleasant idea when considered from that island of tranquillity they called the Amman.

Our newfound peace maintained itself in the room as well, which bore a simple, clean, Old World beauty. Even Lizzie took on a warmer glow in the odd light.

"Would you be a dear, Leo, and fetch me something cool to drink?" Her voice was strange, deeper than usual. I looked twice to see if it wasn't an entirely different person—not Lizzie—sitting on the bed.

The room held a refrigerator stocked with bottles of mineral water. I took one out and handed it to her.

Her lips embraced the container's opening and welcomed the fluid into her mouth. The withdrawal of the bottle was followed by a smacking sound and a gasp.

"You know," she said, "I think we overpaid the cab driver."

"Excuse me?" I asked as I pulled my attention from the meaning of her lips to the meaning of her words.

"How often does a cab ride cost as much as a hotel?"

She was right about the cab driver ripping us off, of course, but I didn't care. All I could think about was her soft round bottom as it cried out to me from the bed. I curled up behind her and reached my hands around to cup her breasts.

"Think of it as a contribution to the needy. A meal for a small, starving child. That sort of thing," I offered between nips of her earlobe.

Her silky blond hair fell to the side as she rotated her head to the beat of my tongue. "Prices what they are here," she managed in a husky, almost unworldly voice, "it's more like a banquet for the entire national football team."

"They should enjoy . . ."

"I say, Leo . . . I say . . ."

They say that love is a many-splendored thing. I now had proof.

THE DAWN

Dawn came. Dawn went. We slept.

The previous evening's passions had taken their toll. I woke in a daze. My chest felt heavy. My stomach warm. Where was I?

I opened my eyes to find Lizzie's head nestled in the fur of my chest. Her breath passed southwards in a warm and steady pulse. Not a bad situation, I thought, for a guy who doesn't know where he is.

I turned my head to get a better feel for my locale. What I got instead was a smack in the forehead. A few moments of blinding pain were followed by the wide-eyed conclusion that I was face to face with a large wooden block.

I pulled my head back to refocus from afar. The block, I found, was actually the leg of a bed as seen from the perspective of a man on the floor. I also found that, except for the covering formed by the artistic arrangement of Lizzie's head and hair around my chest and side, I was completely nude.

The mystery of last night loomed large.

"Lizzie?" I whispered.

No answer.

"Plum?" I called out endearingly towards my shoe.

"Mmmmmmmm?" she purred.

"Darling. Did you sleep well here on the floor?"

"Ohhhhh, yessssss. It was wonderful." Each word passed in slow motion.

"Naturally. I just wish I remembered all the details."

"To what end? To what end?" Reality remained asleep in the guest room of her consciousness.

"None in particular. Call it scientific curiosity."

No response. A new peace held power over her soul. I was not to disturb. I closed my eyes.

NEXT I KNEW

Next I knew, Lizzie's feet were standing by the leg of the bed. She was wearing a bright yellow dress—something she'd picked up on a Greek island—running a brush through her hair and humming to herself. I was where I'd left myself—naked and sprawled on a hotel room floor.

"Time to get up, sleepyhead! It's nearly one in the afternoon."

Long moments passed before I could muster a response. My head felt light—kind of like I was drunk.

"Take . . ." I heard myself mumble.

Take what? What the hell was I talking about? I needed a strong hit of some cold Cairene shower water, and fast. I saw my hand extending to Lizzie. She took it and pulled.

SUDDENLY STRANGERS

"Listen," I said about one hour later from beneath the canopy in front of the Amman. "What say you to a slight change in this morning's tour schedule?"

"Whatever are you talking about, dear boy? It's already afternoon. For all we know, the tour to Giza's already returned."

"True, true," I answered. Hmmmm, I thought, first light remark of the day crumpled up and tossed to the dogs. Lucky I hadn't ventured a full-fledged joke. And after last night, too.

"All right," I continued, this time smiling. "How about flagging a camel and burning some hoof down to the museum?"

Lizzie looked at me with a puzzled expression that seemed to ask: "Poor child, what *shall* we do with you?"

Distance fell between us. British and Americans—two people separated by a common language. Was it true? The humanitarian in me cried: "No! Human nature is the same all the world over." My inner voice, on the other hand, weak and timid from years of neglect, squeaked: "Yes, yes, yes!"

I cast a longing glance up towards the hotel. Hadn't it been just this morning, just a few short hours back, that we'd urgently wrapped our perspiration-soaked bodies one around the other? Hadn't the storm of passion raged through our blood, while the poetry of love sang from our lips?

Maybe yes. Maybe no. Here on the sidewalk in front of the Amman, humanity took a backseat to heart. And heart spoke. And it said: "Face the music, Jack. You're Leonard Robert Gold and she's Elizabeth Anne Bruback Simms. The music you make is out of tune. The opera is over. The fat lady has sung."

But last night! This morning! The floor! It had all been so mathematically correct! This can't be, I thought. It just can't be.

But what did I know? I was young. I'd been in Cairo less than twenty-four hours.

2

Fire of the Gods

TAKING AIM

We began the afternoon by wandering the streets of Cairo. We were not without aim, just misguided. Or more accurately, our aim (the Cairo Museum) became corrupted (and I know this sounds paranoid—but you'll soon understand why I say it) by evil forces bent on our bad fortune.

If only I'd recognized the signs of impending trouble. God knows, they were there. Like the hotel receptionist who directed us with Japanese-accented English. He was a *definite* tip-off.

"Cailo Mooseum? You lookin' fo Cailo Mooseum? Go stlait down stleet to blidge. Closs blidge. Go, go, go, go to big open. People, people, people. . . ."

He accompanied these incomprehensible directions with a well-worn Arabic language map of Cairo. I initially balked at taking the map because I neither spoke nor read Arabic. But Lizzie insisted I "make a go of it," and I acquiesced, saying: "Yes, dear."

Not surprisingly, the map proved completely useless as a navigational tool. More critical than where to go, was the compelling issue of how to use it. I finally decided to hold it with Cairo's white-colored districts on top because white is the color of cold, cold is the temperature of north, and north is the direction of up.

But this didn't seem to help either. So I fiddled with the map, I did a few spins, I even checked once more to see if the Arabic hadn't miraculously turned into English. But it hadn't. So I did the next logical thing: I crushed the map into a little ball and "made a go of it" into the trash. This I did, with the words "Real tourists go with the flow, not with the map."

Lizzie wasn't impressed.

DR. HADDI

Dr. Haddi entered our lives some two hours later. He did so quite casually, really. Just pulled up alongside as we crossed the clerk's "blidge" (I think) and said, "Hello."

The voice was soprano, and it came from below. It belonged to a four-foot-tall black man wearing sandals and an ankle-length, long-sleeved nightshirt with buttons down to the waist. I'd learned in Jordan that this type of stylized gown was very popular among the Arab set. They called it a galabia.

"I know, I know," I said by way of answering his greeting. "Welcome to Egypt."

"Ha, ha, ha! Very good! Where are you from?" He spoke in unaccented American English.

"I'm from New York and she's from London."

"New York? Too cold in the winter, of course, but certainly the most exciting city in the world. And London, you say? Well, I'm not as familiar with London as I should be. My schedule never permits more than a week for visiting some dear friends and catching a show or two. . . ."

He went on like this for some five minutes or more. A black Egyptian dwarf in peasant garb with the vocabulary of a professor and the taste of a millionaire. On and on he went: about Paris, his love of art, the West, the world.

His name, we learned, was Haddi ("Ha as in ha, ha, ha,

and di as in the fourth letter of the alphabet''): Dr. Haddi. He'd earned a doctorate in philosophy from Columbia University in New York during the 1960s (a very exciting period, he assured us) and returned to his native Egypt to join the family perfume business. He had no choice in the matter, he confided. It was his responsibility as the only son. We also learned that his blackness was Nubian (though his skin tone often caused him to be mistaken for Sudanese), and that the Nubian people traced their ancestry back to the original Egyptians.

It was a great story, if not entirely believable. Something smelled fishy. Perhaps it was that he shouldn't have been telling it in the first place.

But worst of all was Lizzie. She was captivated. Her eyes sparkled with each cast of his line.

"Come now, we've spoken enough. My perfume shop is nearby. I'd be honored if you'd come with me to sample some scents."

Sample some scents? It certainly wasn't *my* thing. But Lizzie lit up.

"Oh, Leo, let's! It sounds fascinating!"

The shop was just a few blocks away on a quiet side street. The name on the window read THOUSAND AND ONE NIGHTS PERFUME. The inside was compact. Two men sat by a single desk surrounded by walls of display cases.

THE RED ROOM

Dr. Haddi nodded to one of the men before guiding us up a steep spiral staircase to the second floor. He waited for Lizzie to reach the landing before taking my hand and leading us through some hanging beads into a small room. He called it the Red Room, and not without reason. Red silk curtains, "imported from India," defined three walls, while a ruby red carpet, "a gift from a friend in the Islamic Republic," cushioned our feet. The ceiling was completed by the waves and folds of elegant red cloth "woven in the Sahara Desert."

As well it must have been, for the atmosphere was that of a desert tent. I had the feeling that a look beyond the beaded entrance would reveal this room as one of several tents dotting an endless vista of rolling sand dunes.

Only the fourth wall, the wall to the right of the entrance, broke the complete texture of the room—the warmth of the fabric and its folds—to provide some hint that we were really on the second floor of a shabby building two blocks from Tahrir Square. This wall was of glass, a large mirror, actually, lined with eight shelves enclosed by sliding glass doors. Each shelf stretched along the complete length of the wall and held a series of delicately shaped bottles filled in varying measure with a clear liquid we took for perfume.

"Please be seated," said our host with a bow and a gesture towards deep pillows of red velvet which lay scattered around the edges of the room. "These, you will be pleased to learn, are locally made from the hands of Egyptian peasants."

Both Lizzie and I squatted, then fell back into some cushions along the far wall. We weren't immediately prepared for the instability we felt as we sank in, but shortly, after some shifting and adjustment, we found a semblance of balance.

"It takes some getting used to, I know, but with time, in a few moments, you will forget how you ever used a chair."

I laughed with him at this small joke, then pulled my right heel beneath my left thigh. There, I thought. Now for the left heel. This too could be pushed into place, though not without serious effort.

"You know, Dr. Haddi," I called out from an immobile posture, "I feel like I'm imitating a pretzel."

"Ha, ha, very funny! You must have patience, Leo, patience. You'll soon adjust. You may even find it comfortable. Perhaps try removing your shoes. It's the only way to fully enjoy the pleasures of the carpet. You too, Lizzie.''

The advice seemed sound, though I wouldn't act before silently calculating the physical and aromatic condition of my socks. The good news was I'd picked them up just before leaving the States. The bad news was that they were in their second consecutive day of service.

Just then, right in the middle of my silent deliberations, as Lizzie was removing her second shoe, I became aware of a low whirring sound. This was followed by a light breeze emanating from somewhere within the folds of the curtained walls.

Dr. Haddi smiled. It was clear he'd read the look on my face.

''Very good, Leo,'' he commended me. ''Most guests are so captivated by the surroundings that they fail to notice the ventilation system. I had it installed to prevent the scents of different perfumes from lingering on after they'd been sampled. The air is carried from the room through a series of discreetly placed air vents.''

He paused a few moments to let the fact of the invisible ventilation system sink in.

''Don't let surfaces fool you,'' he continued with a gesture about the room, ''not only here, but throughout the Middle East in general.''

''Don't worry,'' I assured him, ''I know what you mean. It's like American news shows where information is presented through a surface of entertainment.''

Dr. Haddi took this in. His expression indicated that I hadn't made myself clear.

''That's part of it,'' he said politely. ''But I also meant that Westerners have a tendency to view Arabs as primitive people. They see the bedouin nomad crossing the desert on a camel and think that this is the entire picture. This is a great mistake. What they don't understand is that the Arab affair with high technology is as deep and involved as the Americans'. It's just expressed differently."

"I suppose what you mean is that Americans are somewhat naive," said Lizzie, as I removed my shoes.

"Yes, naiveté. Many Americans are naive, are they not?"

He said this almost to himself, and neither Lizzie nor I responded. Yet I was sure that had she commented, Lizzie's continental sensibilities would have aligned her with Dr. Haddi.

"But enough chatter." Once again Dr. Haddi broke the silence. "We came here to sample the scents of the gods, did we not? Yes. But first, before we get down to business so to speak, I must—and this is a character trait of *my* people—I must offer you a glass of tea. A glass of tea to wet our tongues and help us enjoy what is to come. You would like that, no?"

Lizzie replied first. "Yes, thank you. That would be lovely."

I nodded in agreement.

"Fine," said Dr. Haddi, who then turned to the wall on the opposite side of the room, snapped his fingers twice and called out something sounding like: "Mamud!"

The curtain in the area to which he'd directed himself began to stir. Then from the depths of its folds, from nowhere it seemed, emerged a giant male figure.

Lizzie gasped.

MUHAMMAD

Excepting his size (larger than normal), everything about him spelled peasant. An off-white (from use, not design) turban was wrapped around his head, while a matching galabia outlined a muscular physique. His feet were bare except for what looked like a ruby ring on the pinkie toe of his left foot. Beyond that, his single most impressive feature, at least in the half-light of this tent, was his expression, which projected a natural, animal-like charm. I found this particularly noteworthy because his eyes were hidden in the shade of his forehead.

Dr. Haddi barked a few words in Arabic towards the man, who simply bowed and shuffled from the room.

"He'll be a few minutes in returning, so why don't I begin with a short explanation of the perfume."

"Excuse me, Dr. Haddi," I interjected, as I recovered from the shock of the servant's entrance. "How did that fellow get into this room?"

"Why through the door, of course."

"*Please,* Dr. Haddi, we have eyes, you know." This was Lizzie. "We saw that the man didn't come in through the door." It was fun watching Lizzie attack when she felt someone wasn't playing cricket. Her eyes began to squinch up and patches of pink appeared on her pale skin.

"All right then, you're right," confessed Haddi from behind a plastic smile. "He was here all along. You didn't see him because he was sitting in the folds of the wall drapes. Your problem is you didn't take my warning about the appearance of things seriously."

"Listen, Dr. Haddi," I said, picking up Lizzie's attack. "We came here at your request to sample your perfumes. We took you at your word. Do you intend to tell us now that your invitation was not what it seemed?"

Haddi raised his hands in surrender. "Now, now. Don't become excited. I've sent Muhammad out for some tea. I thought you'd enjoy my little joke. I'm sorry if you didn't. Please don't leave now."

I looked to Lizzie who gave a "one more chance" shrug.

PERFUME

Dr. Haddi read our signal. "Good. Thank you. Now to the perfume. Egypt, you may be aware, has long been involved in the production of perfume. Much of this history has passed within my very own family.

"The production process begins when the perfume essence is collected from specially cultivated flowers. You'll be interested to know that the French use this same essence in some of their most exclusive perfumes.

"The perfume is worn by mixing a sample of the essence with a bit of alcohol, and rubbing it into the appropriate spot."

A jangling of beads interrupted the lecture.

"Ah, it's Muhammad with the tea."

TEATIME

The huge figure passed into the room turban first to avoid the top of the entrance. A delicate tray lay incongruously in a huge right hand whose design seemed more fitting for a wooden hoe than a silver tray. He placed the tray with its three glasses of tea on a low round table in the middle of the room.

The servant gave a deep bow before backing towards the corner of the room. There he sat, disappeared actually, into the same folds from which he'd first emerged.

Haddi continued as if the interruption had never occurred.

"Please. Lizzie, Leo, raise your glasses. Cheers!"

We took up our glasses by their rims to avoid the heat of the tea. Each glass held small green mint leaves he'd called *nah nah*. Haddi was first to taste and first to react to the drink.

"Ahhhhhh!" he cried, as his eyes closed and his lips pursed into a contented smile. "Nothing warms the soul like tea."

"Oh yes! Dr. Haddi, quite," Lizzie joined in. "There's something unmistakably unique about this tea. Very good, really. Very good."

The eyes of the room passed on to me.

I took a sip of my tea. It was kind of minty and overly sweetened in a Middle Eastern sort of way. Good, though nothing worth getting teary eyed over. Still, if everyone was making commercials, I'd give one too.

"Tea with *nah nah*," I said, with all the conviction I could muster. "Just what a man needs after a long morning on the streets of Cairo."

Lizzie shrank back in horror at this defamation of the teatime convention. "Really, Leo, must you be so crass?"

Dr. Haddi was more understanding. "Very good, Leo! Don't worry Lizzie, I think Leo was entertaining us with an imitation of American commercialism. Am I right?"

I nodded, pleased with his reaction but shamed by Lizzie's.

"I knew it! I knew it!" Haddi showed satisfaction from his recollections of the good old days in New York.

"Come, now. So long as our tongues agree on the pleasure of the tea, let our noses enjoy the similar delights of perfume."

OF VIRGINS AND WHORES

Dr. Haddi turned, lifted himself by his toes, and picked two bottles from the shelf behind him. One was short and round with a long-stemmed neck. The other was tall and thin like a twelve-ounce bottle of Coke.

"This," he said, holding up the shorter, more elegant bottle, "is perfume essence. The source for the essence— the flowers—is grown in the southwest region of the Sinai Desert. Not far, I might add, from where Moses encountered the burning bush and later received the Ten Commandments. The essence is quite pure—free from all contaminating elements like alcohol. Here, I'll show you."

He placed both bottles down, picked up and struck a match, then dropped it, still burning, into the bottle of perfume essence. The match went out as soon as it touched the liquid.

Lizzie and I shook our heads in unison. We knew a successful demonstration when we saw one.

Dr. Haddi summarized the results of the experiment we'd just witnessed with the comment: "You see? It's pure." Only it sounded like: "Check my sleeves. Nothing hidden there."

"Hold on to your watch," I whispered to Lizzie.

"Shhhhh!" came the reply from the believer.

"What was that?" asked Dr. Haddi.

"Nothing," I answered. "I'm simply curious. What's in the second bottle?"

"I was just getting to that. The second bottle contains alcohol. Just don't ask me to throw in a lighted match to prove it. Ha ha. Perfume is created by mixing the essence with a bit of alcohol."

He picked up the smaller bottle, poured a measured amount of the essence into his hand, then added a touch of the alcohol, and mixed the two.

"Give me your wrists."

He applied a bit of this newly concocted substance to the inside of Lizzie's left wrist and my right.

"Allow me the pleasure," he began with a flourish, "of introducing a scent I call Maiden's Bath. It's a delicate fragrance for the woman of refined manner. The true secret of its power is that it is only noticeable from close up. I like this fragrance because it doesn't shout. On the contrary. It's coy and pure."

We brought our wrists up to our noses and inhaled. Lizzie reacted first.

"Very nice, Dr. Haddi. Truly lovely."

Though I had to sniff twice to detect any smell, I felt it my duty to smile appreciatively.

Haddi must have noticed my hesitation, for he reached up to a higher shelf and pulled down a larger, rounder bottle.

"I sense in you, Leo, a man who appreciates strong scents. If so, I doubt you'll be disappointed by this. It's called Midnight because that's when it's used. I'll apply it here to your wrists, but be aware, Lizzie, that a woman may wear it anywhere she wants: behind the ear, along the neck, even further down. It's an imaginative scent for the woman of passion. My wives, I must confess, use it often.''

He applied a bit to each of our wrists. There was no need to bring our noses close. The perfume jumped. If the last one was for virgins, this one spoke for whores.

"Dr. Haddi . . .'' Lizzie was actually blushing.

"You like? I'm happy.''

"It's just that it's so . . . I don't even know if I can express it . . . so full . . . so . . . sensuous. Yes, sensuous!''

"Don't worry, dear Lizzie, you're expressing yourself perfectly. And I think I have just the scent for you. One that reflects that special femininity I feel in your carriage and personality. One moment, please.''

It's part of the game, I thought, this kind of talk. Women buy it by the gallon. Lizzie certainly did. My one hope was that the perfume would give off a better smell.

FIRE OF THE GODS

Haddi, meanwhile, squatted to pick up a square bottle from the lowest shelf. His eyes grew wide as he raised himself and continued to lift the bottle over his head. Its contents glowed red.

"Behold the Fire of the Gods!'' his voice cried out in dramatic pitch. I half expected a crescendo of drums and cymbals to build in the background.

"Fire of the Gods! A fragrance of beauty and form.'' His voice lowered. "A striking scent for one woman alone.''

He removed the top and held the bottle out for Lizzie to smell. Her nostrils quivered as they discovered the fumes. Her cheeks flushed.

The bottle moved in my direction. I leaned forward to meet it. I was surprised to find that there was indeed something special about the scent. It was sweet and left the nose tingling.

"I believe we've found a perfume that even Mr. Gold can appreciate."

There were smiles all around.

"You've both noticed how different this scent is from the others. It has a different color and texture, and even a different method of application. Thus, instead of mixing it with alcohol, I mix it with fire."

I raised my eyebrows.

"That's right, Leo, fire. This perfume is applied warm so that the pores can expand and hold it. Would you care, Lizzie, for a sample?"

"How could I pass up an offer as exciting as hot perfume?"

"Indeed," he said, then took a wooden match and struck it against the table. The fire flared and hissed for a moment before settling back into a steady flame. Haddi extended the fire into the mouth of the bottle. A few seconds passed before anything happened. Then a pinkish-red smoke began rising from within the bottle. The smoke grew heavier as it drifted up to the folds of the fabric above. Visibility deteriorated to near zero within two or three seconds.

Lizzie called out: "Leo?"

I reached over and took her outstretched hand before it completely disappeared into the pink mist. "I'm here," I answered. Then: "What's going on here, Haddi?" There was movement all around. "Haddi!" I called again. And again, he didn't answer.

I told Lizzie it was time to go and lifted her by the hand as I stood. We were moving in the direction of the entrance when someone snapped our hands apart and pushed me in the chest. The force of the attack propelled me backwards and over the table where the glasses of tea had sat. Lizzie called my name, and I hers. The clouds were less dense from the floor and gave me a chance to look around. First I saw Lizzie's feet, then I saw Haddi's, then I saw nothing.

3

Alone

ALONE

Next I knew, I was propped up on a pillow. All was quiet except for my head, which was pounding. The results of the recent tumult lay before me. Shattered glass was scattered all about, a product, I presumed, of my collision with the table which now lay on its side in the far corner. The carpet had taken in a good measure of tea. The moist spots were still warm to the touch. Other than that, everything was the same except Lizzie was missing. And not only Lizzie, but Haddi too.

I went over and checked the folds in the curtain from which Muhammad had once emerged. No Muhammad either.

I rushed downstairs for help, but found that here, too, I stood alone. A glance towards the shop window revealed hordes of shoppers passing beneath the late afternoon sun, oblivious to my misfortune.

I returned to the Red Room in the hope that a brief check might cast some light onto the circumstances of the current circumstances. Nothing methodical, mind you. Not even thorough. Just something to ease my growing sense of helplessness. Something that might lead to Lizzie's return, without, hopefully, exposing me to any more trouble.

I stumbled over to the shelves where the perfume essence stood and began a clearing process which included long sweeps of the hand along the rows, and the picking up and tossing of bottles here and there. A few of the smaller, more elegantly shaped vessels found their way into my pocket.

My frustration mounted. I went over to the curtains and yanked them down so I could check the ventilation ducts. These, I found, were solidly in place. I lunged for the beads by the entrance and began tugging at them in the hope that the action would release some secret, be it door or otherwise. Yet all they did was come off in my fists.

I decided to check the floor. A cloud of dust rose up from my feet to my neck as I threw the carpet aside. Below the wood planking, I thought. Check below the wood planking! So I jumped up and down from one corner to the next trying to detect a hollow. Only there was nothing to find. Nothing at all. Just solid floor from end to end.

"Where?" I called out. My voice sounded shrill as it rebounded off the bare walls.

THE POLICE

I took the echo of my own voice as a sign that my usefulness there was spent. I descended the stairs two at a time, then bounded out through the front door.

The noise of the street came as a shock, as did the dust-scented air. But I kept moving, first in a trot, then in a sprint, as I searched for someone to help me. I pushed through veiled women, galabia-clad hawkers, and runny-nosed kids. I stumbled on a can in the road. Four blocks went by before I came across a white-uniformed, black-capped boy directing traffic in the middle of the street. Bold letters on his shirtsleeve read "Traffic Police." I grabbed him by his label.

"Come," I panted, "with me! There's been a kidnapping at the Thousand and One Nights Perfume shop. Come with me. Come with me!''

I tugged at his arm. I implored, I begged, but he wouldn't move. Cars started honking at us for blocking their way. He was talking at me in Arabic. He was yelling. Then he reached for, pulled out and raised his nightstick. I backed off, read his actions as a sign to leave, and did.

My shirt was soaked in sweat by the time I reached my next official figure. This one's uniform was identical to the first's except it was green and the label on his arm read: ''Tourist Police.'' I took a lesson from my previous experience and approached without grabbing. I was red faced, I knew, and dripping wet.

''Come and help me! I'm an American citizen. My girlfriend's been kidnapped!''

He gave me a strange look, then smiled and held up his hands in a gesture which indicated he didn't understand English. He welcomed me to Egypt.

''Welcome to Egypt? Welcome to Egypt! I've been attacked. My girlfriend's been kidnapped! I need your help, goddamn it! Come with me!'' I gestured for him to follow me and pointed in the direction of the shop which was now some six blocks away. His smile faded when he realized I wasn't looking for the Pyramids. I grabbed myself by the throat with my left hand, bulged my eyes and made gurgling noises. Then I made as if knocking myself over the head with a stick and pointed back once again towards the Thousand and One Nights.

A light took up in his eyes. It was as if he were saying, ''What is it, Lassie? What are you trying to say? Is something wrong? Where's Timmy? Okay, Lassie, you lead the way and I'll follow.''

He pointed to himself then to me, then pumped his arms in a running motion and pointed down the street from which I'd come.

Yes! Yes! I nodded wildly. Yes. Come, I motioned. You and I together.

He began trotting in my direction. I took off a few steps before he reached me. Follow me, I waved. Follow me.

He called out a few words as we passed the guy with the Traffic Police label I'd met earlier. He was still reluctant to join, but fell in behind, after a second, gruffer command from my companion.

We were all three nearly buckled over from exhaustion by the time we reached the shop. Two men were sitting inside. The same two I'd seen earlier. Still, I didn't stop to ask questions. I just took hold of the banister and hauled myself up the stairs to the scene of the crime.

Only, there was no scene. That is, there was no evidence of a crime at the scene. The room was exactly as we'd found it not one hour before when Lizzie, Haddi, and I came up to sample perfume. Everything was in its place. The curtains were hanging. The carpet lay flat. The table stood straight. A check for a spot of moisture on the carpet came up dry. All the bottles, in all their varied shapes and sizes, stood in rows along the shelves in precise order by scent and quality.

I stood motionless at the entrance. My legs grew weak. How could I have expected anything else?

Waves of heat fell against the back of my neck. I turned and found their source in the panting breath of my red-faced tourist policeman who, when he saw my face, gave a comradely smile that said "We made it!" The two men from below were just beginning to mount the stairs when the traffic cop (he'd been standing off to the right) took professional interest in the developing jam by the doorway, and motioned me inside.

I walked over to where Haddi had taken the Fire of the Gods, but found that the bottle was missing. I turned to bring this fact to the attention of the authorities, but found that they'd formed a tight circle with the two men from the shop.

"They'll tell you," I told them. "They can explain everything." But I doubted they would.

Five minutes of animated conversation followed. The police referred to me often through gestures and nods. The two from the shop referred to me, too, though usually in the negative.

The police would say something that sounded like gargling.

And the two would answer: *"la"*—for no—and shake their heads.

The police would follow up by clearing their throats.

"La," the two repeated. *"La,"* and shook their heads.

"They're stonewalling," I said to the cop charged with policing tourists. "They won't talk because they're in on it. They participated in the assault and they probably fixed up the room after I left." I gestured about the room.

The conspirators smiled.

"You bastards!" I spit and lunged at them, but the cops caught me. "Don't you see they're in on it? It's a conspiracy, don't you get it? They've kidnapped my girlfriend!"

The cops began moving me downstairs. An air of hopelessness fell over the situation. I gave up my struggle and decided to avoid arrest by going quietly. They released me on the sidewalk.

"You'll hear from my congressman!"

The tourist cop gave me a long look of apology. He'd done his best. His voice came calling after me as I made my way down the sidewalk.

"Welcome," he said.

MORE HELP

I spent the rest of the fading afternoon at the American Embassy. The response there was not unlike what I'd found with the Egyptians, except the English was better. The problem was that Lizzie, as a British subject, fell outside their immediate jurisdiction. Besides, they said, it was a case for the local authorities.

The British Embassy came next on the list. Only it was closed for the weekend by the time I arrived. A guard stationed by the door suggested I leave a message, which I did. I stated the nature of the emergency as the kidnapping of a British subject. He asked what happened and I told him. He expressed surprise when I described the behavior of the Egyptian police. Then he asked what I planned to do next. When I said I didn't know, he suggested I return to the Amman, clean up and wait for a call from the Embassy, so I did.

I didn't even haggle with the driver over the price of the cab back.

BACK AT THE AMMAN

The front desk clerk commented at once that something seemed not quite right with me.

I answered his inquiring eyes with a brief: "She's gone, she's gone. They've kidnapped her . . ."

"What!"

"Yes," I said, with more than just an air of depression about me. "It's true." Then I took the room key from his hand and headed down the corridor.

"Hold on," he called out. "Have you contacted the police? Come back here, I'll help you."

"Thanks," I said almost to myself, "but don't bother. I already have. The police . . . the police don't understand . . ." I turned and stepped into the elevator.

THINKING

Once inside the room I headed straight for the shower. I needed to think, and that's where I always found the best conditions.

The steam ran thick as I collected my thoughts. My immediate feeling was that Lizzie'd been kidnapped after I'd been knocked out, either by the tea or some blow to the head. I figured they must have taken her from the room through some secret passage. The alternative, down the stairs and out the front door, seemed too pedestrian for a guy like Dr. Haddi. Why, I figured, would he bother with the door if he'd gone to the trouble of filling the room with pink smoke?

And what of Muhammad? It seemed pretty obvious that he was the henchman. I mean, except for the tea business and the servanting, he looked and acted exactly as a henchman should. He probably corralled Lizzie and took her away under orders from Dr. Haddi. And as for his appearance and disappearance through the folds in the curtains, well, this just lent further credence to the hidden passage theory.

SLEEP

How did I sleep the night following the most trying day of my life?

Let's put it this way: Trying times affect different men in different ways, especially in the area of sleep. One type, the go-getter, works through the night in a tireless effort to correct the crisis. This is a foolish approach, because it rarely yields anything more than a ragged body and fatigued mind.

The second type turns this neuroticism on its head. That is, he recognizes the importance of relaxation as a vital ingredient to successful crisis resolution, but can't rest because he's too worried about what he should be doing. This type is worse off than the first because not only is he tired in the morning, but he faces it without a single new idea.

And then there is the third type. This is the fellow who recognizes sleep as the most pleasurable of all human activities. Sleep is not just a goal, but a way of life. This type uses worry and tension as the fuel and engine for a high-powered sleep that enables him to meet the morning sun refreshed and ready to go.

It is with this third type that I identify myself. Moreover, I can honestly report that I spent the night following the day of Lizzie's abduction sleeping like a gas-guzzling, super-charged '67 Caddy.

4

Jihad

JIHAD

Which brings us to breakfast. I must admit that notwithstanding Lizzie's new status, I was feeling very, very good. Almost high. It might have had something to do with getting an unusually restful twelve-hour sleep, or that the hotel had some sort of inexplicable aura about it. I certainly didn't know, and was in no rush to find out.

I felt good in spite of the facts, which, when they spoke for themselves, found not a single decent thing to say. That's what I was thinking when my waiter came up to clear the remains of my morning meal.

"More coffee, Mr. Gold?"

I looked up into the sparkling blue eyes of my ever-attentive waiter.

"No thanks, ahhhh . . . Jihad," I replied with a glance towards his identification badge.

I noticed that Jihad had been ignoring everyone else in the dining room. More than that, he was neat, eager, and efficient, and he spoke with a completely enchanting accent. Looking back, I think that this, more than anything else, was the main reason I decided to use him as a sounding board for my thoughts on the previous day's events.

"Say, Jihad, I've got a problem you might be able to help me out with."

"It would be my privilege." There was a soft musical tone to his voice that went well with his sad, yet understanding eyes. His hair was short, dark, and curly, with sprinklings of gray. His skin was pale. I judged him about forty-five, and you could see he'd once been a very handsome young man. "You grew up right here in Cairo?" I asked.

"Not right here, but in Cairo, yes."

"Then you must know the city pretty well."

"I don't like to brag."

"I can see that. Perhaps you've heard of the Thousand and One Nights Perfume shop?"

"Why do you ask?"

"My girlfriend and I went there yesterday to sample some perfumes. She was kidnapped instead."

"La!"

"I swear it."

"Then why don't you appear concerned?"

"Heck if I know. I think it's got something to do with this hotel, but I'm not sure. Anyway, I've reported the kidnapping to the British Embassy and they're going to get back to me."

"By phone?"

"That's the assumption."

"Don't hold your breath. The Cairo phone system's been dead for the last five hours."

"No kidding?"

He pulled out a gold pocket watch, flipped open the cover and checked the time. "Nope. No kidding. Five hours exactly."

"You were about to tell me about the perfume shop," I said.

"The Thousand and One Nights?"

"Yeah . . ."

"They don't just sell perfume."

"That was my experience."

"And their client list is very exclusive."

"Kind of like yours," I said, referring to the fact that he'd been devoting his complete attention to me.

"Right. Kind of like that." He paused and gave me a sharp look. He was waiting for me to follow up.

"What exactly do you mean?"

He took a long slow survey of the room as if he were searching for someone. Halfway through, his hand brushed against and knocked my napkin to the floor. He stooped to pick it up, and as he rose, whispered in my direction:

"I mean maybe we should continue this talk outside."

ON THE ROAD AGAIN

He directed me to leave through the hotel's front door and meet him around back in five minutes. I did as he said and got there in three. He made it in seven. My euphoric mood passed in six.

"Sorry I'm late," he said rushing up. "I couldn't find my card to punch out."

"Let's cut the small talk, Jihad."

He flinched visibly then shrugged his shoulders. "Okay, we'll do it your way. I may be able to help you find your girlfriend."

"Who says I need help?"

"I thought you said you wanted to cut out the small talk."

"All right, what do you know?"

"Enough to believe your life is threatened."

"How would you know something like that?"

"Because, Mr. Gold, I'm not really a waiter . . ."

"What waiter is?"

". . . I'm actually a private investigator."

I gave him a second once-over. It was obvious now that he wasn't a waiter, his fancy Italian shoes, tight black pants, and fitted silk shirt were evidence enough of that. Yet it wasn't the stuff of a private eye either. Or was it? I decided to hear him out.

"Who says you need help?" he asked, echoing my earlier question. "The hotel receptionist, for one. He came to see me last night—my office is right next door. He said that one of his guests had been kidnapped and that my services might be needed."

"The hotel receptionist? The guy who speaks English with the Japanese accent?"

"English too? I thought it was just his Arabic. You know he's been seeing a speech therapist."

"Really?"

"That's right. Anyway, I'm not talking about that guy. I'm talking about the fellow who works the evening shift. We became friends when this hotel opened up six months ago. We look out for each other."

"You mean he gets you clients, and you send him guests?"

Jihad looked offended. "It's a legitimate business practice. There's no need for sarcasm."

A pretty fishy answer, I thought, though I still didn't know what to make of him. "If you're a detective," I asked, "then why didn't you approach me directly instead of posing as a waiter?"

"I wanted to get a good look at you first. To see you in an unguarded moment."

Now I knew what to make of him. It's called a con man. I decided to let him down easy. "Look, I want you to know I appreciate the trouble you've gone to in order to meet me and I'll report your good work to the private eyes' union. But I'm wary of unsolicited help. I contacted the British Embassy yesterday and I think I'll stick with them on this one." I extended my hand for a farewell handshake.

"I wouldn't wait for the British Embassy on this one," he said, ignoring my hand. "Your chances of hearing from them are very slim so long as you have to rely on the Cairo phone system."

"They'll fix it."

"It doesn't matter if they do. The British won't come up with anything. Neither will the Americans and neither will the Egyptian police."

Though I didn't say it, my instincts told me he was probably right. "But you will?"

"Yes."

"And I should trust you."

"Yes." He sounded quite sure of himself.

"You know the last time I trusted an Egyptian I just happened to bump into, he took my girlfriend."

"Well, now you're talking to one who can get her back."

"You can guarantee that?"

"For a modest price."

"Oh?" I felt my hand take up a defensive position outside the pocket where my wallet was stashed. "And what might that be?"

A sympathetic look crossed Jihad's face. "Let's not talk of money now," he said. "Why don't you just give me a couple of hours of your time? You'll tell me more about the kidnapping. I'll see if it's a case worth handling, and you'll get a better idea of my abilities. If in the end, one of us concludes that it's not a good match, we'll say *MaaSalami*—farewell. You can return to the Amman, wait for the British Embassy or Egyptian police or whoever to ring, and I can go back to my office. What do you say? We can even take in the Pyramids if you like."

I still wasn't the least bit sure about him. He was arrogant and a little too fast with the answers. But then again, his answers were, well, the only answers I was getting. I decided to take him up on his offer. It would give me time to feel him out. Besides, I reasoned, I *had* missed yesterday's tour.

AMMAN AGAIN

We stepped up to the Cairene curb where the morning rush hour passed in chaos. A cab slowed as it reached our position. Jihad hollered a few words in Arabic, but the vehicle kept going.

"In my country," I said, "a simple wave of the hand will do."

"Perhaps. But this is Egypt, and it is *my* country. Here, we call out our destination to the passing taxi. The driver stops if he wants the fare. He keeps going if he doesn't."

Just then a local cab, unsolicited by hand or voice, pulled up to meet us.

"Then there's always the exception," he offered.

He stepped forward to open the door where the words *AMMAN CAB CO.* were written in red. I hesitated.

Jihad sensed my sudden tenseness. "Something's wrong?"

"I've got a funny feeling about this one, Jihad."

GETTING NOSY

"Nonsense. Come, let's go." He gestured that I step in.

I ducked my head and moved to the far corner. The seat had a sticky feel to it. A remnant, I figured, from the time some dirty-faced delinquent let his ice cream melt all over the black vinyl cushions. And how could I blame him? The cab was as hot as a sauna.

I sought relief by trying to open the window but the handle came off in my hand.

"I thought my day was yesterday," I mumbled to myself.

Jihad sat back after passing instructions on to the driver. "Excuse me?" Streams of sweat flowed through the furrows of his brow.

I held up the handle.

Jihad gave an understanding nod and addressed the driver. I assumed he asked if the handle could be fixed.

Though the reply came in Arabic, I figured out fast, this

driver "didn't do handles." He emphasized this by proceeding to verbally beat me with accusations of inchastity with my mother, questions over my lineage, and a few imaginative suggestions about what I could perform with the window handle. That, at least, was the gist of what I took from Jihad's simultaneous translation, though I might have been mistaken, what with all the attention I was giving to the driver's face as reflected in the mirror. It was the kind of face you felt you'd seen before on the screen of some grade-B horror flick. Most impressive was his mouth, which was completely toothless and black inside. Also of note was the empty socket where his right eyeball should have been.

"He's pretty upset about the handle," said Jihad. "I think you'd better put it down."

The next five minutes passed without talk, as both Jihad and I tried losing ourselves in events passing beyond the film of our respective windows. The streets were a carnival of humanity. Dusty children played around the hems of women striding along with huge packages balanced on their heads. Turbaned merchants shook sticks at wild dogs sniffing too close to the merchandise. Cars and camels jostled for space along the road.

But the picture was no match for the heat. My shirt was soon soaked through and sticking to me like flypaper. Make conversation, I thought. It will delay the onslaught of delirium.

"Listen, Jihad . . ." I said as I turned to my right.

"Sir?" He turned from the window and placed his nose within striking distance of my own.

"You said before that my life might be threatened. What did you mean by that?" I tried opening some space between us by executing a discreet backward tilt.

He took a few moments sizing me up. When he spoke, his words were measured. "I said that, yes. But before I say more I have to know more details about the case. The circumstances surrounding the abduction.''

That seemed fair enough. Besides, it would take my mind off the heat. So I told him all about how Lizzie and I had met Dr. Haddi quite by chance, how Muhammad the henchman had brought us tea, and how the Fire of the Gods perfume had gone up in a pink cloud. I also recalled how the police had been of no help in their dealings with the two Egyptians who'd been downstairs during the entire episode, and how the embassies had been equally ineffective.

Jihad nodded as I spoke. His expression was as sincere as it could be while his brow dripped like a leaky faucet.

''Well,'' I asked, ''what do you think now? Is my life threatened?''

''Perhaps, though now I'm not as sure as I was before.'' He didn't say more. He just leaned his head closer to mine.

''It's too hot to be coy, Jihad.'' I proved my point by flicking away the single drop of sweat that had bridged the gap between our noses. ''What are you saying?''

''I'm saying, Mr. Gold, that it's my belief that you and your girlfriend, quite by chance, and through no fault of your own, had the unfortunate fate of falling into the path of a group of very unscrupulous individuals . . .''

''Tell me something I don't know.''

''. . . Moreover, this kidnapping may be part of a much larger scheme which should be of no concern to you.''

''An interesting theory,'' I offered with some relief now that he seemed to be suggesting that my life was no longer in danger. But just to be sure, I decided to play devil's advocate. I pointed out that my status as the only living hostile witness to the kidnapping, made me also, as far as the perpetrators were concerned, a very loose end and therefore a matter of some concern. Jihad listened closely as I made this point. He found the analysis impressive but unconvincing.

''You overlook, Mr. Gold, that they could have had their

way with you during the abduction, yet they chose to spare you. I view this as a sign of your unimportance."

"Unimportance?"

Just then the cab came to a screeching halt. Dust flew up all around.

"But enough business for now," said Jihad to avoid expanding on his last point. "I promised to show you the Pyramids and I will."

"You can't end the conversation like that," I protested.

"Yes, I can, Mr. Gold. Yes, I can. Please remember where you are. This is the Middle East. Matters move at a slower pace here. Be patient. All your questions will be answered in time."

I didn't feel in a position to argue.

Jihad passed some money up front. The driver said something and Jihad said something back. The driver spit.

"What's the matter, Jihad?"

"It's the window handle. He wants you to pay for it."

"What? The thing came off in my hand. Tell him I don't owe him a thing."

Jihad did as I asked. The driver blinked his eye in what looked like astonishment before laying into me with another string of hostile ravings.

"Come on, Jihad," I said as I opened the door. "I knew we should never have taken a cab marked AMMAN."

ARRIVING AT THE PYRAMIDS

We got out into a cloud of dust.

"So these are the famous Pyramids of Giza," I shouted over the sound of the cab accelerating back toward downtown Cairo. "Quite impressive."

"They're over here," responded my guide as he took hold of my body and turned it around.

The image of three huge stone triangles emerged from the fog. "Indeed they are."

Jihad took my hand and began walking. "Come. Let us begin our tour."

I gently removed my hand from his.

"Come," he repeated. "We must hurry if we want to see the Pyramids before the crowds arrive." He referenced a group of sightseers who had moments before walked into the local tourist market where anything from camel rides, to hieroglyphic inscriptions, to models of the Statue of Liberty were available to the willing bargainer. Must be Americans, I guessed, judging from their preference for purchasing over prehistory.

My eyes drifted over to the bus from which they'd recently descended. It was larger than the standard, and its windows were curtained. Large red letters in Latin script decorated its side. They spelled: *AMMAN*.

WILD CAMEL

I was about to bring the matter of this unholy coincidence to Jihad's attention when a bloodcurdling cry went up from within the group. The tourists began scattering away from the center that had moments before held their attention, until all that was left was the source of the disturbance and her entourage of two. Three if you counted the camel. A grandmotherly tourist, now overripe with fear, was surging to and fro from atop a wild camel, in what was obviously a pleasure ride gone sour. The camel was followed by a huge Arab making spastic grabs at the beast's tail in a failing effort to halt the rampage. Following the Arab was a desperate-looking older man who waved his hands and wept pathetically.

"Stop! Stop you wild beast. Oh, my God! Hold on Sophele! Hold on!"

"Herman! Herman, my dalink," cried the grandmother. "Save me!"

The crowd was now well away, packed once again in a tight ball of flowered shirts and Bermuda shorts. They viewed the tumult with fear and awe, though the more level-headed among them had the presence of mind to unholster their cameras and pose their loved ones between their lenses and the action.

Meanwhile, the Arab, his turban now fallen to his nose, managed to grip the animal's tail with one hand and strike its side via a long stick with the other. He spoke to the animal through hissing sounds, but was still far from mastering the situation.

The foursome went into a spin. The frantic grandmother held on for dear life as the camel executed an unnatural tap dance designed to free its tail. The old man stumbled up in its wake, red faced from exertion, and nearly lost of hope.

"Oy! I knew we should never have left Brooklyn. Forgive me, Sophie. Troubles like this we should never have known! Why didn't I ride the animal instead? Oh no, oh no!"

The grandmother wasn't much better. "Help! Help us, somebody! Help my husband. Herman, are you all right? Stop running, you'll give yourself a heart attack! Helllllp!"

Just then three nearby merchants dropped what they were doing to come running. One grabbed the camel by its muzzle, while the others took hold of the saddle. The whole thing was under control within a few moments.

The grandmother was lifted shaking from the saddle and brought safely to the ground.

"Hermile!" she cried.

"Sophele, you're alive!"

They exchanged tears of joy from the comfort of each other's arms.

THE PYRAMIDS OF GIZA

"We've been witness to good fortune, Mr. Gold. How do you say? All's well that ends well?"

"That's how we say it."

"Very good. Now come with me. It will be best if we

arrive at the Pyramids before that group." Jihad walked me in the direction of one of the Pyramids.

"This is the Great Pyramid," he said, pointing up ahead. "It was built by a king called Cheops about twenty-five hundred years before Christ. More than two million blocks averaging two and a half tons each were used in its construction. It is the largest stone structure in the world."

He took my hand once more in his and began to pull me along. "Now the second Pyramid was built by Chephren, Cheops' son. It's slightly smaller than the Great Pyramid, and is distinctive for the substantial portion of limestone facing preserved near its peak."

I tried unsuccessfully to shake my hand free.

"Finally, the third and smallest Pyramid was erected by Mycerinus, Chephren's successor. Let's try to get there before the crowds so we can enjoy a trip inside."

He didn't wait for a response. He just released my hand and motioned for me to follow him to the Pyramid standing about a hundred yards to our right.

"It's hard to believe they did all this so long ago. Wasn't engineering a problem?" I called this out to Jihad's back. He seemed very anxious to get to the third Pyramid.

"There are many theories about the construction of the Pyramids," he called back as he walked. "None of them have been confirmed since no records have been found. It is said that the Great Pyramid took one hundred thousand workers twenty years to build. One possibility is that the work proceeded in stages during the three summer months when the flooding Nile turned the valley into a huge lake. Limestone blocks would be transported up the Nile on papyrus boats and dragged by men or oxen up to the site."

"The slaves built them, didn't they?" I was still two steps behind.

"That's the popular belief, though it's not universally accepted. An alternative theory holds that the overriding importance of the afterlife in ancient Egyptian culture, along with the pharaoh's importance as God's representative on earth, made the work a sacred chore for each member of the population. This hypothesis rejects the assumption that the building work was carried out by Hebrew slaves.''

He completed this sentence from the base of Mycerinus' Pyramid. I reached him about ten seconds later.

''After you.'' He extended his hand and gestured up the staircase leading to the entrance. I reached the top and peered down into a narrow passageway.

''It's dark down there, Jihad.''

''Don't worry, there's a light at the bottom.''

''Will we see anything that can't be explained from up here?''

''You're not afraid of the dark, are you?'' His voice was challenging.

''Of course not,'' I lied.

''Then come now.'' He gave me a gentle but firm push downward.

The trip to the bottom passed without event, though I continually checked for Jihad's silhouette outlined against the light of day shining in from above. The room at the bottom was a lot less impressive than the triangle above it, for except for a lightbulb, there was nothing else to see.

''Impressive. No?'' Jihad spoke with pride.

''Amazing.'' I didn't want to offend him.

''Would you like additional explanations?''

What I wanted was out. The room was confining and even stuffier than the taxi. And the smell! The smell made it clear that this ancient king's tomb was today often used as a tourist rest room. Yes, I wanted to tell him to let me out, but all I could manage was ''Please . . .'' The problem was, it must have sounded like I was breathless with anticipation, when in fact I was choking.

''The ancient Egyptians believed that even after he died, the pharaoh became a god of the underworld who could affect life here and now. Since the underworld was the other half of a single reality, the dead man would have all the same needs as a living human being.''

Jihad moved slowly through the small room, tapping the walls, kicking at stones, examining the lightbulb.

"All this meant," he continued, "that the body would have to be carefully preserved, and its needs met. For just like the living pharaoh himself, his soul would need boats for traveling, the choicest foods and wines for dining, and a bevy of servants for helping out. This last requirement meant that the pharaoh's family and servants would be buried in a group of smaller pyramids constructed nearby. You did notice them outside, didn't you?''

I conserved energy by nodding.

"In short, the tomb was a place where the dead man could receive homage and nourishment, as well as make a successful journey to the afterworld where he could radiate blessings back to his people.''

Jihad paralleled the lecture with a continuing inspection of this small, dank room.

"The sad truth is that that tomb theory was inconsistent with human theory. Thus, despite their intimate relationships with the gods, the gold-draped, gift-showered bodies of the pharaohs were vulnerable to grave robbers looking for riches. So vulnerable, in fact, that each and every pyramid was eventually broken into and robbed of its wealth. Not even the body of the pharaoh, whose organs were often replaced by precious jewels, was left undisturbed. . . .''

". . . which explains why the room is empty. Okay, let's go up.'' I spit this out in a single breath.

"Just a minute, Mr. Gold. I brought you here for a reason.'' His eyes grew serious. "I want to continue our earlier conversation. I want to know more about your girlfriend.''

"Again?''

"Not again. But in more depth. Something about your

history together. Come now. We had a deal. You promised to tell me about your girlfriend if I took you to a tourist site.''

"All true. But must we speak down here?''

"From what you've told me, this Dr. Haddi is a serious man. I am sure he would stop at nothing to put an end to any investigation. I am very concerned with security. This thorough examination I've just carried out was not for nothing. I was searching for bugs.''

"If you're so concerned with security," I pointed out, "why did you speak so freely in the cab?''

"The driver had no idea what we were talking about. The man couldn't read Arabic, much less speak English.''

"To be quite frank, Jihad, I'm having a little trouble breathing down here. I feel like I'm going to be sick.''

"I understand your problem, and I wouldn't ask you to remain here if it weren't of the highest importance.'' He took my hand and gave it an imploring squeeze. This, along with the stench of the air, was putting me in great physical discomfort. I suppressed a burp.

"I'm not telling you anything down here, Jihad. And I've got two reasons.'' I spoke in a whisper. "First is this location. You've sure picked a funny place for an office. This stink could choke a mummy. I couldn't talk about my girlfriend down here even if I wanted to.'' I covered my mouth with my free hand and took another breath. "And second, I don't want to. By that I mean, I like you personally and I'm considering taking your help, but I have to know why you think my girlfriend was kidnapped.'' A chill ran down my throat. I swallowed. "You said before that her kidnapping might be part of a larger scheme. You must tell me what it is.''

In actual truth, I wanted out more than I wanted to hear about Jihad's investigative theories, and might even have told him what he wanted to know had he met my request for fresh air. But Jihad couldn't read my thoughts. All he saw was a man who couldn't be pushed. He decided to talk.

"I didn't want to tell you this. I thought it best you didn't know. But now you leave me no choice." He paused here and looked to me for a reprieve. The poor lighting gave him the sorrowful look of a bloodhound. His lips quivered with emotion. The power of this moving scene was almost, but not quite enough, to make me change my mind and tell him what he wanted to know.

"All right," he began reluctantly, "I'll tell you what I think. Though first you must understand that my conclusions are based on intuition alone. I have no proof. Is that clear?"

I nodded.

He repeated it once more for emphasis: "I have no proof." Then: "With that understood, all my information seems to point in one direction—to something that's really quite common in these parts. It indicates that Dr. Haddi, your perfume salesman and your girlfriend's kidnapper, is masterminding a ring that trades in women. A ring that buys and sells women as slaves."

What happened next was inevitable. I'd tried to warn him but he wouldn't listen. He'd been more concerned with the implications of his own conclusions than the very real sufferings of his listener. This, more than anything else, explained his confused expression when I answered his declaration with a deep rumbling belch and the reappearance of the half-digested remains of my morning meal.

Confusion turned to shock as Jihad released my hand and flew back against the far wall of the tomb. His white silk shirt was now untucked—a used canvas for the horrors of my stomach.

I didn't stick around to clean up.

5

On Violence

LIZZIE A SLAVE?

It was crazy. I could no more envision Lizzie a slave than my own father and mother making hot, wet love.

"You'll have to do better than that, Jihad," I said when he finally emerged from the bowels of the Pyramid looking haggard and pale. It was clear he'd used our time apart to make some additions to my earlier inspiration.

"I'm afraid I can't," he said. He reached down to where I sat and took my arm. "Come. Let's walk. You'll feel better."

"I feel fine," I informed him as I stood. "Now." In fact I was thrilled to be free from the tomb—something I'd expressed moments earlier when I fell to my knees, lowered my head and pressed my puckered lips to the ground.

"Then maybe you'll look better." He handed me a handkerchief. "Here, wipe that sand off your face."

I let him guide me towards a remote location about six hundred yards from the Pyramids. A very short time passed before the two of us were very much alone, far from any prying ears, real or synthetic. An air of resignation hung about Jihad as we walked. It was as if he was sorry for having mentioned the slavery thing. I knew he wouldn't have told me without my prompting, but now that he had, I knew I was aligned with him. It was a relationship I was ready to accept, though I was fuzzy on its implications. So I spoke of other things.

"But a slave? She's so unsuited. She's so . . . so . . . British. Who would want a British slave anyway?" I shook my head.

"You can never account for taste."

"What will she have to do? Cook? Have sex? Dance?"

"I think meals are provided."

"What about training? Is sex like a laboratory course?"

"As I understand it, they keep the girls in a group, like a harem. They work together practicing the skills they'll need in the field."

I tried to imagine the training sessions. The utter repulsiveness of it attracted me.

"She'll never do it," I declared. "Lizzie's a very moral person."

"It's been said that man is an immoral being at heart. That morality must be taught. If that's the case, they'll just encourage her to unlearn some old habits."

"Lizzie . . . my Lizzie . . ." I was without words. I was in shock.

"I know this must be hard for you, Mr. Gold." Jihad brought a comforting arm around my shoulders. "It will be all right."

I felt small, helpless, and lost.

"Why don't you tell me more about Lizzie," he continued. "Don't leave out the smallest detail. It might just be the clue that breaks this case."

"All right," I said, as I felt my composure returning. "But let's sit down first. This is a long story." There were two flat-topped boulders nearby. I walked over to one and sat down. Jihad took his place on the other.

IN THE BEGINNING

"I met Lizzie about two months ago in Paris," I began. "I was in a secondhand record and CD store I'd found about two weeks earlier. The place was one block down from my hotel in the Latin Quarter, and had a terrific collection of rock and blues artists—B. B. King, Jimi Hendrix, The Allman Brothers . . . you name it, everyone. Anyhow, I soon found myself in the habit of dropping by at the end of the day.

"Lizzie was another regular. She'd usually come in a few minutes after me and browse nearby. We shared the same taste. Anyhow, one day she came up and asked me a question about Roy Buchanan. Now I'm no expert on Roy by any stretch of the imagination, but she was so pretty, her eyes so bright, that I was ready to tell her anything just to keep her in my sight. Fortunately, things clicked. I learned she was traveling alone. We decided to team up—to travel together."

"You began going out . . ." Jihad clarified.

"Well, yeah, in a manner of speaking. You see, I'd been in Europe for a month by then, traveling by myself trying to recover from the fallout. It was a chance meeting, really . . ."

"Fallout?"

"Right. I'd been working in New York as a marketing consultant for the Fruit Squares breakfast cereal campaign when our market analysts discovered that kids preferred loops to squares. A serious flaw, I'll admit, but not uncorrectable. Unfortunately, word of our engineering difficulties leaked to the press before we could make the necessary product adjustments. Most of the investors were gone within two weeks. The company held on for three. My job, as you can imagine, fell through somewhere in between. That was the fallout.

"Looking back, it couldn't have happened at a better time. I was burnt out from overwork, and ready to get away from it all. So I got myself a passport, bought a ticket to Europe, and went.''

"Just like that?'' He was astonished by my boldness.

"Well, I put my newspaper subscription on hold first.''

"So you met''—he searched for her name—"your girl-friend in Europe?''

"Lizzie,'' I reminded him. "Her name was, is, actually, Elizabeth. Lizzie's a shortened version of Elizabeth. Like a nickname. Her full name is Elizabeth Anne Bruback Simms.''

Jihad nodded. "Yes, Lizzie. Two months isn't a very long time. I guess I imagined that your relationship was much more developed.''

"My relationship with Lizzie? You could say it was developed for what it was. We were travel companions. We got along well, at least in the beginning. But if you're asking if we were 'deep'? I'd have to say the answer is no.

"The point is, I traveled with this woman twenty-four hours a day for two months. We shared everything. I mean *everything.* We were responsible for one another. Was it love? No, not in the sense that we planned to get married. But it was a love that grew from a mutual respect and need to work together. A respect that continues even now that she's missing.''

Jihad held up his hand. "Fine. But what I don't understand is, if this friendship was only *casual* . . .''

"Listen, Jihad,'' I interrupted. "Try to get this straight: I care about Lizzie. I care very much about what happens to her. That's why I tried to report the kidnapping to the police and why I went to the embassy. That's also why I've hired you . . .''

Jihad's eyes widened at my presumption. I realized that I hadn't yet taken him on officially.

". . . if forty dollars a day is all right.''

It was, I thought, a very generous offer, though Jihad didn't exactly jump at it. My original assumption was that his shocked expression resulted from the abrupt way I'd changed the subject. But once he spoke, I wasn't too sure. "Sorry," he said, "my usual rate is seventy-five . . ."

This, naturally, sat as uneasily with me as my original quote had sat with him. I told him that that seemed high and that my offer was firm at fifty. "About the only other concession I can make is to cover your expenses." I extended my right hand to show there were no hard feelings— that business was business.

He considered my offer. "I don't know . . ." he said. "I don't usually do this . . . but since you're a tourist—a guest in Egypt—I'll make an allowance in your case . . . I'll take sixty . . . with one week up front."

Though he presented it as a compromise, the effect of this latest proposal was to put significant strain on the unspoken bond I felt we'd formed following the vomit incident. My hand fell to my side.

"I'm worth it," he continued, sensing my doubt. "I'll find the girl."

It was a questionable claim, I told him, considering he came without references. We finally agreed on fifty-seven a day, two weeks paid in advance.

MORE ON LIZZIE

"Now, where were we?" I asked, anxious to continue now that my money was his.

"You met Lizzie in France."

"Right. We met in France and decided to travel together. We spent one week in Paris and another week bicycling through the Loire Valley."

"Wasn't that difficult?"

"For me, yes. I was more used to traveling on subways. But Lizzie had no trouble at all. The whole thing was her idea. We rented bikes in Paris, took the train to Versailles and made a circuit that included Chartres, Orléans, and Fontainebleau. We slept in a tent, cooked over a small gas stove and stopped in every village pâtisserie we could find."

"So it turned out all right."

"Pretty much so, although we did have our moments . . ."

Jihad prompted me for more.

"It's really a personal matter, Jihad."

He reflected a moment, then said: "I understand. And after the bicycle trip . . ."

"Things were not going so well at that point. I was tired of France. I didn't feel comfortable with the people. I wanted a change, so I suggested a safari in Kenya."

"Kenya? Why Kenya?"

"I liked the idea of going somewhere totally out of the way. I was getting into the freedom of travel. Lizzie'd introduced me to the wilds of nature with the bicycle trip, and I saw the Kenyan safari as a natural progression."

"Wasn't it expensive?"

"I didn't mind paying for her."

"What happened then?"

"Nothing. We toured. Saw some great wildlife. Hung out on the beach. We even took a side trip to Mount Kilimanjaro. All told I'd say we spent about four weeks in the region."

"And then . . ."

"Greece."

"How was that?"

"Fun. But once again, too many people. Not the Greeks, but the tourists. So we decided to go to Jordan."

"Jordan? Isn't that a somewhat unusual choice for a vacation spot?"

"More unusual than Kenya? Than France? Than England? Not for me. You're talking to a guy who used to think the world ended at the Jersey border. I thought everything outside New York was one big wasteland. Then I started traveling and discovered the world. It was like waking up after years in a deep sleep. It was . . ."

"So you decided to go to Jordan." Jihad cut me off here, for fear I was about to repeat the entire story of Rip Van Winkle.

"Huh? Uh, yes. Right. Greece was just too crowded. We even tried biking again, but it just wasn't right."

"Too many people on the roads?"

"Not only that, but between Lizzie and I. So I suggested we go to Jordan. To really get away from it all. Lizzie was against the idea. She was tired of roughing it. I'm sure she regretted that original bike trip in France. Besides, she said, Jordan had absolutely no appeal to her.

"But I insisted. 'For the relationship,' I said. I reminded her of how good things had been in the beginning. She finally agreed."

"How did you end up in Egypt?"

"Jordan was slower than anticipated. We started getting on each other's nerves. So after five days, Lizzie suggested that we go to Egypt. She'd heard about it and was curious. The Jordanian food had put me in a humble mood, so I agreed.

"We arrived here the day before yesterday and went to the Amman at Lizzie's suggestion. We stayed up late that night and went out the following morning—yesterday—after having slept through our wake-up call for an organized tour. That's when we bumped into Dr. Haddi—while we were wandering around on our own."

The story continued for another half hour, including another rendition of our experiences in the perfume shop. I stuck to the details and kept it short. The hour was nearing eleven and it was getting hot. Jihad listened without comment.

A BREAKTHROUGH

Then I saw him. He was about fifty yards away. I wasn't sure at first, as his face was obscured in the shadow of a camel. But when his eyes remained hidden in the shade of his forehead even after the camel had moved, I knew in that instant my luck had changed: Muhammad was back in my life.

The sparkle of the ring on his pinkie toe clinched it.

I had no idea what he was doing at the Pyramids. What's more, I didn't care. It was enough that we were both there together. My heart began pounding. I felt a mixed bag of emotions. Joy, fear, rage, anxiety, hate, you name it, the whole gamut. Joy was strongest, of course, but hate was right up there.

"Hey, Jihad," I whispered, "good news."

"Yes?" He asked innocently.

"Shhhhh!" I brought my arm around his shoulder. Our eyes faced the earth.

"Remember the henchman I described to you? The guy who brought the tea in the perfume shop? Muhammad?"

Jihad nodded.

"He's here. Nearby. I can see him now."

Jihad picked up his head to look around. I pushed it back down.

"Be cool," I hissed, "you'll tip him off. We have to be smart."

"Do you see Haddi anywhere?" he asked.

I kept my face parallel to the ground while my eyes scanned the horizon through the tops of my eyelids.

"Negative," I reported. "What do you want to do?"

"Capture him."

"Right here? In broad daylight?" Pretty gutsy, I thought.

"Absolutely. I won't be able to stand like this until dark."

A PLAN

Jihad came up with a plan. It was as brilliant as it was simple. We would charge Muhammad in unison, with Jihad on the right, myself on the left. The first one to reach him would hold on until the other arrived.

"Have you got a weapon?" he asked.

"Just this." I picked up a stone and shook it menacingly to show him that hate was overtaking joy as the dominant emotion.

"What about one of these?" He removed what looked like a compact ivory handle from his pocket. He held it out for me to inspect, before bringing his thumb down on a small button. A sharp blade shot out from the top.

I'd never before been handy with weapons and didn't think this an appropriate time to start playing. What would happen, I thought, if the thing accidentally opened in my pocket? I picked up another stone and shook it menacingly in my other hand.

"This is all I need," I sneered. "Let's do it!"

CAPTURE

We took off on the word "Go!"

Muhammad was standing alone about twenty-five yards from a camel that stood between him and us. Any of his prospects for help stood about five hundred yards behind us. I took Muhammad's isolation as a sign that he'd been searching for a spot to defecate. I hoped he'd found a good one. I really did. Because we intended to kick the shit out of him unless he told us what we wanted to know.

The animal screened our approach until we were within thirty-five yards of our prey. We knew he'd finally seen us when he opened his mouth as if to scream but couldn't make a sound. He just stood his ground with his mouth ajar as the two of us charged past the camel. Only then, when we were sure he'd seen us, did we start yelling. This, to instill within him the fear of Allah.

Fear proved a fine stimulant. It made him run fast. The distance between us grew. I sensed Jihad was tiring when he grabbed at his chest in pain. I attributed my own freedom from cramps to the bike trips. Lizzie'd been right when she told me I'd thank her one day for making me pedal uphill. I was now in shape to run down her kidnapper.

The problem was, Muhammad showed signs he'd done a few circuits of the Tour de France himself. The gap between us grew from ten yards (moments after we started yelling) to twenty-five (moments after I realized that yelling was sapping my energy) and was now a constant twenty. My breathing steadied as I adjusted my pace for the long haul. I looked behind and spotted Jihad walking about fifty yards back. His face was red and he was doubled over, gasping for air.

Muhammad and I headed into the desert. Ours was now a private battle to see who would fade first. I vowed it wouldn't be me, though I'd never been one to keep vows. Maybe it was enough that we'd spotted him. After all, now that we knew his general whereabouts, we could just lie in wait by the nearest watering hole or surprise him when he sought out shade. In fact, the alternatives to running were wide and probably a lot more comfortable. Still, I kept going.

I noticed that Muhammad was barefoot, and hoped that the heat or the rocks would slow him. Then I remembered the rocks in my hands. I realized they were probably slowing me and doubted I'd ever get a chance to use them at a closer range than this. Their time had come. I imagined myself an Olympic javelin thrower running down the track preparing to heave my spear. I let go and watched as the stone flew well over Muhammad's head. Too much, I thought, but at least I'm on the right line. I transferred the second stone to my left hand and let go again. This one caught my target in the ankle, causing him to stumble and fall.

I was on him moments later, panting for breath and pummeling him mercilessly. I hit him in the stomach when he guarded his face, and reversed my strategy when circumstances dictated. I hit and I hit and I hit and I hit, until Jihad appeared and forced me to stop.

ON VIOLENCE (A NOTE)

I'm not a violent man by design, just by nature. I spent many years hiding this fact from my peers and myself. But now I know it to be true.

Nonviolence is a funny thing. It goes a long way in theory. I can recall attending many demonstrations against the war, against the death penalty, against seal hunting, against violence against women. I stood against physical cruelty in all its forms. This I did for many years with no apparent effect.

Wars continued to be fought, the state continued to kill, seals continued to be slaughtered, and women continued to be violated. I can't even claim that I became a more sensitive or considerate person.

Having said that, I can now state, with a complete heart and clear conscience, that being violent is much more enjoyable than being nonviolent. Which is not to say that watching can't be pleasurable too. It can. But for sheer out-and-out fun, nothing delivers like pure, personally offered, unabated violence. This, at least, is what I learned during those moments of bliss when the flesh of my fist met the ever-softening cheek of that scoundrel, Muhammad. I know this sounds brutal, if not completely out of character from the mouth of a nice Jewish boy, but if the truth's to come out, then let this be the place.

I don't know why I attacked Muhammad as savagely as I did. It wasn't bravery. At least in any conscious sense. No, I didn't feel brave.

I could say I did it for Lizzie, or because that damn Amman business had started getting on my nerves. I could even say I did it because "a man's gotta do what a man's gotta do." I know I could use any of these explanations and be justified. I could, but I won't, because none of them really cuts to the heart of the matter.

It goes deeper. I think it has to do with stupidity.

FEEL NO EVIL

Whether through stupidity or not, Muhammad was mine!

All right, ours.

I dismounted the beast on Jihad's command. I was struck by the tone of his voice, which was now devoid of any of its previous music. I looked up to a face that was also transformed. Features that had been round were now angular. His expression was cold. The creases along his cheeks were filled with dirt.

"Turn him over," he commanded. "And bind his hands with this." He removed his belt.

I rolled Muhammad onto his face, brought his arms together behind him and secured them with Jihad's belt.

I stood up. "What do we do now?"

"We'll find out where they're keeping Lizzie."

Jihad called out a few phrases in Arabic. Even though I didn't understand a word he said, it was clear that "please" had not been among them.

Muhammad nodded vigorously, but said not a word.

"Come on you. Speak!" Jihad launched his foot into Muhammad's side. The prisoner coughed up some dirt but said nothing.

"This is going to be tougher than I thought." Then he switched to Arabic and said something like: *"Wen al mara!"*

Muhammad continued his silent ways.

"Must you be so rough with him?" I asked. A lot of the momentum from my earlier exercise had passed. Hitting a man you'd caught in a chase was one thing. Torturing him as he lay tied at your feet was quite another.

"I asked him where Haddi took your girlfriend. He's not talking, and I don't think he will until he's convinced we mean business."

I gave him an expression of doubt.

"You don't believe me? Listen, I understand this kind of man. He only responds to power. This is what we've got to do if you want to see your girlfriend again." He gave a kick that sent Muhammad's turban flying.

"He looks pretty beat up," I observed. Blood was dripping onto the sand from Muhammad's mouth.

"Don't give me your soft Western sensibilities. I'm only doing this for you!"

"For me? You're only doing this for me? Christ, that's just what my father used to say when he whipped me." I was dumbfounded.

"Listen, Mr. Gold, time is not on our side. Either we find your girlfriend soon, or she's going to find herself cleaning some desert prince's tent. That's a fact. Now hold this monster's legs while I cut off his balls."

"Excuse me?"

"You heard me! Now!"

He spoke and I obeyed. I never dreamt, even as I'd pounded away at Muhammad myself, that I'd ever participate in a deed as dirty as this. That's why I was so surprised to see my very own hands around the ankles of a man about to lose his manhood. Events were definitely out of control. Jihad was pulling all the strings now. I just wished he'd let go of mine.

A lot more tough talk was directed towards Muhammad, who maintained his silent story. He looked stunned. I doubted he could speak even if he wanted to. Jihad took out his ivory handle. It opened with the sound of metal speeding through air. The blade glistened under the sun. More talk, no answers. Jihad brought the knife to Muhammad's eyes. Muhammad shook his head. More talk.

"The only reason I'm giving him this chance," said my partner with his back to me, "is because of you."

I was about to thank him for the courtesy, when he continued. "Now we do it my way."

He came to where I was holding Muhammad's ankles, nicked the hem of the galabia and began slashing upwards. He hollered as he cut. Muhammad's face was a mask of silent terror. I was too frightened to do anything but tighten my grip.

Jihad arrived at Muhammad's undergarments and cut them off. He gave Muhammad one more chance before digging the knife down between his legs. I looked away and strengthened my grip in anticipation of some orgasmic-sized convulsion. But there was none. I let a few more moments pass before turning back to Jihad. He was looking down towards Muhammad's ass. He appeared confused.

"Something's wrong," he said. "Flip him over."

We worked together on this one because there was no way I could handle the task on my own. Muhammad was just too big.

I resumed my station by his ankles after we'd managed to roll him over. I noticed that his pinkie toe was bare now, absent of the ring, and that his arms were pinned beneath him and formed a kind of platform for his back and pelvis. Jihad couldn't have asked for a better table of operation. This time he slashed up the front of the galabia. Remnants of undergarments came away with a delicate tug. This was where I closed my eyes and held. Everyone was silent. I gripped tight in expectation of convulsions which never came. Sixty seconds passed before I found the courage to open my eyes and look to Jihad.

He was on his knees by Muhammad's midsection. His shoulders were slumped and his arms hung limply. His jaw hung too.

"What is it, Jihad? What is it?" I asked.

He didn't answer at first. He just maintained the same

dumb look. Then slowly, ever so slowly, the edges of his lips turned up and he began to chuckle. Then he shook his head and began to laugh.

"Come on, man. What is it?"

Jihad was really laughing hard now and shaking his head.

"For the love of Allah," he said. "For the love of Allah. We're late! Someone got here before us!"

WE'RE NOT IN KANSAS ANYMORE

"What do you mean 'Someone got here before us'? What kind of people live in this country anyway?" I clasped my hands unconsciously over my groin.

Jihad was having trouble regaining his composure. He wiped tears from his eyes. "Very good people, thank you." A hint of his former courtesy was back in his voice.

He returned his attention to Muhammad, who was struggling along the ground.

"Look at him," he said to me. "He muddied the ground." He pointed towards a spot where Muhammad had lost control of his bladder.

"It wouldn't surprise me if he'd laid fertilizer," I commented.

Jihad thought about this, then said: "He had no reason to. He had nothing to lose."

"You're saying he was lucky someone got to his jewels before you?"

"Just a minute here. Are you feeling sorry for this *thing*?" He gestured towards where Muhammad lay on a patch of dry dirt. "I don't understand you. First you catch him and beat him to the edge of consciousness, then you reproach me for prompting him for the information we're after."

"Prompting? You call castration prompting?" I shook my head. "No way, man. That's torture. Look, I want that information as much as you. I want Lizzie back unharmed.

That's why I caught him and beat him up. But I didn't intend to torture him.''

"You shouldn't have started a job you couldn't finish."

"Torture is immoral."

Jihad made a face like I'd said something vulgar. "Torture is immoral?" His expression turned to disbelief as he shook his head. "You've got a lot to learn, Mr. Gold, and you've got to learn it on your own. But if you're going to start making judgments about what is moral and what is not, then I suggest you examine your own backyard before judging mine.

"Each country, each place, has its own standards for morality and behavior. Let's talk about what you'll need to know to survive here. Start with a look about." He gestured around the area. "What do you see? Some stone pyramids? A few guys dressed like their ancestors. People riding camels to work? A eunuch? Think about it. We're assaulting a man within sight of the most popular tourist attraction in Egypt, and no one is coming out to see what we're up to. Doesn't that strike you as strange?"

I didn't answer.

"Go to the center of town," he continued, "and you'll see people jumping on and off of moving buses. Take a trip down south and you'll see whole villages without a single electric bulb. Visit a farm and you'll see irrigation techniques that haven't changed since the time of the pharaohs. How do you think these people deal with the moral issues of our time? The same as you?

"Do you know, Mr. Gold, that many Egyptian families give the father license to kill his daughter if she loses her virginity before she is married? That's right. Family honor is very important in Arabic culture. Restoring lost honor is justification for murder. In your country, a man who kills for honor is sent to jail. Not necessarily here.

"And if you want to talk of brutality . . ." He lay his foot into Muhammad's side. "Brutality is an Arab specialty. Which doesn't mean you Americans are far behind. You're just more random about it. Here, a person will attack you for a reason, not just because he's bored or because he got the idea from television."

He looked at me close to see if I was following. "Do you get my drift, Mr. Gold? You're not in Kansas any longer."

"I understood that Arabs were a culturally advanced people." I avoided, out of politeness, any reference to his cowardly attacks on America.

"You understood correctly. It was the Arab, you'll recall, who carried the torch of enlightenment through the Middle Ages. And it was the Arab who invented the modern numbering system, and developed some of the most fantastic architectural styles known to man. Finally, it was the Arab who brought the concept of hospitality to the level of art.

"Yes, what you've heard is true," he continued. "And that is the paradox. For at their best, none are greater than the Arab people. But at their worst, none are lower." He indicated Muhammad.

I was astonished. "How can you say such a thing about your own people?"

"How can I not? Let me fill you in on another great Arab talent: the talent for story telling. In this they are truly without peer. The problem is, their love of fiction seeps into their ability to read and understand reality. Arabs have a tendency to fool themselves. How else, I ask you, could they have misjudged their abilities so completely when they involved themselves in the 1967 war with Israel?

"No, Mr. Gold, I don't disparage my people out of hate. I do it from love and from frustration. I do it because I see what they are and what they can be.

"Now if you please, we can't go on neglecting our guest like this." Jihad took a few steps over to where Muhammad was quietly pushing himself.

"Look, he's so bored he's trying to leave. Come back here, you." He spoke in a gentle voice. "You simply can't leave until you tell us where Dr. Haddi has taken Miss Lizzie.'' He said it as if he were talking to a child. In fact, he was talking to me.

SPEAK NO EVIL

Jihad continued speaking in English, though it was clear Muhammad didn't understand.

''Now I've had a talk with Mr. Gold over here, and he tells me I'm acting harshly. He's from an advanced culture, you see. He's from the people who gave the world the atomic bomb, pornographic films, and fast food. Too bad you don't live there, Muhammad. If you lived there, you wouldn't have to say a word unless you wanted to.

''Not true here. Here, you must pay if you don't talk. Here, the price for silence is your tongue.''

Uh oh, I thought, here we go again.

''And consequently, since it's Mr. Gold's girlfriend we're after, why don't we let him do the honors?'' He turned to me and held out the knife.

''Thank you, Jihad, but I already told you torture's not my thing.''

''This is not torture, Mr. Gold, this is reality. Remember when I asked if you wanted to be involved in this matter, and you said 'yes'? Well, you've got your wish.'' He began moving towards me.

''You also said this would be a day of fun at the Pyramids.'' I began backing up. My hands were up and I shook my head no.

''I'm having fun.'' He actually smiled.

''I'm not.''

''Take it!'' The voice of command returned. He slapped the knife in my hand, grabbed my wrist, and brought me over to Muhammad. He started questioning Muhammad harshly. He probably explained what would happen if he didn't talk. Muhammad kept his mouth sealed. With good reason, I thought.

It happened with little warning really. He just said: "Get ready, Mr. Gold . . ." took my arm, straddled Muhammad's chest and collapsed. This knocked the wind out of Muhammad and brought me down to the ground.

"This is your chance," he told me. "Go for it!"

This was about as sticky a situation as I'd ever been in. My waiter had gone nuts and I was being ordered to cut out the tongue of a stranger. I considered my options. I could refuse to do his bidding, break free, and run. Or, I could refuse to do his bidding, stab him, and run. Or, I could refuse to do his bidding, stab myself, and die. Or, I could do his bidding, get it over with, and live.

I immediately discounted the first two because I felt too weak in the knees to run anywhere. Number three was out because I wasn't ready to die. Which left number four. What's the big deal if I cut out his tongue, I rationalized. Muhammad had never been a big talker.

"I'm ready," I said without enthusiasm.

"That's my boy," said Jihad like a proud father. "Now force his mouth open and cut away."

I did as I was told. I crawled through the dirt to the place where his head rested, then brought my thumb and index fingers against both sides of his mouth and pushed.

"Please open wide," I said, figuring if it worked for my dentist, why not for me?

He did as instructed and revealed before me the wonders of his mouth.

I'd seen better. Most of his teeth were missing. Those that were there were brown from years of neglect. He had lots of sores between his lower lip and his gums.

I was about to raise the knife when I noticed that his eyes were on me. This made me feel very uncomfortable, so I covered his eyes with my other hand. I rationalized my action by saying that he shouldn't see what I was about to do. My new physical position had its limits, though, because it didn't leave me a hand for my knife. I solved the matter by picking up some dirt and throwing it in his eyes. Then I picked up the knife, positioned it above the open orifice and began searching for my target.

It was very hard to find. I recalled all the biology I'd ever learned in the hope that it would help me track down Muhammad's tongue. I even laid the knife aside and stuck my finger down his throat to see if he'd swallowed it. I found that he hadn't. It was a puzzling situation. His tongue was definitely missing. I thought about it a good while. I consulted with Jihad. Then it struck me. Muhammad's tongue had gone the way of his testicles.

I felt grateful. I'd been spared.

6

Muhammad Speaks

MUHAMMAD'S JOB

I picked myself up off the ground and gave the knife back to Jihad. Muhammad lay unconscious about two feet to my right, a victim of the heat, Jihad, and myself. He looked bad.

"Pretty messy," I said. "What do you make of him?"

"That's just what I'm trying to figure out."

I dusted myself off while Jihad thought. I knew he'd reached some kind of conclusion when I saw his eyes flash and heard him say: "I think I've got it. And it's so simple."

"Nu?"

"So simple." He was smiling now. "It just confirms my earlier assumption. Muhammad works with the harem. He's a professional eunuch!"

I saw what he meant. "So he won't spoil the merchandise, right?" Though I wondered how the professional distinguished himself from the amateur in this field.

"That's right."

"And they removed his tongue for the same reason?"

"What?"

"You know, so he wouldn't kiss the women?"

Jihad thought this over. "I think castration took care of

any drive he might have had towards the opposite sex. No, it's something else. Someone, probably Haddi, didn't want our friend here"—Jihad kicked Muhammad's leg—"talking to anyone about the things he's seen around the harem."

This struck me as particularly low. "That's disgusting," I said. "Really disgusting. Even if I can understand why he'd cut out the guy's crotch, I can see no justification for removing his tongue as a preventative measure. That's just plain barbarism." I spit on the ground.

"I know what you mean. Almost as bad as slicing off a man's tongue for refusing to talk."

A COURSE OF ACTION

I sought to deflate this undignified reference with a suggestion that we take a few moments to reevaluate the situation.

Jihad agreed that it would be a good exercise.

We came up with two major conclusions. First, that Muhammad was ours, at least what was left of him. And second, that Muhammad was invulnerable to torture, considering what was left of him. We both agreed that having a prisoner was a good thing. Jihad said it gave us credibility. I didn't understand this, but figured he knew what he was talking about.

We split on the issue of Muhammad's invulnerability. I said this was good. Jihad looked sad. I didn't press for an explanation.

Our minor conclusion was that Jihad's harem theory was correct. We were also convinced that Muhammad knew where the harem was quartered. The question was how to get him to talk. So to speak.

I tried lifting Jihad's spirits by reminding him that the affair seemed to be moving forward in a nontrivial manner. Muhammad's capture was proof of that. Jihad remained unmoved.

"We'll never get anything out of him," he whined. "We might as well leave him here to die under the hot desert sun."

All this talk of torture and killing was beginning to plant some doubts in me about my partner. He had a volatile nature and a proven ability to hold me under the sway of bad influences. I felt this made me liable to commit acts for which I was both physically and emotionally unfit.

I also considered what I thought to be Jihad's major asset: his knowledge of Egypt and detective work. This exclusive information could not be found elsewhere. So he said.

"You're putting too much faith in torture," I said, in an effort to open his mind to alternative paths. "There are other ways to get information. Besides," I reasoned, "killing him won't bring us any closer to Lizzie."

Jihad seemed to consider my words. I took this opportunity to propose a course of action. I told him to put the murder issue aside for a few hours. "Let's continue questioning him," I suggested. "It's a no-lose proposition. Succeed, and you find Lizzie. Fail, and you get to kill Muhammad. Who knows? With luck, you'll do both." I added this last item as a sweetener.

The idea appealed to Jihad as I thought it would.

"All right," I said as I continued on my roll. "Let's concentrate on getting Muhammad away from the Pyramids. We need a more suitable location for questioning. Do you know a place?"

Jihad said he did and that we could get there if we carried Muhammad on the back of a camel. We tracked down the one we'd sprinted by earlier, and brought him over. "This must be Muhammad's camel," Jihad hypothesized. "He and the beast share the same nose."

I noted the resemblance as I took Muhammad by the shoulders and helped swing him over the animal's hump.

IN THE SHED

We arrived without incident at a windowless old shed on a vacant lot. It was nearly five P.M. We hitched the camel to a large stone and approached the structure. Jihad gained entrance by breaking a small lock that secured the door. The inside was furnished with a rickety table surrounded by four termite-ridden chairs.

Jihad picked up a box of candles he found on the floor, removed a candle and lit it. He dripped enough wax onto the table to create a small pool, then stuck the candle in the hardening wax.

"I wonder why they lock it," I asked as I surveyed the barren room.

"So it won't be stolen." Jihad answered as if "it" were obvious.

"So what won't be stolen?"

"The lock, of course."

I didn't know if he was kidding or not. I gave him a "come on" kind of look, but he didn't bite. I tried another approach.

"What kind of place is this? It's not what I had in mind when I asked you to bring me to another setting for questioning."

"I'm sorry. It's the best I can do under the circumstances." His voice was hard. I doubted he was really sorry. "This is a workers' hut," he continued. "Men who work in the lot take their breaks in this shed. It gives them shade in the summer and protects them from rain in the winter."

I surveyed the lot from the perspective of the door. The place was barren except for a few bottles littered about. "What kind of work do they do here?" I hoped they weren't in the lock business.

"I think they watch the lot. Their job is to make sure nothing happens to it."

"But why?"

"For money. Why else?"

"What I meant was, it doesn't look like anything ever happens in this lot. Why do they watch it?"

"Of course nothing happens. They're doing a great job."

I looked at him long and hard. Then I said: "Let's eat dinner."

DINNER

Jihad reached into a small sack and took out some fresh pita bread and a can of hummus we'd bought along the way. He opened the can with his knife, spread some hummus onto the bread and gave me half.

"Bon appétit!" he said.

It was the first thing I'd eaten since breakfast. I finished it fast, then helped myself to a second sandwich.

"Where's the drink?" I asked as I chewed.

"Right here." Jihad unscrewed the top of a one-liter bottle of Pepsi and handed it to me.

I gulped some down and handed it back to him. I looked out the door to check on Muhammad. He was still slung over the camel. "Don't forget to save some food for Muhammad," I said.

"You're not going to feed him, are you?" Jihad's voice was flat with undertones of hostility.

"We agreed to do it my way," I began, hoping not to upset him further. "Muhammad needs food. We can't work with him if he doesn't have strength."

Jihad took a swig of soda. "Soft," he said. "You're too soft with him." Then he wiped the bottle neck and handed it back to me. A smudge of dirt was visible where he'd wiped.

I drank anyway, to prove I wasn't soft.

POOR MUHAMMAD

There was a stirring outside. Muhammad was waking up.

"Let's bring him down," I said.

We brought him in and sat him on the chair by the side of the table farthest from the door. He was groggy and completely passive. Jihad insisted on securing him to the chair. I offered no objections, though I noted that with his size, Muhammad could probably shatter his bonds without much effort.

"No matter," said Jihad. "Just belt his legs to the chair."

I did as he said then offered Muhammad a piece of pita with hummus. He bit in hungrily, and chewed long and hard with his back teeth before he could swallow. It was apparent that eating without a tongue was quite an effort. I passed him the soda which he drank with relish. I think it helped him swallow too.

He ate like that for about twenty minutes. I sat with him at the table while Jihad stood by the door with his knife at the ready. It was my first chance for a sustained look at Muhammad.

The first thing I noticed was his forehead, which was indeed large, though not as big as it appeared when his turban was in place. I also got my first good look at the hair on his head, which was jet black and thickly curled. It offered a nice contrast to the hair of his beard, which was about two days old and caked with dirt and dried blood. Some of the blood had come from his mouth and some had come from his nose. The nose, by the way, was wide and flat, though it seemed to me it had once been narrow and tall. His eyes were visible through narrow slits of swollen eyelid that bore a striking resemblance to his thick and severely chapped lips. It happened more than once that liquids which didn't make it directly into his mouth, passed to the outside world through the deep cracks in his lips.

I wanted to laugh, but I felt like crying.

This was Muhammad. Big, ugly Muhammad. The personification of the blues. A guy that only a mother could love, provided he didn't live at home or ask for money. A person who wouldn't get two sniffs from a scroungy dog.

FRIENDS?

I realized we needed a special strategy for questioning this man.

One that would tell us what we wanted to know without inflicting any more damage on our source or ourselves. Something hate-free and humane, with a touch of understanding. Something built on trust. Something like friendship. I gave it some additional thought and concluded that the friendly approach was not without strategic justification.

Especially in light of the alternative. I was convinced that coercion was a dead strategy. Muhammad's immunity proved that torture and the threat thereof were tactically unsound. He could take the pain. And even if he couldn't, there were some very real physical limitations which prevented him from running on at the mouth.

I examined the moral implications of befriending Muhammad. He was, after all, the man who'd kidnapped Lizzie. The same one whose tongue I'd tried to remove, and a fellow without balls. I figured there had to be something immoral about cozying up to this kind of man, though I couldn't think of what it was.

I even considered his interrogators' lurid pasts. I had to admit that my behavior with the knife, did not, in retrospect, fill me with pride even if it had been for Lizzie's good cause. I was reluctant to see a repeat of this approach by myself or Jihad.

Having thought of all these things, I decided to listen to the word of my heart as I heard it in that old shed. I heard the word and it was friendship. Guilt and pity were part of the equation, but friendship was definitely the word. I grew more enthusiastic. Friendship would bring the answers, I said to myself. Muhammad would tell me what we wanted to know after I made him my friend. He'd do what we wanted, I was sure. Okay . . . confident. Okay . . . hopefully optimistic. I was hopefully optimistic he'd tell me what we wanted to know. I really hoped it too. Because if he didn't, I'd have to let Jihad kill him.

I shot a glance over to Jihad, who was cleaning his nails with the knife. You'll see, I thought, you'll see.

IDEAS

Maybe.

There remained the question of how to make friends with a mute Egyptian peasant. It was a very big question for which I had no ready answer.

This in itself surprised me because I usually overflow with ideas about everything. That's what I used to produce. That's what people paid me for. I was best at fads. It was a specialty. Remember when all the kids were riding around with multicolored bicycle tires? That was mine.

I had people pay me for advice on fashion, interior design, auto mechanics, high tech, the Internet, astronomy, astrology, psychiatry, and neurology. I even sold ideas about film, television, theater, literature, advertising, jogging, swimming, aerobics, baseball, health, dieting, local politics, world affairs, race relations, acid rain, sex, drugs, rock and roll, travel, flying, boating, snowboarding, driving, and cooking.

To name a few.

If I had a shortcoming, and I know that I did, it was probably this: that my ability to translate an idea to an activity was a little weak.

I think it's understandable. Not everyone can realize an idea, just like not everyone can come up with one. Anyhow, that was my weakness.

That's also why I was so concerned over how to go about translating the friendship idea into action. I was all theory and no experience. I had almost no idea how to go about making Muhammad my friend.

A FRIENDLY CHAT

One possibility was to do Muhammad a friendly deed. Something endearing. Something to make him want to do a friendly deed for me. Like fill me in on Lizzie's whereabouts, for example. That was the general idea.

I realized that the friendliest thing I could do for him would be to restore his manhood and get him a woman. That would be very friendly.

Replacing his tongue would also be a step in the right direction.

As would introducing him to the secret of time travel.

I also considered options within the realm of the possible. Among these were the temptations of good food. What man, after all, is ill-content after a free meal? Not a one. The food idea seemed like a good one. I decided to run with it. I looked at the empty can of hummus and the half-eaten pita on the table.

"Ask him if he's had enough to eat," I said.

"Your will is my way," replied a sarcastic Jihad before relaying my question from his perch in the door frame.

I was somewhat disappointed with the way he did my will. He spoke without sensitivity.

Surprisingly however, Muhammad responded by lowering and raising his head.

"Good." I stood up, gave Muhammad a smile and patted him on the back. "Now ask him where they've taken Lizzie. Ask nicely," I added. "Ask as a friend."

Jihad asked this too, though in the manner of an acquaintance.

Muhammad shook his head from side to side.

It struck me that he couldn't tell us if he wanted to. That finding a way for Muhammad to communicate would have to be our first priority. So I looked around until I spotted the cardboard box where the candles were stored. I picked it up, emptied it out, and unfolded it by the seams so it could lie like a piece of paper in front of Muhammad.

I asked Jihad if he had a pen. He said he did, but didn't see the point in giving it to an illiterate. I took the pen from his hand and gave it to Muhammad.

"Ask him again," I said, as I gave Muhammad a friendly look.

Muhammad sat stone faced for this and the next twenty-five questions. The situation did not look promising. Neither of my Egyptians were cooperating. I plunged my hands into my pockets and began pacing. I needed a new approach.

Then it came.

Something that often worked for me in New York. The kind of favor that made me many friends.

MUHAMMAD SPEAKS

"Ask him if he wants a bribe. Offer him *bakshish*."

Jihad said he was tired of humoring me. I told him he could take a nap after making the offer. My intermediary addressed Muhammad. He accompanied his words with the local sign for the greasing of the palm: the rubbing of the thumb against the middle and index fingers.

Muhammad didn't react.

Maybe the intonation of his fingers is wrong, I thought.

I decided to make the offer personally with a nonambiguous international sign. I took out my wallet, removed a one-hundred-dollar bill and placed it on the table.

"Ask him again."

Jihad didn't hear me. He was too busy admiring Benjamin Franklin's ascot.

"Jihad! Ask him again."

He didn't have the chance. Muhammad grabbed the bill and crumpled it into his pocket. Then he picked up the pen like a person picks up a stick, and began drawing on the cardboard. He began with a crude, downward pointing triangle. To its left he drew a box. These two objects touched at the triangle's upper left and the box's upper right corner.

He continued this burst of artistic inspiration by drawing a "Y" within the box. It began about one quarter of the way in from the right border, and stretched from the box's base to its top.

Next, he pointed to Jihad, myself, and himself before making a dot close to where the "Y" split. He looked up at us to see if we understood. We didn't. He shook his head and did it again. This time Jihad understood.

"It's a map," he announced. "A map of Egypt. The box is the mainland, the 'Y' is the Nile, and the triangle is the Sinai Desert. He's trying to say that we three are in the dot. The dot is Cairo."

"Ask him if that's what he means."

Jihad spoke and Muhammad nodded.

"Now ask him where they've taken Lizzie."

Jihad made another dot near the bottom of the triangle.

"They're keeping her somewhere in southern Sinai."

"Where exactly in Sinai?"

Jihad relayed my question.

Muhammad brought his index finger to his lips. It was a secret.

"He doesn't know or won't tell us?" I asked.

Jihad passed my query along.

Muhammad shook his head before bringing his right hand up to his brow like in a salute. He began looking around as if he was searching for something. Then he pointed to himself and nodded his head.

"It seems like he knows where they are," I said. "Ask him if he'll guide us there."

"You mean *tell him* to guide us there." Jihad corrected.

"No. I'm still paying for this party. Ask him."

Muhammad listened attentively as the request was translated. His response came immediately. He took up the pen and drew a dim replica of a dollar sign followed by the number 100. He followed this with a smile. Some of the scabs on his lips cracked and bled.

"Let's kill him now," said Jihad.

"Tell him we'll pay him when we arrive. Not before."

This brought a rise in Jihad's left eyebrow. It wasn't just that I'd acquiesced to Muhammad's terms, I was sure, but that I'd given him a better rate.

"It's a fixed rate," I explained. "You've got a long-term contract."

"There's no need to explain," said Jihad just before transmitting my agreement to Muhammad. "It's your money."

Muhammad sealed the deal with a nod.

Jihad turned to me and said: "You overpaid, you know. He would have taken us there for fifty."

SECRETS

"What's a hundred dollars between friends?" I asked rhetorically. "Besides, now we know where they're holding Lizzie, and we have a guide to get us there." I was feeling pretty proud of myself.

"*We* have a guide?" He emphasized *we* as if it didn't include me.

I answered without addressing his undertones. "That's right, he's sitting right here." I motioned to Muhammad, who bowed his head in acknowledgment.

"You don't intend to make the trip down to Sinai, do you?" Now it was in the open. He wanted me out of the picture.

"*I* wouldn't have hired him if *I* didn't intend to go." This was my message to him: I draw the pictures.

"It will be a dangerous trip."

"Especially for Muhammad if he goes alone with you."

"Let's be *realistic,* Mr. Gold. You're in no shape for wandering through the desert."

"No shape? How do you think I caught Muhammad? Besides, I come from a people with forty years of experience in that wilderness."

"Much has changed in the last three thousand years."

"That's right, and I feel nostalgic for the old neighborhood."

"What do you want, Mr. Gold?" His eyes were hard.

"What do you mean, what do I want? I want Lizzie. Isn't that clear from the way I've been throwing money around? And by the way, if you think I've been dishing out all this loot just so you and Muhammad can wander off on your own, you're nuts. Because I may be stupid, but I'm not dumb. So just think of it this way: We're a team and I'm the owner. Get it?"

I paused here to study the effect of my words. Jihad still looked arrogant. Muhammad, a little worried. I decided to conclude with an offensive parry: "The real question is—what do you want, Jihad? Why don't you want me around?"

Jihad weighed my ability to handle his new information. Then he spoke. "I want to solve this case, Mr. Gold. I want to find this Haddi and your girlfriend too. Do you know what that means?"

I imagined the worst. "Could it mean that Muhammad and I might get hurt?"

Jihad answered with a grim expression.

"You can be a pretty scary guy, Jihad . . ."

He nodded.

"Is that really it? You don't want me around because you don't want to see any blood, possibly mine, shed? Hmmm. I can appreciate that. Thanks for the warning." Then I let my voice go deep. "But I can take care of myself."

I waited for a reaction and continued when none came. "But maybe that's not everything. Maybe you have your own secret agenda that you don't want me knowing about. Is that it?" It was a stab in the dark, but when Jihad flinched ever so slightly, it occurred to me that I might be onto something. Just what, I wasn't sure, and frankly, wasn't interested in finding out, given that I was paying him to solve my problems and not the other way around. So I let it go. I told him he didn't have to "share" if he didn't want to. The important thing was "that you still need me as much as I need you."

Jihad made a face.

"That's right, you need me, so don't make faces. You need me because you need Muhammad. Muhammad is mine because, one, I caught him, two, I bought him, and three, he likes me more than he likes you. This I know because he told me so." I smiled to Muhammad, who, amazingly, smiled back.

"I'm only considering taking you along on our trip to Sinai because I'm still waiting for a return on my investment in you. That's all. Because truth be told, I haven't been terrifically impressed with the investigative skills you've displayed so far.

"So here's my proposition. Help me find Lizzie in Sinai. Do that and you'll have fulfilled your obligation to me. I'll pay you the balance of whatever you're owed and you can proceed with whatever secret agenda you might have. Sound fair?"

Jihad took his time thinking it over. He definitely didn't like me calling the shots. But he definitely had no choice.

"I accept your proposition, Mr. Gold," he said without cheer. "Though I can't say I admire your foolishness. Do you mind if I ask why you'd endanger your life for a *woman* when you could leave the job to a professional?"

I answered the remark with my own version of the death stare. Then I said: "You're not the only one carrying a secret here, Jihad."

LYING AND CHEATING

Over fifty million people live in Egypt. Many occupy themselves with politics and business. I figure this says two things. First, that many people earn their daily bread through lying and cheating. And second, that most of them

SEE NO EVIL   79

have secrets. This was what I meant when I said "you're not the only one carrying a secret *here*."

Because the truth was I didn't think twice about going down to Sinai. Lizzie was there and she needed to be saved. The day's successes had built up my confidence to the point where I felt immune to any threat of potential danger. It was like being high on cocaine without the runny nose.

Yes, I lied to Jihad when I told him he wasn't the only one with a secret. I did it to get him off my back. Besides, he wouldn't have understood if I told him how I felt. That wasn't his style. So I implied I had a secret. That was the kind of talk Jihad understood.

What I didn't know was that my lie had not been far from the truth. There actually was a secret. I'd learn about it later. It belonged to Lizzie.

I'd also learn that coke heads come down hard.

7

Going Up South

PLANNING THE TRIP TO SINAI

We planned the trip to Sinai right there in the shed. Jihad figured that Haddi was watching all the conventional routes to southern Sinai. This meant that a gentle car ride across the Suez Canal and down the Sinai coastal road was out, and that an overnight train to Luxor, followed by a bus to the coast, followed by a ferry across the Red Sea, followed by a jeep to our destination, was in.

That was the plan. It would preserve the element of surprise. A train was leaving for Luxor that evening. We hadn't a moment to lose.

PREFERRED SCENTS

We arrived at the station some twenty minutes after the train was to have left. Boarding took place one hour later.

Our compartment was furnished by a cushioned seat running down the side perpendicular to the door. The wall across from the seat held a small mirror. The fourth wall, the one opposite the door, had a window. Jihad and I sat on the seat while Muhammad squatted on the floor.

It was only after we'd shut the door behind us and settled back for the evening's journey that Muhammad's strange odor really made itself felt. It was not, I might add, a pretty scent. I considered what I might do to offset Muhammad's effect on the rapidly deteriorating environment. I recalled the perfume essence I'd taken from the Red Room.

My hand came over my nose as I stood to open my pack and remove one of the bottles. I sprinkled some essence into my hand with a single shake. The accompanying alcohol was missing of course, but I didn't care. I patted my cheeks, inhaled deeply and smiled. I extended the bottle to Muhammad and motioned for him to follow my example. What he did instead, was take the container from my hands, hold it out at arm's length and shape his mouth into a cry of anguish before rushing from the compartment.

He returned moments later empty-handed.

I commended myself for having saved two more bottles.

Jihad got up from his seat with the words: "You two smell like camel's breath," and excused himself from the compartment. He said he'd be in the snack car if I needed him.

THE NOTEBOOK

That left Muhammad and me alone together, each in his own carefully defined space and scent. Muhammad began rolling a cigarette. I took out a small notebook I'd found on the station platform.

"Don't pick that notebook up," Jihad had said. "You don't know how long it's been lying there."

I peeled the gum off its cover. "It looks okay to me," I said. "The last five pages are still unused."

TAKING NOTES

The notebook's previous owner had been a scrupulous note taker. Each new date was inked in red, while the text of his Arabic penmanship was in smooth, unedited blue. I ripped these pages out and put them in the trash. Then I uncapped the pen Jihad lent me earlier and began to write. I called my first note: "On Violence."

My second note was less philosophical. It covered all our activities between the shed and the train. I kept it short and to the point as I had only four pages left.

CLEAN UP (A NOTE)

We decided to clean up back at the hotel before heading off to the station. Jihad flagged a cab. Muhammad paid.

Jihad showered first and emerged sixty minutes later looking as neat and clean as he had this morning when he first served me coffee in the hotel dining room. Muhammad went next, though insisted—via mime—on a bubble bath. Jihad gave his okay on the condition that I bathe Muhammad. He said this would move things along. I liked the idea too. I figured it would boost our budding friendship.

"Come on, pal," I said as I sprinkled some bubble mix into the water.

Muhammad cooperated in full. I had him out and dry in forty-five minutes—a pretty good time considering how messy he'd gotten during our "encounter" by the Pyramids.

Though Jihad was in a mellow mood (a quality I attribute to the strange atmosphere of the Amman Hotel), I showered as fast as I could to prevent the development of any unpleasant incidents between my partners. I learned that my worries were unwarranted, however, when I entered the bedroom to find Jihad and Muhammad engaged in a game of backgammon. Muhammad had just thrown double sixes and was clearing his pieces from the board. Jihad took the defeat philosophically.

"It's in their blood," he said.

I wondered who they were.

I commented that Muhammad's shredded galabia was inappropriate for a long train ride. Jihad agreed (due, I figure, to my good influence, not that of his heart) and decided to take Muhammad shopping in a clothing shop off the lobby while I settled matters with the front desk.

I'd just finished checking Lizzie's luggage and paying the bill when they returned. Muhammad was wearing a white galabia with gray trim and a matching turban. His feet were outfitted in black rubber slippers. It was, Jihad assured me, the very latest in bedouin fashion.

Not to be outdone, Jihad had his shoes polished and treated himself to a new shirt and slacks. He looks quite dapper.

AT THE STATION (A NOTE)

There was a brief moment of fright when Muhammad got lost on the way to the ticket window. Jihad went off to track him down and returned fifteen minutes later with his man by the collar. He'd found him, he said, in a garbage Dumpster. It was obvious. Muhammad really stinks now. So much for the bubble bath.

SECURITY (A NOTE)

Jihad decided to share his concerns about Muhammad with me just after I picked up this neat new notebook. Muhammad was occupied rolling a cigarette at the time.

I was cautioned to remain alert. Muhammad's innocent attitude, Jihad warned, could be a very sophisticated cover. He reminded me that Muhammad used to and might still be working for Haddi.

"You mean he could be a double agent?" I looked to the subject, who was at that moment using his upper lip to wet the glue on his rolling paper.

"Anything is possible."

I'm wondering now if this could be so. I have to assume, if Muhammad's behavior is to be believed, that his loyalty to me springs from his roots as an insecure, downtrodden, simple peasant, who seeks to ally himself with the current boss, whoever he is. Before he was with Haddi. Now he is

*with me. I give him food. I provide shelter. I supply his
wardrobe. For now.*

*Neither possibility: Muhammad as opportunist, nor
Muhammad as agent, fills me with confidence, as they leave
his loyalty open to question.*

*I'm going to do what Jihad said. I'm going to keep an eye
on Muhammad.*

GOING UP SOUTH

Jihad took over the Muhammad-watch about twenty minutes after I closed the notebook. He said the snack car was
filling up with American tourists and suggested I check it
out. It might be relaxing, he said, "from a cultural point of
view."

The place was festive. Frank Sinatra tunes blared from a
portable tapedeck. Beer and wine flowed freely at the
"standing room only" bar.

"Excuse me, sonny, would you be a doll and pass me the
nuts?" It was an older woman's voice trying to make itself
heard above all the racket.

"No problem," I said, and slid the nuts down to an
overly rouged grandmother with salt and pepper hair pulled
back into a bun. Her name tag read: "Sophie Binsberg,
Brooklyn, New York."

"Thanks, dalink. You're a sweety."

"Don't mention it," I said, and turned back to the action.

"So you're going to Upper Egypt too?"

I turned to face her again. "What's that?" I asked. "No,
I'm heading south."

"I know that, honey, that's what I said."

I took a closer look at her face. It was vaguely familiar.

"You asked," I informed her, "if I was going to upper
Egypt. I said: No, I am not going to upper Egypt. I am
going south along with the rest of this train."

She took my forearm in her vein-mapped hand and shook
her head. "That's the same thing, you silly boy. Upper

Egypt is southern Egypt, and Lower Egypt is northern Egypt. It's the *same* thing.''

This didn't make a grain of sense to me, and I told her so.

"Let me start again." She looked towards the ceiling as if she were trying to remember what she'd learned. "Egypt is actually two separate regions, Upper and Lower. Upper Egypt begins in Aswan in the south and continues to Giza in the north. You know, with the Pyramids in Cairo?"

I nodded.

"Lower Egypt, on the other hand, goes from Giza to the Mediterranean Sea where the Nile fans out like a V. Are you following me?"

I thought so.

"So what's actually the north is called Lower Egypt, and what's actually the south is called Upper Egypt."

"I think I'm starting to understand this country."

"I learned it from our guide, Salim. He also said that the Nile was important to the ancient Egyptians because it was the main north–south highway. The people moved north from Aswan by drifting with the river, and came back by sailing against the current. This they could do because the wind from the north was very strong."

"You mean the Nile flows from south to north?"

"Sure. Isn't that what the guide told us, Herman?" She addressed the short balding man to her right. He was eating some pretzels and watching one of the younger women in the car. I had the feeling I'd seen him before too.

"Sure," he agreed absently in what was clearly a trained response.

"Who would have thought?" she continued. "These Egyptians, they do everything backwards. Imagine, without the Jews, the Pyramids would have come out square." She started laughing and poked her husband. "Isn't that right, Herman?"

"Absolutely," he said, and joined in the laughter.

"You know something?" said the old man once he'd

regained his composure. "You could do to put on some weight. Here, have a pretzel." He pulled one from his jacket pocket and handed it to me.

"What's the matter, your wife doesn't feed you?" Now it was the old lady's turn.

"I'm not married."

"That explains it. Doesn't that explain it, Herman?"

"It sure does." He patted his stomach and gave me a wink.

"So where are you going anyway?" the grandmother asked.

"To Sinai."

"Sinai?" She didn't seem to have heard of it. "Herman, do you know Sinai? Is it near Aswan, Sinai?"

"The Sinai is a peninsula," I informed her. "It's a desert."

"Sure," Herman jumped in. "From the Bible. The Jews got the Ten Commandments in Sinai."

"That's right."

"And the Israelis won it in the late 1960s," he added.

"I think so."

"I'm a great Zionist." He was proud of his knowledge.

"I can see that."

"Young man." Sophie began pulling at my arm to get my attention. "Young man. I'm not sure you're on the right line. I'm not at all sure this train stops in Sinai." She was worried for me.

"You're right, it doesn't," I told her. "The Sinai Desert lies across the Red Sea. I'm going to take a boat."

"A boat! How romantic. Remember when we took a boat to Cuba, Herman?"

"How could I forget." He put his arm around her. "For our honeymoon. Almost fifty years ago. We sailed into Havana. A great city then. Alive with excitement. We had a terrific time. This was all before the communists, of course."

"You were a dalink then, and you're a dalink now." She gave him a loud smacking kiss on the cheek.

"You see, son. It pays to have a wife."

"Maybe we can fix you up with someone." Sophie was thinking again. "We have a few widows in the group . . ."

"Leave him alone. What does he need with old ladies, Sophele?"

"I'm just trying to help."

"I'll bet he has a girl, anyway. Right?"

"That's right. I'm on my way to see her now."

"She's in Sinai? Nice girls live in the desert? Is she an Arab girl?" The old woman seemed shocked.

Herman's attention, meanwhile, had drifted to the far corner of the car, where a group of people were gathered around a table. He left to join them.

"She's British," I answered.

"That's nice." She seemed relieved. "Is she staying in a hotel? I didn't know they had hotels in the desert."

"I'm not exactly sure where she's staying."

"You're not sure?" she looked confused. "Do you have a phone number?"

"No."

"You don't seem very well prepared to me. How do you expect to reach her?"

"I have a guide."

"Oh." She wasn't sure what to make of this. "That's good . . ."

"Look at this, Sophele. . . ." Herman was back from his trip to the table with some balloon skins in his hand. "The group leader gave these out." He took a red balloon and began blowing.

"Stop that, Herman." Sophie grabbed the balloon from her husband's mouth. "A heart attack, you want to get? And here in Egypt? I don't think there's one doctor in the

whole country. Here, let this nice young man blow it up."
She handed me the balloon.

I put it to my mouth and began blowing. It inflated without much difficulty. I could see some black writing growing on the far side.

"Look at him," Sophie said admiringly. "Such strong lungs."

The balloon inflated to almost twice the size of my own head. I was about to knot it when I turned it around to see the message on the second side. It read: "Amman Tours."

The balloon shot out of my hands and sailed up and out of control.

"What a shame," said Herman. "You really had it big. Try this one." He held out another balloon. A green one.

I wasn't there to take it.

"What's wrong?" called Sophie as I ran to the door.

Then I heard Herman observe: "He didn't even say good-bye."

COINCIDENCE?

I slid open the compartment door and found the light off. Muhammad and Jihad were squatting on the floor, asleep.

"Jihad!" I whispered with urgency. "Jihad! Get up!" I shook him by the shoulder.

"Huh? What is it?"

"Jihad! Remember the old lady and old man we saw at the Pyramids? You remember? She was riding that camel gone berserk, and he was chasing them. Remember? Some merchants helped bring the animal under control? Remember that, Jihad? Remember?"

He looked at me blankly. He was disoriented. He didn't remember.

I kept trying. "And remember, how their tour bus was labeled 'Amman'? *Amman,*" I repeated with emphasis. "You know, like the hotel I stayed in, and like the cab that took us to the Pyramids. You know?'' I felt my eyeballs extending from their sockets. I was nodding my head rapidly and breathing almost as fast.

"Turn on the light and get to the point." He was standing now. I finally had his attention.

"The point is . . . The point is I just met them again, this old lady and her husband in the snack car. They're with an American group called Amman Tours.'' I paused to let this news sink in.

It didn't.

"Doesn't that seem strange to you?'' I helped out. "Isn't it just a little too coincidental?"

He thought it over and came to the conclusion that it wasn't.

"What do you mean: No? It's downright weird, if you ask me. And suspicious too."

"How do you mean?"

"First of all, that hotel. The Amman Hotel. Did you notice how everything seemed too nice in that hotel? Kind of pleasant for no good reason? Like when Lizzie and I checked in. There'd been this undercurrent of tension between us for nearly a week, since before we arrived in Egypt. Before even Jordan . . .'' I had a revelation. "Christ, we'd been staying in *Amman,* Jordan!''

"Calm down, Mr. Gold. Here, have a seat.'' Jihad sat me down and brought his arm around my shoulder. Muhammad was awake now too. He took out his tobacco and papers.

"I can't calm down. Don't you see the connection? Jordan, that hotel, the Amman Tours group at the Pyramids? Everywhere I've turned!"

"Get control of your breathing, Mr. Gold. Try to swallow."

I did as he suggested. I took a few deep breaths.

"Don't worry,'' I said after a time. "I'm all right, though

I think Muhammad needs a light." I pointed to our compartment mate who was holding up his cigarette. Jihad took out a match and lit it.

"Okay," I continued. "What about the way we got to the Pyramids in the first place? Huh? There you are trying to flag a cab. Only you can't get one until a guy comes by in a cab labeled Amman. And not only that, the guy pulls over without a single word from you. He just pulls over and *stops,* something unheard of in Cairo. It was as if he'd been waiting just for us. Had you even heard of Amman Cabs before then?"

"I don't think so."

I started shaking my head. "You see! And then we're at the Pyramids where you're going crazy over security. We rush to the farthest Pyramid so we can have the whole place to ourselves. You start pressuring me to talk so you can learn something about Lizzie. Only the place makes me sick. So we come up, and what do we sec? A bus from Amman Tours. Ever hear of them before?"

"We saw that bus before we went into the Pyramid."

"What? Before? After? Who cares! That's not the point! The point is that now we're here on an overnight train going down to Upper Egypt, so we can take a boat over to a desert that's a simple bus ride away from Cairo, and who do we bump into? A grandmother and grandfather blowing up balloons printed with Amman Tours. Don't tell me this isn't as weird as a donkey in Bermuda shorts on skis, Jihad. Don't tell me it's just a coincidence."

Jihad was listening closely. I felt I was finally getting through until I heard him speak. "You've made a number of good points, Mr. Gold, though I can't say I'm completely convinced . . ."

My jaw dropped.

"Now hear me out," he said. "About the hotel, how did you end up there in the first place?"

"Through Lizzie," I answered. "She'd found it in a tour book."

"So you basically arrived there at random. What I mean is, the name probably appealed to her. After all, she'd read about it while in *Amman,* Jordan."

I was listening.

"Now as for our cab to the Pyramids, I have no explanation, except perhaps that it belonged to the hotel's private fleet."

"Does the hotel have such a fleet?" I asked.

"Not that I know of. But not that I don't know of."

"What . . . ?"

"Now as for Amman Tours," he continued. "They seem like the kind of group you'd see at any tourist site like the Pyramids. Even on this train, for that matter, as it's primarily used by tourists going to the ancient ruins down south. Places like King Tut's tomb. In this sense, their presence on this train is not the least bit suspicious.

"Finally, on the possibility that these people are spies, and you did, I believe, infer that they were spies; have you ever seen a spy with dentures? Or, in the case of that driver from Amman Cabs, a spy with one eye? Have you heard of such a thing? I haven't. I've never heard of a spy with anything less than twenty-twenty vision."

He motioned with his hand that he was done. Muhammad stamped out his cigarette. I didn't know what to think. He'd taken some of the wind from my sails, that was true. But I still wasn't completely convinced.

"I'm surprised at you Jihad. I thought you'd be more concerned about security."

He brought his hand up as if to caution me. "I am concerned, Mr. Gold. More than you realize. That's why we've taken this roundabout route to Sinai. I'm just not convinced that there's been a breach in security. But if it will make you feel any better, I'll take a look down in the snack car."

He got up and moved to the door. "You just wait here with Muhammad."

I looked to Muhammad. Muhammad waved back.

THE PARTY'S OVER

"The party's over," said Jihad on his return.

". . . And the snack bar's closed, right? And everything's cleaned up like no one was there, right?" I was through being surprised.

"A few people are sitting around listening to soft music and playing cards," he reported. "But most of the crowd is gone, including all of the older people. . . . And there weren't any balloons," he added as an afterthought.

"And you don't believe me." I wasn't through being disappointed.

"Don't pout like a child, Mr. Gold. Of course I believe you. I believe everything you told me about the gathering and the people you met there. That's why I went to see for myself. What I don't happen to agree with, is your conclusion that every Amman label is associated with this conspiracy theory. I don't, and it's my prerogative.

"There's one thing I'd like to know, however," he continued. "If you were so suspicious of these people, Mr. Gold, why didn't you confront them yourself? Why did you run away? Were they bigger than you? Stronger?"

I didn't like his tone. "Don't attack me, Jihad. And speak softer, Muhammad is trying to sleep."

"What do I care about Muhammad?" He pushed the squatting Arab to the floor. "Did you care about me when you woke me with your tales of conspiracy?"

"I . . ."

A MORE CARING JIHAD

"Grow up!" he shouted before I could respond. Then in a lowered voice: "I'm not attacking you. I'm working with you. We're working together. Remember? I warned you from the start that this would be a difficult mission. I advised you against coming—saying I would do the mission on my own. But you wouldn't listen and now you're here. Now *we're* here." He gestured to the three of us. "It's a dangerous situation and we need the most from everybody."

This was about as sensitive as I'd ever seen Jihad. As unnatural as it was, it brought with it reassurance. I wanted to tell Muhammad: "See, he's not such a bad guy." But the mute wasn't listening. He was too preoccupied with the growing bump on his head.

"So here's my advice for the rest of our time together," concluded Jihad. "You can even use it when we're apart: Always maintain your honor and keep your head about you. It's important that you remember this, because it's going to get worse."

I made a mental note to keep my head about me when it got worse. About the honor bit, well, I took it as some sort of Arabic cultural affectation not meant to be taken seriously by Westerners.

LION

"That's it, Mr. Gold," he said as a closer. "Now get some sleep."

"Look, Jihad, there's no need for that 'Mr. Gold' stuff anymore. I mean, if we're going to be working together . . ."

"Sir?"

"And throw out 'sir.' It's too formal. My name is Leo. I'd appreciate it, Jihad, if you'd call me Leo from now on."

"If you insist."

"I do."

"Isn't Leo another name for a lion?"

I thought of the astrological sign. "Yes, I think so."

"That's funny, because I don't think of you in that way."

"Maybe if you saw me in my home territory, in New York, you'd think differently."

"I don't think so, Leo. I find that people maintain their character wherever they are. A crook remains a crook, and an honest man remains honest. It's just the circumstances that change. A man either meets the challenge of his environment or he doesn't."

It was strange to hear him say my name.

"But on the other hand, maybe you're right," he continued. "Perhaps I've misjudged you. Maybe you're really a caged lion just waiting to break out. Maybe you just need a little encouragement. You did, after all, show glimmers of strength out there by the Pyramids." He was smiling.

"That wasn't the courage of a lion, Jihad. It was the wild beast in me."

"Not wild, Lion, just untamed."

That was the first time he called me Lion.

A POEM

Jihad switched off the compartment light before squatting with his back against the compartment door. "Just in case your friend Muhammad decides to go sleepwalking," he explained.

I took out my notebook some thirty minutes later and wrote the following poem under the glow of my flashlight.

LULLABY FOR A TRAIN (a note)

The light of the sun has long since passed.
The night is in the next day.
Three of us rest as the train moves south
with creaks and a gentle sway.

"Sleep if you can, dream long and dream deep,"
comes Jihad's voice from the side.

*"You too," say I, with hope that by dawn,
some rest will soften our guide.*

*That leaves Muhammad, locked with his thoughts,
curled on the floor that's his bed.
"Sleep well," I whisper, "and dream in peace."
His answer, it goes unsaid.*

8

The Wilderness of Sinai

UPPER EGYPT

Muhammad, Jihad, and I watched scenes of Upper Egypt pass outside our compartment window as the sun broke over the horizon. Bright colors offered a rich alternative to the grays of Cairo. The train passed through a valley of contrasts. Lush green fields of corn spread west in the wake of the Nile, while a parched yellow desert extended out towards the east.

Our gently rocking car carried us through small villages of mud huts connected by a network of green fields. Narrow canals of Nile water irrigated fields tended by peasant farmers, *felaheen,* as Jihad called them, who moved through the corn and the sugarcane on the backs of water buffalo and harvested the crops with wooden machetes.

The Nile itself was alive with activity. Women laundered their clothes and bathed their babies. Children, their faces painted with screams of delight, splashed one another with the cooling waters. Rainbow-colored boats with their sails stretched full ferried goods and people between the shores. "Those are the *feluccas,*" Jihad explained. "I'll take you out on one when this is all over."

The train arrived in Luxor near ten o'clock. The station

was packed with tourist buses spewing noxious fumes. I observed that the inhospitality of the air seemed incongruous against the beauty of the land.

Jihad answered that this was good preparation for Sinai.

THE WILDERNESS OF SINAI

The historic implications of the impending trip to Sinai loomed large in my mind. I thought of my ancestors, the ancient Hebrews, and their own experiences moving from slavery to freedom. I recalled their good fortune vis-à-vis the ten plagues and how they'd come through the Red Sea dryshod and all, while the Egyptians had not. Everything had gone their way until Sinai. Then an unwise decision here, a bad judgment there, and suddenly, all original slaves were doomed to death in the wilderness.

I didn't want to repeat their mistakes.

I reviewed the trials my ancestors had faced, and considered how I might use their experience as a lesson for my own successful passage. I enumerated the factors working for me: First, foremost and almost only, was the fact that outside of a few emotional balls and chains, I knew that I wasn't, at least in a technical sense, a slave. This meant I could be flexible in new situations, something my ancestors could not.

And that was all.

It wasn't much, certainly, but it was all I'd have to bring the freedom I sought. And if not Lizzie's, then at least my own.

TRAVELING, EGYPTIAN STYLE

The next two days confirmed two personal theories about traveling off the beaten path in Egypt. First, that rush or no rush, it's always no rush. Second, that first or second class, it's always third class.

I first mentioned these theories to Jihad during our second hour without seats on the bus from Luxor to the coast. He called me a spoiled American.

"What do you mean, spoiled American? I paid good money for this trip."

"What I mean," he answered sharply, "is that I'm tired of listening to you whine."

I thought his answer harsh, and told him so in no uncertain terms.

"Watch your mouth," he retorted. "You want to bicker? You want to complain? Do it in Muhammad's ear, not mine."

His point of course, was that the use of expletives wouldn't ease the inconveniences of life on the road in Egypt. So I held my words about having to stand on that bus for six hours, and I pretended not to notice when the air conditioning failed or when Muhammad threw my second bottle of perfume out the window. I didn't make an issue of any of these annoyances though I would have been justified.

THE VIRUS

What I did do was find a few choice words for the Egyptian people, who, if good cheer was a disease, would all be hospitalized. Each and every one of them. Their most overt symptom was a compulsive need to sing the "Welcome to Egypt" refrain over and over. Only it didn't stop there. The friendliness virus also revealed itself through acts of generosity and selflessness. Among these was a strange need to press their children in my arms, and have me pet their chickens.

I resolved to adapt. To try and get along. So I smiled at stories I didn't understand, and ate food I shouldn't have swallowed. I even photographed on command, long after my film ran out. Only I drew the line (I knew I had to somewhere) when a one-legged beggar offered me her seat.

THE FERRY RIDE ACROSS THE RED SEA

The ride from the coastal port of Hurghada to Sharm el-Sheikh in Sinai went as well as could be expected. I did, after all, have a seat, and it was on the ferry. My fellow passengers kept to themselves, and the service was down to standard. If there was anything to complain about, and hours before I would have thought that there was, I would have said the boat was standing a little low in the water. I might even have asked the captain to check if we were sinking. But I kept my mouth shut because it didn't seem to worry anyone else. Besides, the proximity of the waterline made it possible to enjoy an underwater parade of multicolored tropical fish escorting us out of port.

SHELTER FROM THE STORM

We slept that night in Sharm el-Sheikh and set out the following morning in a roofless rented jeep.

Muhammad took over as chief guide since Sinai was his specialty. Jihad even let him drive.

It was a rough debut. We hit a sandstorm about an hour out of Sharm. Swirling sands cut visibility off at the edge of the jeep, while howling winds reduced Jihad's shouts to whispers. Through it all, Muhammad drove as well as could be expected and no one held him responsible for drifting onto the rocks by the side of the path (we'd long since left paved highways) and puncturing our tires one by one. It was unanimously agreed that the situation was out of hand when we could no longer see the jeep. Muhammad brought the vehicle to a halt.

"Jihad!" I called out. "Where are you?"

"Get out of the jeep! Go into the tent!" came the reply.

"Tent? What tent?"

"Follow Muhammad!"

"Muhammad? Where's Muhammad?"

A pair of hands pulled me from the jeep shoulder first. We went about ten steps before I bumped into a wall of rough fabric. The hands continued towing me along the surface of this flexible barrier until we reached an edge and I stumbled around it.

The roar of the wind grew muffled when the flap we'd pushed through fell shut. I rubbed the sand from my eyes and looked around. Muhammad, Jihad, and I were in a large (30 feet by 30 feet, I'd estimate) tent. Carefully laid mats removed any hint that the floor beneath our feet belonged to the desert, while long wooden poles lifted the roof well over our heads and provided little knobs from which kerosene lamps hung and cast their yellowish light over walls of coarse brown material I took for camel hair.

A very exotic atmosphere, all in all, and one I might even have appreciated had there not been two very suspicious-looking characters by the multi-stemmed hookah pipe on the tent's far side. I say suspicious because the look on their bearded faces revealed that we were not just unexpected, but indeed, unwelcome.

Jihad read their wariness. *"Al-salaam aleikum,"* he said as he held up his hand.

"Wa-aleikum esalam," responded the galabia-clad men though without the accompanying gesture of peace.

Silence returned. The men continued sizing us up through the mist of the sweet-smelling pipe smoke I took for the source of their evident paranoia.

Yes, I recognized the scent. It was hashish.

One of the men rose and addressed Jihad. Though I had no idea what he was saying, I could feel some easing in the general tension as he spoke. Jihad listened closely then directed his response to the second man—the one sitting cross-legged before the pipe. I figured he did it because this man's beard held streaks of white while his companion's did not. That's what I figured, but who knew for sure? The point was that anyhow, somehow, Jihad knew just what to do.

We were invited to sit on the cushions by the pipe.

The younger man boiled water for tea over a small gas camping stove. Muhammad drank his right up, while I sipped mine and Jihad spoke with our hosts. The conversation continued for fifteen minutes. At one point Jihad turned to me and said: "In case you were wondering, these men are bedouins . . ."

I nodded. "I figured," I said. "The tent gave it away."

Jihad continued as if I hadn't spoken. ". . . I told them that I'm a tour operator from Cairo, and that you are an American tourist who's hired me to take you through Sinai. Muhammad is our mute driver. I explained that we became lost in the storm and that we'll be leaving as soon as visibility picks up."

WEDDING BELLS

The atmosphere lightened even more when the gray-haired man made a comment with a gesture towards me. Jihad and the younger man laughed. Muhammad made soft choking sounds.

I smiled sociably.

Suddenly, the older man reached over, stuck his fingers into my mouth and spread my lips wide.

"Hey!" I pushed his arm aside.

Jihad was still laughing when he touched my arm and said: "Watch it. Remember, he's our host."

"What do I care? This is my mouth." I waved off additional attempts to touch my face. "What's this all about, Jihad?"

"He wants to know if you have a daughter."

The older bedouin nodded his head and smiled.

"A daughter? How could I have a daughter? I'm not even married."

"He doesn't know that. Most bedouins are grandparents at your age."

I stood up and addressed the bedouins. "Please excuse us. Jihad, come here." Jihad rose, made a few remarks in

Arabic and followed me to the second side of the tent. The others watched as we huddled together.

"What do you mean, grandparents?"

"The man with the white in his beard is the other one's father. He wants to know if you have a daughter between twelve and fifteen years old. A young girl of marrying age for his son." His expression said he wasn't kidding.

"And then what? What does he expect? That if I had one, I'd give her to him?"

I glanced over to the bedouins and Muhammad. The three of them looked on expectantly.

"Look," said Jihad, "there's something you have to understand. Bedouin cultural norms are not the same as yours . . ."

"I'm figuring that out."

". . . And that how they meet and marry, is different, but no less valid than how people meet and marry in your culture."

"When you say different, what exactly do you mean?"

"What I mean is, well . . . the woman's place in bedouin society is very low. This is the first thing you have to understand."

"How low?"

"Very."

"Is it a secret?"

"No, it's not a secret, it's just that as I said, bedouin culture is different from yours, and I don't wish to offend you."

"Jihad, I'm an educated man. I understand there are many different ways of life and I accept people's rights to live as they choose. Don't worry about offending me."

"As you wish. The bedouin woman's place is on par with that of a goat. About the best I can say is that she has absolutely no legal rights."

"That's the best? That's shocking!"

"I warned you."

"What else?"

"Every woman is controlled by a man called her 'willie,' or guardian. This man is usually her father, and in the absence of her father, her brother, or her father's brother. One of the willie's responsibilities is to arrange the girl's marriage."

"How does it work?"

"Very simple. Most marriages are exchange marriages. That is, the willie will trade the girl for money or material goods—like a camel. In some cases, he may even exchange his charge for another girl to marry himself or his son."

"And what if the groom's side is too poor to pay, or if they have a girl but she's too young to marry?"

"Marrying age, as you just discovered, is quite low. Yet since eligible women are in demand, most bedouins would be prepared to wait for an underaged girl to mature if her hand was promised for a later date."

"That's crazy!"

"Calm down." Jihad turned, smiled to our hosts and said something that made them laugh.

"That's crazy, Jihad," I repeated. "I mean I've heard of that kind of arrangement in sports. Like trading one player for another to be named later . . . but in marriage?"

"That's not all. The willie's supreme power over a woman's destiny continues even after she's married."

"Are you saying that a woman would leave her husband if her willie told her to?"

"That's what I'm saying."

"And what if her husband locked her in the house and refused to let her go?"

"That would be cause for a blood feud."

"A what?"

"A blood feud. That's when one family feels justified in killing one or more members of another family over a matter of honor."

"This still goes on today?"

"Today and every day."

"But Jihad . . ."

"No buts, and don't get me wrong, but I think we're going to have to cut this chat short. Muhammad doesn't look like he's keeping up his side of the conversation with our hosts. Let's go back. I'll explain that you don't have a daughter. That should settle the matter."

Jihad turned to go. I took his arm. "Just one minute, Jihad."

"What is it?"

"Don't you think there's something weird about all this?"

He waited for me to continue.

". . . I mean here we are in the middle of some of the most backward country in the world. I mean a place where the moral majority would feel slightly left wing. And there you have Lizzie, somewhere nearby, practicing sex slave techniques and who knows what else. Doesn't that seem weird to you? I mean, doesn't it?"

Jihad nodded his head. "I have news for you," he said. "I wasn't going to say anything, but that's not the only thing that's weird around here."

"It's not?"

"No, it's not. And please don't act alarmed when you hear what I'm about to tell you. In fact, it's best if you smile, because they're all watching."

"All right, how's this for a smile? Now tell me what's so weird?"

Jihad brought his face to my ear. "What's weird is that there's a concealed gun beneath the older bedouin's galabia. I think it's a shotgun. You can see the edge of the barrel by his foot."

I discreetly shifted my glance towards the old man. Jihad's claim was correct.

I laughed nervously. "What should we do?"

"Nothing. Just sit down, smile and enjoy the tea. Being

bedouins, these men are obligated to take care of us while we're in their tent.''

"And after we leave?" I grinned and waved as we approached our hosts.

"The obligation ceases."

I tried to do what he said. I sat down and smiled. I drank more tea. I didn't, however, relax.

PARTY TIME

The bedouins didn't sense our heightened tension. In fact, the younger one greeted our return by placing a fresh piece of hash in the bowl, lighting it up and extending one of the hookah stems in our direction.

Muhammad was first to refuse. Jihad followed. *"La,"* he said. *"Shukran."* While I understood Jihad's reaction—fun was not his thing—Muhammad's was more puzzling. I could have sworn he was the partying type.

I was still considering this point when the stem appeared before me. I welcomed the offer. It was just what I needed following the unsettling news of the shotgun. I reached out through the blue haze of the hashish smoke. The stem was nearly in my grasp when Jihad's hand took mine. *"La,"* he repeated graciously. *"Shukran."*

This really annoyed me. "What's this *'la, shukran'* business, Jihad? I decide whether I smoke or not."

Jihad's face showed concern. "Didn't your doctor warn you that smoking could be hazardous to your health?" His voice was soft and understanding, and in complete contrast to the message expressed by his viselike grip. The message was: "Don't touch the pipe if you know what's good for you."

"Why, thank you for reminding me, Jihad. I'd nearly forgotten."

A CHASE

The wind stopped howling outside the tent about an hour later. Jihad rose and addressed a few words, first to our hosts and then to me. "It's time to go," he said. "We've got a lot of territory to make up."

I gave Muhammad a hand, thanked my hosts and walked outside.

"Hurry up!" ordered Jihad as he wiped a layer of sand from the jeep. "Let's go!"

We resumed our former positions with Muhammad behind the wheel, myself to his right, and Jihad in back.

I turned to Jihad after we'd been driving for about ten minutes. "What was that all about?"

"Smuggling," came the reply. "Those two are drug smugglers. We shouldn't have seen what we saw."

"Should we tell Muhammad?"

"No. There's no need. Muhammad pointed out the shotgun to me just after we entered the tent."

The jeep turned sharply and headed down a narrow canyon. "That must have been why he refused the hash," I observed.

"That's right. He's obviously aware of his brain's limited capacity and figured that drugs at this time wouldn't be wise."

I took Muhammad's lead and ignored this insult. Instead, I raised a question that cut to heart of the matter at hand. "Are we in trouble, Jihad?"

Jihad nodded and turned his head towards the path behind us. I followed his eyes and focused on a white pickup truck that had just entered the canyon and was barreling down the gravel path towards us. The truck's cabin held two bedouins, the two we'd just left in the tent. The father drove. To his right sat his son with the shotgun cocked and ready.

"Yes," said Jihad. "It looks like we're in trouble."

"What about their obligation to protect us?"

Jihad directed a few words to Muhammad before answering. Muhammad checked the rearview mirror and floored the gas.

"Their obligation ended," explained Jihad, "the moment we left the tent."

The bedouins were gaining. "Muhammad!" I called. "Can't you make this thing go faster?"

Jihad answered for him. "Not with two punctured tires, he can't."

Muhammad began weaving the jeep from side to side in a desperate attempt to frustrate the marksman. It was an admirable yet dangerous tactic, for it brought us within inches of the narrow canyon walls.

The pickup pulled up along our right side, putting their driver between the gunman and me. What a fool, I thought, he's blocked his own man's line of fire. I stuck out my tongue and laughed.

The truck turned sharply and banged into our jeep. "Hold on!" cried Jihad as Muhammad fought with the wheel. The jeep scraped against the canyon's left wall. A large boulder appeared in our path. Muhammad swerved to avoid it.

The old bedouin prepared to bump us again. Jihad called up to Muhammad. The truck came crashing once more into our side. I fell over against Muhammad, who struggled to maintain control. I looked back and saw Jihad stand, grab hold of the tailgate, and throw himself into the back of the bedouins' truck.

The bedouins saw this too. The gunman smashed the glass that separated the rear of the cabin from the bed of the truck. I saw the gun barrel poke out through this jagged hole. Jihad struggled to rise.

"Watch out!" I cried.

The sound of the shotgun going off thundered through the air moments after Muhammad swung the jeep into the pickup. Jihad fell over the side. The pickup scraped the canyon wall, rolled up a medium-sized boulder, and flipped over on its head.

Muhammad hit the brakes and pulled hard right on the steering wheel. The jeep performed a one-hundred-eighty-degree spin before coming to a halt. Muhammad shifted into first, then sent waves of gravel shooting into the air as he jammed the gas pedal into the floor.

The wheels of the pickup truck were still spinning in the air as we passed it on our left. I could see the younger bedouin crawling through the shattered windshield while his father exited by the window.

Muhammad slowed as we searched the area for Jihad. I signaled for him to stop while I jumped off to check behind a couple of boulders.

Muhammad honked his horn. "What is it, Muhammad?" He pointed up ahead. I looked and saw Jihad. He was standing in the middle of the trail looking neat and groomed. I ran up to greet him.

"They missed . . ." he said. These were his first words.

I clapped him on the back.

". . . but I'll never forgive them for making me scuff my shoes."

"Forget about your shoes. We're alive! Think about it! And all because of Muhammad's driving and your bravery."

I turned to Muhammad who'd just pulled up and was stepping out of the jeep.

Jihad was less impressed than me. "He saved his own life," he said. "You just happened to be in the passenger's seat."

What could I say to that? Nothing, certainly, to Jihad. Muhammad had saved my life, and he'd done it without a word of reference to my own shameful behavior at the Pyramids. I felt grateful and wanted to express it. I turned to Muhammad and stepped forward. He blinked his eyes and stepped back. I continued my approach. He bumped into the jeep. I wrapped my arms around him. He froze uncomfortably. I hugged him deeply. He remained frozen. I released him. He walked away.

I asked Jihad what this meant. He said it meant Muhammad regretted saving my life.

"Stop kidding," I said.

"I'm not," he answered.

MUHAMMAD REVISITED

We passed the rest of the drive in silence. It's not that we didn't have what to say about the day's events. I for one would have been happy to talk had circumstances been right. But they weren't. We were tired. And our bodies ached as much from the drama of the chase and escape as from the discomfort of riding on two flat tires. So I kept my observations to myself. Most of these concerned the pleasant discovery of Muhammad's iron tough will. I scolded myself for failing to recognize this characteristic at the Pyramids when I took his refusal to talk as a physical problem alone.

Now I realized how wrong I'd been: that the strength of his inner resolve had as great an influence on his behavior as any physical impairment. For there he'd been, driving through the most difficult of weather conditions with punctured tires on a gravel road. He didn't have a map, and was dependent for support from two men who'd recently tortured and beat him, while shotgun-bearing bedouins tried to crash him into a rock wall. Through it all, he harnessed his concentration to meet the challenge.

I asked myself how this could be, and concluded that it had to do with living a life of tragic proportions. Any man who'd suffered and survived the kind of abuse Muhammad had, could not help but to have established extraordinary reserves of character.

INFORMATION FOR HIRE

Both the moon and sun were in the sky when Muhammad stopped by a canyon wall and maneuvered the jeep until it formed a V-shaped barrier with the rock. Jihad suspended a roof over this space by fastening one end of a large blanket to the jeep's door, and the other end to a bush growing out of the canyon wall.

We sat down by the remains of the right front tire. Jihad said that the day's events proved there was no guarantee that Muhammad—or any of us—would live through this trip, and that he wanted Muhammad to tell us where he was taking us. Muhammad had promised, he pointed out. The time had come to deliver.

Muhammad answered with an impassive stare. I found this disappointing for two reasons. First, because it revealed that the bonds we'd built up during the course of the day had not been enough to instill a degree of trust in our guide. And second, and most important, because I worried that Jihad was running low on patience and would call for another round of torture. So I cautioned him to stay calm. I told him everything would work out, though I had my doubts.

But Jihad said: "Maybe you're right," and directed my attention to the way "the mute's" right hand played in his lap. I looked where he advised but saw nothing of note. Jihad said I was missing the message. I looked again. Muhammad's thumb and index finger continued rubbing one against the other.

Then I understood. It was *bakshish* time again.

I pointed out that we'd agreed to pay him after we reached our destination.

Jihad was exasperated. "I already told you, Muhammad's a bedouin. All he knows is self-interest and survival. Loyalty . . . honesty . . . these mean nothing to him."

I took offense at his cynicism.

"Don't be offended," he replied. "Just pay Muhammad whatever it takes."

I let the tension build a few moments before acquiescing.

"All right," I said. "Explain that I've got fifty dollars now if he tells us where he's taking us, and fifty more after we arrive."

The deal was struck. The money put up.

GETTING CLOSER

Muhammad gave us the information we needed through the employ of a simple game. Jihad called out the names of different places until Muhammad signaled a hit. It came on the fifth try.

"Hal Doktor Haddi be Wadi Firan?"

Muhammad shook his head no, held up a semifist, and spread his thumb and index finger a short distance apart.

"What did you ask him?" I asked.

"I asked if Dr. Haddi is in Wadi Firan. Muhammad says no, but that he's near. Now I'll ask if that's where he's taking us."

"Important to know," I observed.

Jihad agreed, then turned to address Muhammad: *"Hal Satahuzhuna le Wadi Firan?"*

Muhammad nodded.

"Le ein nakhnu zaheboon min hunok?"

Muhammad raised his right arm as if he were asking permission to speak. He didn't hold it straight up, but at an angle of one hundred thirty degrees. Then he took his index and third fingers from his left hand and began walking up this slope.

I didn't like what I saw. "What did you ask him, Jihad?"

"I asked where we'll be going from Wadi Firan."

"And the answer?"

"It looks like we're in for some mountain climbing."

9

✤

Holy War

A FAMILY AFFAIR

There's nothing like a day in the dust to fuel a deep sleep. Muhammad proved this after lowering his arm and curling up into a fetal position. The sound of gentle snoring commenced shortly thereafter. Jihad said we'd be smart to follow his example since according to Muhammad's last estimate before closing his eyes we'd be upon Dr. Haddi's harem in two or three days. The rest would do us good.

"True," I said. "But look, it's just dusk. Wouldn't you like some dinner before sacking out for the night? I mean, we'll also need our strength."

Jihad answered with a growl from his stomach.

I took out my gas stove, filled the pot with water, and waited for it to boil. "Tell me a little more about yourself," I said by way of making conversation.

"What would you like to know, Lion?" There he was again with that inappropriate nickname. I hoped he saw something I couldn't.

"What about you?" I asked. "Do you have a nickname?"

He paused before answering. "My father used to call me tracker." He said it low, as if he were ashamed.

"Tracker? How did he come up with that?" I noticed that the water was starting to boil and took out a package of French onion soup mix.

"It's a long story."

"That's all right. We haven't even started on the main course." I ripped open the package and poured it into the water.

"I guess he gave me the name because he wanted me to develop tracking skills. It was his way of encouraging me."

"Why would he want you to do that? To be a tracker?"

"Tracking had been in the family for many generations. My father was the first to break the tradition. He wanted me to pick it up again."

"But tracking? Is that a marketable skill?" I looked from Jihad to the pot and began stirring.

"It is," he replied without enthusiasm, "if you're a bedouin."

ROOTS

I removed the spoon from the pot to consider this headline. Jihad? A bedouin? Like Muhammad? Like the two hashish smugglers? But hadn't he always spoken poorly of bedouins?

The implications were pregnant with meaning.

Jihad saw my calculations and tried to change the subject. "How's the soup coming?"

"The soup? The soup's ready. I'm a little shocked. But the soup is fine."

Jihad let out a short laugh. "Then let's eat."

I poured out three portions, handed one to Jihad, and nudged Muhammad awake. He sat up quickly, then waited for me to offer him a cup.

"So let's hear it, Jihad," I said between sips.

"What?"

"The story of your bedouin roots."

"I'd be boring you." He tried to sound modest. In fact he was putting me off.

"Nonsense. Nothing could interest me more." I poured more soup for myself and settled back.

"All right," he gave in. "Just make sure you don't finish all the soup while I'm talking."

I held up the pot to show him that plenty remained.

"My father grew up in a bedouin village in northern Sinai. He moved to Cairo during the Second World War where he was employed by British intelligence. It was there that he met my mother. A short romance ensued, they married, and I was born. He left us when I was ten to return to the desert."

He reached over for the pot and refilled his cup. I waited for him to continue, then spoke up when he didn't. "That was a fast tale."

"Experience has taught me that he who talks most eats least."

"A very graceful exit."

Jihad nodded his head.

"I'm sorry about your father," I added.

"No reason to be. I'm not."

"You never tried to get in touch with him? Never wanted to see him again after you grew up?"

"My mother went after him. She left me in an orphanage while she traveled to Sinai to convince him to keep the family together. She told me she'd either be gone for a short time or send a sign that I should follow. That sign would be a ruby ring. A family heirloom. She said she would find a way to send it, and that I should take its receipt as a sign to come to her in the desert. Only neither she nor the ring ever came back. A letter arrived nine months later. It said she was dead."

"Jihad, I . . . I'm sorry."

"It all happened a very long time ago. Anyway, that's when I decided to drop his name from mine."

"You mean your name is just 'Jihad'?"

"Not just. But not more."

HOLY WAR

I kept on the subject of his name. "About your name. It's a special name, isn't it? Doesn't it hold some meaning in Arabic?"

"You might say that. *Jihad* is the Arabic word for 'holy war.' It's said that every Moslem is duty bound to wage holy war against the nonbelievers."

He gave me a long purposeful look through the last of the day's fading light. I didn't know what he meant, but it made me feel uncomfortable. He'd given me the same feeling in the cab on the way to the Pyramids, and in the Pyramid itself. I became conscious of the wind whistling outside, and how dark it had grown beneath the cloth roof. I got up and went to my pack which lay in the back of the jeep, opened it up and took out my flashlight. It was a sturdy flashlight that could also be used to defend my life. I sat down with it in my lap.

"It also means to struggle," he continued. "We Moslems are meant to struggle for our religion."

Something didn't feel right and I didn't know what it was, though I now regretted making that original inquiry into the meaning of his name. The atmosphere of warmth and camaraderie had long since faded. In its place, I felt only threat. I switched on the flashlight and turned it towards Muhammad to see if he felt the same. The beam caught him protecting his soup cup beneath his left arm. His mouth was open wide in protest and his left hand was raised against the light. He tried kicking some dirt in my direction. Clearly, Muhammad didn't feel right either. I moved the light to the ground in front of me before checking my apprehensions: "Ever get into any fights over it? You know, with nonbelievers?"

"Not too often really. I only know believers." He said it cold.

A drop of sweat ran down from my armpit. I waited for him to say something reassuring like: "Don't worry, you're okay for a nonbeliever." But no, he stayed silent.

My heart began pounding against my ribs. I tried to swallow, but couldn't. Keep calm, I told myself. He's your friend. My grip on the flashlight tightened as I decided to confront my fear. "Y-y-you know Jihad, I'm not a believer."

My first feeling after making this admission was that I'd made a terrible mistake. Sometimes, I thought, you're really better off keeping your mouth closed, fear or no fear. I raised the flashlight slightly.

But Jihad spoke without surprise. "I know that," he said.

"Y-y-you d-d-do?" I whispered.

"That's right, I do. And it's okay." His tone was completely natural. "So you can wipe that look of terror off your face and stop making sounds like a panicked nonbeliever in the presence of a duty-bound Moslem."

I felt myself blushing. I coughed.

"Look, Lion, it doesn't concern me that you don't believe in the Prophet Muhammad. Everyone has his own beliefs, and that's fine with me. Islam is a very tolerant religion . . ."

"Sure, Jihad. I know that." I wiped the dampness from my forehead. "That's why your name is so . . . unusual. *Because* Islam is so tolerant." I asked myself how I could have doubted him for a moment.

". . . if you don't break the law." His voice was suddenly cold again.

"Jihad?"

I directed the flashlight towards his face and saw that his eyes were pointed towards the darkness beyond our makeshift tent. I turned the light through the tent's entrance to see what it was he saw. A gust of wind sent sand particles swirling wildly in the beam.

"What is it, Jihad? What's wrong?"

The wind began howling again. Jihad didn't answer. Our roof flapped so hard I thought it would fly away. I had the feeling he was thinking about how his father had left him—that maybe this broke some bedouin law.

"Jihad?" I needed him with us. "Jihad!"

My second call seemed to reach him. "I'm sorry. What did you say?" He looked towards me. He shook his head.

"What were you thinking about? Were you thinking about your father?"

"I don't remember."

DRESSED FOR SUCCESS

The wind died down about ten minutes later. Muhammad cast a suspicious glance toward Jihad before making himself comfortable by the canyon wall. All grew quiet. The steady rhythm of Muhammad's breathing indicated that he was asleep again. I moved over to where he lay curled with his forehead pressed against the canyon wall and covered him with a sleeping bag. His thumb was secure in his mouth.

I went over to my own sleeping bag and got in.

Jihad still sat with his back against the side of the jeep. His darkened profile was framed against the glow of the moon. Thirty minutes passed. Jihad didn't move. I decided to see if he'd returned yet from the dead.

"Hey, Jihad," I whispered.

"What is it, Lion?" The outline of his nose disappeared as he turned his head towards me.

It was good to hear a direct answer. It justified taking a stab at dialogue. I asked what he thought of Haddi—what he thought could possess a man to want to manage a harem—though I realized it might be considered a foolish question.

"Dr. Haddi . . ." said Jihad as his head began nodding. "This Dr. Haddi might have been a Moslem once, but that had to have been a long time ago." I strained to hear his voice. "I wouldn't call him a Moslem now."

I sat up on my elbows. "I don't understand. What has he done?"

"That's a difficult question, Lion. You'd be better off asking what hasn't he done." He picked up a long stick which lay by his side and began tapping it on the ground. "Let's start with the most recent. Kidnapping. The man kidnapped your girlfriend. How's that? Want more? Okay, he sells women as slaves. That's not enough? He castrates men . . ." The stick tapping picked up speed with each new offense.

I whispered the question: "Castration?"

"What do you think? Muhammad did it to himself? Why, I wouldn't be surprised if this Haddi drinks alcohol and eats pork."

"Pork? What are you saying, that he's Jewish? Listen, Jihad, I don't think you're being fair to the Jewish people. I mean, sure they circumcise newborn boys after eight days, but they just take off a little piece. It's nothing like castration . . ."

"What are *you* talking about, Lion? Jews aren't the only ones who don't eat pork. True Moslems don't either . . ."

"Huh? Well sure, Jihad. I knew that."

But he continued as if I hadn't spoken. "The question is, what wouldn't a man like this be capable of? Would lying, stealing, and slander be considered crimes?" He was off with the stick again. "How about adultery? Is sleeping with a married woman not a crime?" Jihad's breathing grew heavy. His head moved back and forth.

"Jihad . . . calm down."

"What crime wouldn't be known to this devil? Extortion? Rape? Murder?" He cracked the stick with each crime. "They'd all be within the repertoire of a man like Dr. Haddi."

"Even torture?" I asked out of curiosity alone, to see how he'd answer in light of his own experience with Muhammad.

"Torture's not always a crime, as you know. But in Haddi's case, yes."

I silently wondered how he differentiated between Haddi's case and his. "Could he be involved in anything else?" I asked.

The answer came quick: "How about selling stolen goods? That's a possibility. How do you think Muhammad got this ring?"

He held something aloft in the dark.

"You took Muhammad's toe ring?"

"And I'll bet he's even into drugs too," he continued. "From marijuana to hashish to cocaine to heroin. Yes, even heroin."

"All those things? That's incredible. What about the perfume shop? All that perfume I saw? Where'd he get all that stuff? What would he do with that?"

Jihad thought for a moment. "No, the perfume shop would be legitimate. As a cover."

"The Thousand and One Nights is legit? Why would someone with a record like his even bother?"

"Why bother? To maintain a foothold in legitimate business, that's why."

"If you call using the premises for kidnapping, honest," I pointed out.

"You see."

"You've portrayed him as a thoroughly evil man."

"Through and through. But you asked, Lion. I'm sorry if I've frightened you. Just know that these are the kinds of people you meet in my line of work."

"Sure, I understand. Like if you're in an orchestra, you

have to meet the other musicians you're going to make music with."

Jihad gave a hard look in my direction, sighed, then said: "Good night, Lion."

JIHAD'S ANGLE

I wished him a good night for the second time that evening, and for the second time that evening, I didn't go to sleep. I was too caught up in his stories. I had the feeling they held the key to Jihad's motivations. His angle, as it were, in his search for Haddi's harem. Too many things just didn't add up.

Like this bedouin business. If it was true that Jihad was an urban bedouin, then was detective work for him the equivalent of tracking? And if so, exactly how much experience did he have as a detective? I mean I couldn't say he'd been wowing me with his ability to analyze the facts dispassionately.

And what about his relationship with his dad? My instincts told me his feelings towards his father for his treatment of his mother (forcing her to leave her son) might not be unrelated to his feelings towards Dr. Haddi (who had taken my woman away from me). I also figured that entering the desert into which his parents had long ago disappeared was also stirring up lots of bad images in Jihad's mind. Yes, Jihad's mind was definitely infected. This much was clear from the strange ways his mood had begun shifting as we neared our target in Sinai.

Which brought me to Jihad's mysterious goals. What would he do when he found Lizzie? Kill Haddi? Ask me for more money? The more I asked, the less I felt I knew.

Finally, I asked myself how Haddi would respond to our arrival. I tried to place myself in his sandals. I imagined myself a drug-dealing pimp with a fondness for lying and kidnapping, as well as dealing slaves, robbing, slandering, extorting, raping, and adultering (adultery?). I realized I wouldn't be favorably disposed to any outside interference.

This was how I spent the night. Question after question. Answers came slower. The best I could conclude was that Jihad's past was catching up with his future.

IS LIZZIE WORTH IT?

Which brought me to my own quest for Lizzie. Haddi's new image cast the whole escapade in a much more serious light. It raised the issue of whether my attendance at the rescue was required or optional.

The answer, I realized, could be found in the determination if Lizzie was worth it. If *we* were worth it, now that *we* were just *me*. I reviewed the facts.

Fact 1: I didn't love her. I thought.

Fact 2: She didn't love me. She thought.

Fact 3: We weren't in love. Maybe.

Fact 4: She said she understood me. I knew she didn't.

Fact 5: I said I understood me. I knew I didn't.

Fact 6: I respected her.

Fact 7: We fought a lot (especially in Jordan).

Fact 8: We laughed a lot (occasionally before Jordan).

Fact 9: Her life was in danger and I was the only one who could help her.

Fact 10: I'm often stupid and sometimes brave.

Fact 11: I'm a very selfish person.

Fact 12: I don't want to be.

Fact 13: But you are!

Fact 14: No I'm not!

Fact 15: Rational decisions do not exist. Only rationalizations.

Here was my decision: I would continue after Lizzie. I would rescue her. Don't ask me why.

10

❖

Strange Ideas

DAYBREAK

Day broke over the Sinai interior. Everything was covered with a thin film of dust, including our sleeping bags and ourselves. Jihad was still sitting propped against the jeep. I was about to wish him "good morning" when I noticed he was asleep. He hadn't moved since last evening.

I stepped out of our makeshift tent to survey the emerging day. The air was fresh and clean. The sky, without clouds. Muhammad was already awake and squatting by a small fire of twigs he'd built to prepare some fresh-brewed coffee. He saw me and waved, then motioned to the pot.

"Good morning," I said. "Coffee? Sure, thanks."

He poured out a cup and handed it to me.

"Thanks Muhammad," I said. "Do me a favor, will you? Tell Jihad when he wakes up that I've gone for a walk."

Though he waved once more as I went off, I doubted he'd remember my message for Jihad.

CANYON ART

The morning light brought out many enchanting aspects of the desert environment. Most impressive were the canyon walls, which glowed red, orange, yellow, and gold as the sun crept down their slopes. It was like multicolored paint dripping down a highly textured canvas.

I pointed this out to Jihad after my return about an hour later. He nodded his head and corrected my use of the word canyon. "This isn't a canyon," he said, "it's a wadi," and went on to explain the difference. Though I didn't really understand him, I decided to call all canyons "wadis" from then on.

WADI FIRAN

We arrived at the place called Wadi Firan after a three-hour drive through some of the most inhospitable territory I'd ever seen. Many spots were as I imagined the face of the moon. We traversed lifeless plains and passed through hills where plants found root in the cracks of rocks.

Among our little group, Muhammad maintained his post at the wheel while I passed the time talking to myself as Jihad pretended to listen. I could tell he was preoccupied with his impending business on the mountain. It was obvious from the way he shouted at me in Arabic.

I decided not to let his peculiar behavior disturb me. I concentrated instead on the adventure before us. I felt like we were the cavalry riding to rescue a maiden in distress. It was a good feeling. It was unreality. It was just what I needed to continue moving forward.

Wadi Firan appeared out of nowhere like the desert oasis it was. Just like Las Vegas, I thought, only without the electricity.

The palm trees. These were what struck me the most. They were everywhere, lining and filling the full two miles of this narrow, winding canyon/wadi, bringing a carpet of green to the floor beneath the yellow, orange walls of rock. There was a feeling of life here. Endless life, at least in this one spot. It was better than Las Vegas, I decided. It was

Emerald City, the home of the Wizard. I shared my impressions with Jihad.

"The Wizard was a fake," Jihad reminded me. "Just like the opulence of these harem guys." I was facing his back when he said this. He was looking up to the mountains, searching the folds and the bluffs. "The Wizard was a fake," he repeated. "Just like Haddi."

This was just another indication of the direction his mind had taken.

"Yeah, right, Jihad. Speaking of some of our favorite people, who lives in this village?" I needed him speaking of the here and now. I wanted him back with me or at least in a complementary orb close to the realm of reality. This was where I wanted him. I figured it was best for us both.

My heart lit up when he started talking about the place. I encouraged him to share everything he knew. "Firan is the largest oasis in southern Sinai," he explained. "It is also home to the main bedouin community in this region and more than five thousand date trees . . ."

The story went on and on. And on. And on. I would have interrupted with questions if I could. I even tugged at his arm to say that's enough, but went unheeded. I realized I hadn't succeeded in bringing him back as I had hoped. Jihad was as remote as ever. Only now his distance was cloaked in conversation.

STRANGE IDEAS

Jihad walked off a few minutes later in search of the village dignitaries. This left Muhammad and me to pass the late morning in the company of twenty-five laughing bedouin children who helped themselves to anything not tied to my body.

Jihad returned an hour later. He explained that his talks with the local powers had confirmed Muhammad's main mime that Haddi and his group were quartered on a nearby mountain. Wadi Firan was the end of the road. That is, the road ended in Wadi Firan. The mountain was closed to jeeps.

"All right," I said, ready to put some distance between myself and the kids. "Let's rent some camels and be gone."

"Not so fast, Lion," Jihad cautioned. "This terrain is too rough for camels. Anyone going up is going to have to carry all his gear on his own back." The implication was that *anyone* who couldn't carry his gear up the mountain would have to wait below. It provided an easy out for someone with doubts.

I asked for more details on the trip itself.

Jihad said he'd learned that Haddi's camp was on top of the first mountain after "the hill." He pointed up to a huge geological formation and said: "This is the hill." I realized then that the mountain would be, well, mountainous.

The villagers also told him it would take one day to pass the hill and another to climb the mountain. There wasn't any organized trail as such. It was just a matter of climbing.

I noted that Jihad avoided anything outside the first person singular when describing the climbing party.

"And what of the villagers?" I asked. "Can we get any of them to accompany us?" I emphasized "us."

Jihad said no, he'd asked. His feeling was that something was going on between Haddi and the people of Wadi Firan. They didn't want to jeopardize that relationship.

"What kind of relationship?"

"They didn't get specific. They just said they didn't like the idea that I was going after Haddi, and they made it clear that they wanted me out of the village."

"They said *we* should leave?"

"As soon as possible. They even packed *me* a box lunch for the road." His meaning was clear.

"You're talking as if Muhammad and I aren't coming."

"You're hearing correct. I want you to take Muhammad

back to Cairo. I can't have him reporting to Haddi before I arrive. I don't want him ruining the element of surprise.''

My answer was immediate and surprisingly—even to me—strong. ''Now we've been through this before, Jihad, and I'll tell you again: I want up this mountain. As for Muhammad . . .'' I motioned towards Muhammad, who was sitting beneath a palm tree smoking cigarettes with some of the kids. ''. . . you don't have to worry about him. I'll make sure he doesn't get a chance to warn Haddi.''

Jihad wasn't about to buy this. He said: ''Let me make sure you understand me.'' It was his command voice again. ''This is where we split up, Lion. This is the end. I'm going up to get Lizzie. Me alone. Without your help. Without Muhammad's. I'll take care of Lizzie for you. I'll bring her down.''

''Jihad . . . no. It doesn't work that way.''

''I'm afraid it does, Lion. I'm ordering you . . .'' He checked himself. ''. . . I'm asking you as a friend—go back in the morning. The bedouins will let you stay here tonight. Lizzie and I'll meet you back in Cairo when this is over.''

''Is that so? Well, thanks but no thanks. I had enough bedouin hospitality yesterday. Besides, you think I came all this way just to wish you well on your trip up the mountain?'' I heard my voice rising. ''If that's what you think, then you're the one who doesn't understand. Because, let me tell you something, Jihad, you would never have made it this far without me. You know it and I know it. So let me make this clear to you: I'm not going back without Lizzie.''

Jihad decided to take a new tack in the face of my new resolve. He would level with me.

''Look,'' he said softly. ''Kidnapping and slavery are just a small part of the story here. That's what I was trying to tell you yesterday. Meeting Haddi on this mountain only puts your life in danger. I can't let you do that. I can't. I can't let you end your life on this rock. It's just not worth it."

"And your life is worth it?"

"I'm not going to die," he responded. "Martyrs for Allah live for eternity."

That's what he said. I swear it. And it made me think that as well as I thought I'd gotten to know Jihad until this point—including all his crazy rantings about Haddi—this was just so far out, so beyond what I thought him capable of thinking, that I realized I'd never *really* known him at all. Not in the least. This was what I thought when Jihad gave me that malarky about dying so he could live forever.

I answered him in the only way I knew. In a way, I realized, that probably caused Jihad to conclude that he'd never really known me either. "Don't talk like that, Jihad," I said. "This is the twentieth century."

To which Jihad responded: "Don't *you* presume to talk about things you can't begin to understand. You have to pass through the first nineteen centuries to get to the twentieth, my friend."

The situation was deteriorating. Not only didn't I know him, but he was starting to exhibit Lizzie traits. Traits like relating the unrelated. I felt sure he was about to tell me that twentieth was a nine-letter word.

I needed him back. I needed him back now. "Look, Jihad, this is the way it is. I appreciate your concern, but I'm going up thet mountain to get my girl. *My girl,*" I emphasized. "The one who was kidnapped."

"I have my doubts."

"Doubts? Doubts about what? What are you talking about?"

"I mean I have my doubts that she was kidnapped."

"It's not open for doubt," I stated. "It's a fact. I know she was kidnapped. I was there. I saw the whole thing." I couldn't believe I was getting into an argument about a basic truth.

"Haddi's not a kidnapper . . ." Jihad's conviction equaled my own.

"That's not what you said yesterday."

". . . and I doubt he's running a slave trade."

"Are you crazy? What have we been talking about for the last few days?"

"We've been talking about a lot of things, Lion, but none of them cuts to the heart of Haddi's intentions."

"Really? Then it's about time we started discussing them."

My persistence was getting to him. That, at least, was my impression when he said: "Yes, you're right. Maybe you should be aware of everything."

"I'm glad you're finally seeing it my way."

"Just this once, Lion, and only in the hope that in the end you'll see things my way. Maybe then you'll realize that coming up is neither in your nor Lizzie's interest.

"Now to the point," he went on. "You should know that the ultimate goal of a man like Haddi does not lie in enslaving women. And it isn't extortion or selling drugs. None of these crimes is an end for him. That should be clear from the outset. They're all means to an end."

"And the end?"

"I'm not sure how to explain this to you. It's not so concrete. It reaches closer to the essence of evil."

I waited for him to continue.

"Surely you're familiar with the story of Dracula, the vampire who lived from the blood of men."

"I am."

"This is Haddi's story too. Haddi gets his strength from bringing out the evil in each man."

"You're right, it's too abstract."

"Haddi's goal," Jihad explained, "is to create hell right here on earth. A hell that's built and fueled by a pool of corrupted souls. He does this by punishing the good and elevating the evil. He turns everything on its head. Like polluting in the name of purity, and lying in the name of truth.

"This is Haddi's evil," he continued. "This is his crime against Allah and Islam. This is the reason he must die."

There it was. Jihad's intention to murder Haddi. I might even have understood him if he'd justified it on a concrete basis. Like as retribution for kidnapping, or for forcing Lizzie into slavery. Something like that. But sentencing a man to death for first degree evil? Even *my* questionable moral code wouldn't sanction that.

If only he'd alleged that Haddi did it all for money. To get rich! That I could understand. Anyone could. Greed is a real-world motivator. Very civilized. Very white collar. But just for evil? This was hard to swallow. "Let me get this straight. You're telling me that Haddi does all these evil things, the stealing, the extortion, all that stuff, basically just for fun?"

"No," he answered, "not for fun, yet not for the money. Destroying people's souls is not something one does for money. That would make it meaningless. I doubt Haddi's that way. No, he would be a man of principle. A man of ideals."

He was trying to get me into a philosophical discussion over the ideal involved in destroying a man's soul. I refused to bite.

"I'm sorry, Jihad. I can't buy it. And even if I could buy it, I wouldn't. For me, Haddi's ends begin and end with Lizzie's kidnapping. That's it. All that other philosophical razzmatazz, with the means and the ends, and the principles and the shminciples, well, it doesn't speak to me. All I know is Haddi's kidnapped my girlfriend. Period. What he's doing with her, I don't know. It's not important now. All I want is to set her free. That's all I want to do.

"You," I continued, "seem to be taking this case a little too personally and I think its affecting your judgment. It's making me reevaluate whether you're worth all the money I'm paying you."

Jihad considered my speech. I think I'd taken the wind out of his sails. Or maybe he just finally understood my perspective. In any case, he seemed to have a change of heart.

"It's your choice," he said, and turned and walked over to where we'd parked the jeep. "You're the boss." He sounded resigned. He put his hands into the backseat and started organizing his gear.

"What does that mean?" I asked.

"It means we go up together. That's the best strategy. That way I can keep an eye on you and make sure you don't ruin my plans with any foolishness."

"Muhammad too?" Unlike Jihad, I felt Muhammad was on our side.

Jihad finished securing a few items before answering with a look that called me a fool. Then he sighed and said: "Muhammad too. Just don't say I didn't warn you."

I didn't answer.

"I also want you to know that you can turn back whenever you wish. You don't have to be embarrassed . . ."

"I know."

". . . I'm told —— is a tough climb."

He mumbled something I took to be the name of the mountain. I thought it sounded familiar, but couldn't really hear it. It was as if he hadn't wanted me to.

"How did you call it?" I went up to where he was still playing with his pack and pulled him around by his left shoulder. "What's this mountain called?"

"You didn't hear?" He had this look of feigned innocence. "The villagers claim that Haddi's renamed the mountain. It used to be called Jabal Sirbal. Jabal is Arabic for mountain. But now it's changed, at least from Haddi's perspective. He calls it Amman. Jabal Amman.'' His lips turned up as he said it.

I took this as one last effort to scare me out of coming. It wouldn't work. I was too concerned with Jihad's deepening insanity to give a damn about the name of the mountain.

11

Rock and Roll

CLIMBING

We left Wadi Firan without any further ado in the company of the village elders and a group of muscular bedouin youths. Our escort broke off at the edge of town. This was the edge marked by the first incline of the hill they called Menaje. The village group watched our progress as we began our climb up the steep path. They watched until we were out of sight. And then, I suppose, they watched some more.

The early part of the climb wasn't too bad. The ever-expanding view of the area below was our incentive to move forward. The higher we rose, the more Wadi Firan looked like a giant green snake slithering through a deep crevice.

As for the rest of the climb, I haven't much to say, for my thoughts grew smaller and shallower as the difficulty of the climb increased.

Facts come easiest. Like how I walked. I mean strode.

I strode from boulder to boulder, rock to rock. My hands came into play too. Together, my hands and my feet worked my body up the hill. They moved me along in a traversing pattern, back and forth, up the mountain's steep face.

As for what I saw, I can only say that the limited view from this angle complemented the scope of my thoughts. That is, my field of vision was confined to the one or two yards directly before me. This scenery often included the feet of the person, usually Muhammad, occupying that space.

Injuries were common. Scraped hands, bruised shins, and strained backs most of all.

It was immediately obvious that Muhammad had prior experience in the field of climbing. He could balance himself on a crack the size of a beetle's back, and hop from rock to rock with the assurance of a mountain goat. And all this in bare feet and with his pack on his head.

I decided to copy Muhammad's technique. Jihad said this was dumb, but I insisted. So I took off my two-hundred-dollar hiking shoes and placed my pack on my head.

I'm not sure whether this helped matters or not, though I admit I didn't think too clearly from that point on.

CAMP

We reached Menaje's peak in the late afternoon. I sat down to rest against some stones. Jihad warned me not to get too comfortable because we still had to climb down the second side. I told him there was nothing for him to worry about because I wasn't at all comfortable.

We hit bottom three hours later and continued one more hour before arriving at the area Jihad called camp. The last half hour was a struggle even after putting my shoes back on.

"Look up and feast your eyes on Jabal Amman," said Jihad by way of welcome.

I raised my head in the direction of a multi-peaked, red granite monstrosity. "How do you know this is it?"

"The villagers said it was the only mountain in this area with five peaks. Count 'em yourself."

I did.

"Besides," he continued, "look at Muhammad's reaction."

I turned around to face Muhammad. He was squatting on top of the only boulder positioned in the middle of our little clearing. His arms were wrapped around his knees and his eyes were glued to the shadowy peaks of Amman. Tears rolled down his face.

Jihad displayed his usual sensitivity. He called Muhammad "a lizard," then went off to make a fire.

I called it a day, then went off to go to sleep.

A DREAM

I dreamt I saw two shadows. One was higher than the other and seemed to be floating in the air. The other was wriggling in place on the ground like a constrained worm. I couldn't exactly make out what they were doing, though it seemed like they were fighting. The airborne shadow circled its larger and bulkier reflection with the quick, rapid movements of a boxer in the ring. It danced and jabbed, approached and retreated, in continuous motion against the larger, slower opponent. The ballet was accompanied by whispered threats I couldn't make out.

Then the higher shadow backed away to allow the grounded one to rise. This looked like a major strategic mistake to me, because it was clear now that the second shadow was larger than the first. Much larger.

The smaller shadow maintained its retreat until it crouched down right near me. It was like they were reversing positions, with the big shadow up and the small shadow down. Except the big shadow never approached.

The small shadow seemed to be working with a large bag. I couldn't identify the bag because it was also in the dark. The best I could do was make out the sound of a zipper opening. The shadow was looking for something in the bag, and this took some time to find.

The shadow finally rose and approached the giant shadow

which had waited in place all this time. Watch out, I thought, the big guy's going to squash you now. "Take guard," I called out.

The small shadow stopped in its tracks, turned towards me and waited. "Good," I told him. "Watch out. He's bigger than you." Actually, I'm not really sure if I gave this last warning voice, or just said it in my head, since the smaller shadow turned its attention back to its opponent.

The smaller shadow strode up to the larger one, handed it a few small, flimsy objects and whispered some more taunting words until the larger shadow began walking away. It hadn't moved three feet when the smaller shadow took a step forward and kicked it in the behind. It was as if it were saying "and don't come back!"

This was the end of the dream.

ROCK AND ROLL

I was thinking about the dream and what it might mean when I opened my eyes and saw a man standing over me. He had a large rock in his hand. It wasn't a boulder—I don't want to exaggerate—but it was no pebble either. It was about as big as a medium-sized honeydew. And it was poised over my head.

"Good morning, Jihad," I said as I began hustling out of my sleeping bag.

"Don't move," he warned. It was that command voice he tended to use from time to time. Usually, I noted, when he was feeling violent. I figured he had something more to say and decided to hear him out.

"You're not coming any further." Again, the command left no room for discussion. It was as if we hadn't talked at length the day before.

"What's the matter? Get up on the wrong side of the gravel this morning?" I said this loud in the hope that Muhammad would wake. I knew he was my only chance and I knew this meant my chances were slim. Muhammad just wasn't one to mess with an agitated Jihad. Best bet was he'd capture Jihad's attention by running away. I wouldn't have complained.

"I'm going to have to put you out." There was regret in Jihad's voice. A regret, I was sorry to note, overshadowed by determination.

I looked around. "But I'm already out." I practically yelled it.

"You know what I mean."

Indeed I did. Still, I thought it best he reconsider his decision. I said: "Let's not be rash, Jihad."

"I'm not being rash. This is for your own good. That mountain is much too dangerous for you. Believe me, anything I do to you here, is nothing compared to what can happen to you there."

This was not the first time he'd made this point, though it was the first time I was in no position to argue. The worst part was, I should have believed him. I should have thanked him for the well-intentioned warning, collected my belongings, and left. That's what I should have done because later events were to prove him correct.

But I didn't listen to him. No, I did the very worst thing I could have done. I said I'd take my chances. Don't ask me why I said it. I can't say for sure. I certainly wasn't feeling as bold as I'd felt in Firan. It's possible I was still delirious from the previous day's hike.

"No, you won't," he said. "You won't be taking any chances."

It was a serious moment. I needed a way out. Where was Muhammad? This conversation had been going on too loud and too long for him not to have heard us. I looked around to see what he was up to. I shot a quick glance over to where he'd lain his sleeping bag. It was there, but it was empty. I whipped my head around to the other side to see if he was occupied over there. He wasn't. I decided to take a chance by raising my head to get a better perspective on the camp. I took in a three-hundred-sixty-degree view. All I saw were the surrounding hills, our smoldering fire, and Jihad's rock. Muhammad was not around.

"Where's Muhammad?" I asked. I tried to sound casual.

"Muhammad's gone."

"I noticed," I said with regret. Pure regret, overshadowed by nothing. "Did he happen to say where he was going?"

"He won't be back."

I feared my second worst fear.

"Is he dead?"

"No."

"Did you two have words?" I knew this was unlikely, but I didn't know what else to ask. It turned out to be the right question.

"*I* had words, *he* listened. I told him he wouldn't be continuing up the mountain, that I'd kill him if he tried. I told him he wouldn't be warning Haddi about my approach, that I'd kill him if he tried. I told him he wouldn't be hanging around the camp five minutes longer, that I'd . . ."

We finished the last phrase in two-part harmony.

"And he left just like that?"

"I also gave him two hundred dollars."

"Two hundred dollars? Where'd you get that kind of money?"

He didn't answer.

"Jihad, that's stealing."

"The end justifies the means."

I was about to tell him that this was the type of thing a guy like Haddi might say, but decided to put it off until my circumstances improved. Right now I had to talk him out of doing what I knew he was capable of doing. I started getting out of the sleeping bag again.

He raised the rock.

I returned to the protection of my cocoon. I decided to appeal to his sense of fairness.

"I want you to think about this, Jihad," I said. "I'm defenseless here." I held up my arms.

He said, "I know," yet the rock remained in place.

I appealed to his sense of pity.

"You know it's not one of those things where it's going to hurt you more than it's going to hurt me. That's just not the case. It will definitely hurt me more than it's going to hurt you."

"I know." Again.

He said he knew. He kept saying he knew. Yet my heart told me to doubt him. It said keep doubting him, and maybe then your doubt will become his.

I appealed to his sense of friendship.

"Come on, Jihad, let's talk. This is me! Leo . . . Leo the Lion! Come on man, tell me what's really bothering you."

He didn't answer. I had to get him talking.

"It's your parents, right?"

I knew I'd struck a chord when he didn't react.

"I knew it was your parents. I knew it. You still haven't resolved that stuff about your mom following your dad into the desert and not sending for you. I knew it. It's hard, I know, you missing out on a family and all . . ."

"My father was a bedouin." This was Jihad.

I didn't know what he was getting at, but at least the subject was turning from me. "That's right," I agreed. "And I know that's hard for you. But think of him. He had no choice. He was born that way. It was a burden he had to bear his entire life . . ."

A distant look took up in Jihad's eyes. My words were falling on deaf ears.

"I'm sorry, Lion," he said. "I know you mean well, but this is the way it has to be." He raised the rock above his head. I saw the situation spinning rapidly out of hand. I needed to get through to him, and fast. I appealed to his sense of reason.

"Jihad! Jihad! Stop! Think about what you're doing!"

"I have," he monotoned.

I had the feeling I'd run out of appeals. I couldn't think of anything more to say. So I said "Oh."

Then the lights went out.

OUCH!

I woke later that day with a splitting headache. The first thing I did was thank God for keeping me alive. The second thing I did was curse him for taking away my sight. Then I apologized and turned my anger towards its rightful recipient—Jihad. It was, after all, his rock that had rendered me blind. This was something I doubted I'd ever forgive him for, even if it had been, as he had said, in my own best interest.

Luckily, neither my migraine nor my fury kept me from realizing that I needed to come to grips with the source of my blindness. Where had the rock fallen that it could do such damage? I felt around on my head for a clue. I found two: my eyelids. They were filled with blood and swollen closed. I never would have thought that news like this would lighten my heart, but it did. It meant that my blindness might be temporary.

The solution was as obvious as it was gruesome. I'd drain the blood through man-made punctures. This seemed like the logical thing to do, and I congratulated myself for having thought of it. Which is not to say I would have rejected a second, more authoritative opinion had one been available.

The operation was scheduled for immediately in order to get at the blood before it clotted. I felt around on the ground for my pack which I knew contained the proper tools for the surgery. I went over to where I'd remembered leaving it, but found it missing. I held my eyelids open for a look around. Rocks were everywhere but the pack wasn't among them. Jihad must have taken it with him. The creep.

I realized I'd have to perform the surgery with man-made implements gleaned from the elements. Like the two sharp-edged narrow stones lying nearby. They could be used like razors to slice open a hole in my eyelids through which the blood could drain.

This was the idea. Implementation was trickier. It took an hour or more of scraping and pinching (I never realized how tough my eyelids really were) to break skin on my right lid. The pain notwithstanding, I never felt more pleasure making violence on myself than at that moment.

I went for the second lid. This one splattered after a quick twenty minutes. I was developing into a specialist.

Blood was everywhere. I rejoiced at the sight before considering how I might stop what soon seemed like an excessive flow. The idea of a tourniquet popped into my head. I ripped a piece of cloth from my shirt and fastened it around my neck because this was where I believed I'd find the main artery passing blood to my eyes. This solution proved infeasible early on. I decided to take my chances with bleeding to death.

All in all, aside from the mess, I was very pleased. The operation returned my sight in full.

Another happy side consequence of the activity was its meaningful contribution to a theory on the nature of violence I was developing. For I'd now had the unique opportunity to simultaneously give and receive pain on my very own body. I made a mental note. I said that as pleasurable as it is, giving and receiving pain at one and the same time just doesn't pack the joyful punch of inflicting pain on another.

CLIMBING JABAL AMMAN

The ability to see cast the entire situation in a new light. It left me free to choose between following Jihad's knowing advice or my own already discredited instincts. I decided to listen to myself and turn uphill.

The climb up Jabal Amman was not unlike the climb up Menaje the day before in terms of degree of difficulty. Scratches remained common and knees continued buckling. Yet there were also some differences. Like it was overcast. This kept me from overheating. I was thankful for that. Another difference was the empty feeling in my stomach. This was as much a result of navigating alone on a giant rock in the middle of nowhere, as having missed breakfast.

The absence of my pack was also a big change. It made the top of my head feel a lot better. And while this didn't completely compensate for the continued pounding I felt from within, it was, I knew, a step in the right direction. Another positive change concerned the matter of my feet, which were now happily secured within the golden laces of my overpriced, brand-name footwear. Let Muhammad go barefoot, I thought. I am who I am.

Beyond that, there's not much to say. I hiked for hours. Up, up, up I went. Over rock and shrub. Toward something I didn't know, away from something I didn't understand.

THE DIARY

I was near the last peak when I spotted the diary. Only it didn't look like a diary. Just a few scraps of paper scattered randomly about. I wouldn't even have looked at them if I hadn't been so close to the top of the mountain, but I thought it best to settle myself before moving on to meet my fate, and reading generally relaxed me.

Looking back, I should have taken them as a warning and acted accordingly. Of course, looking back, I should never have entered that Parisian record/CD shop. But that's another story altogether.

The fact is I picked up the papers.

There were five pages in all. Some whole, some ripped. Each one numbered, dated and inscribed in a clear Latin script by a hand well tutored in the ways of elegance and style. I ordered them chronologically and began to read.

What I read appears below. I've refrained from making any editorial comments since I find, and I think you will too, that these pages speak very loudly for themselves. My single insertion is to indicate each entry's relative date or some other essential fact. These are noted within parentheses.

Diary Entry 1
(Dated two months before my arrival in Egypt.)

I've just returned from the Amman Corporation where I interviewed a young bulky peasant for the task I'd discussed with Assad. The job is simple enough. The peasant's to ''play'' my bedouin servant in the shop while I sell perfume to Miss Sherman. I offered him a salary of four hundred pounds, which he took.

In fact he mentioned that the fee was rather generous and said that while the money was welcome, he couldn't help but wonder if it didn't imply a second performance of which he was not yet aware. I, of course, complimented him on the question and said that yes, there might be more, though any specific discussions were premature. I added that the fees for these additional services would be separate from those he'd already received.

My goal is to represent the work as less than it is while making it clear that there is much more here than meets the eye.

Diary Entry 2
(Dated one week later.)

I sent Assad to find the peasant this morning to ask that he come down for a meeting. He arrived promptly at ten and was ushered into my office. The meeting lasted fifteen minutes. I told him I was very pleased with his performance through all of the rehearsals, and wanted to know if he thought he could handle an expanded part. I described it as a very demanding role for which he'd have to undergo cosmetic . . .

(The page was ripped in half at this point.)

Diary Entry 3

(Dated my second day in Egypt.)

The curtain has risen. The first act has played. My part went quite well, as did the entire operation. The peasant did well too—which was something I couldn't depend on after the operation. But he seems to have overcome any ill will he must have felt on learning the truth. I think the additional work he's had on the mountain has helped that. And in any event, I kept his role small, just calling on him to serve tea and clean up. Everyone else was fantastic too—especially Miss Sherman and the men downstairs, Umar and Aledeen. I'm looking forward to the days ahead.

(Two missing pages between this and the next entry.)

Diary Entry 4

(Undated)

I've just met with Assad for a report on all that's transpired during the last twenty-four hours. I must admit that we—myself and the entire Amman staff—seem to have considered everything. We've met each of Jihad's challenges, including, I am relieved to add, the attempted castration and tongue severing.

This Jihad is as brutal as I believed he'd be. He is determined to do his job and will stop at nothing toward this end. The peasant seems to have done his part by giving Jihad the information he needs without making it seem too easy.

This Gold is something else entirely. He is completely ignorant to the danger around him and refuses to heed any of his partner's sound advice. Most ridiculous of all is that he seems to be trying to befriend the peasant. I won't go into all of his many ploys, but leave it to say that he has gone so far as to bathe the giant in bubbles. Were it not so pathetic, I'd be tempted to laugh. Picture, if you will, an underweight, balding American tourist bathing a three-hundred-pound eunuch! Something, no?

Lastly, and perhaps a little too sentimentally, I must comment on the most tragic element of all in this whole bitter opera. It is that Gold risks his life for a woman who finds him contemptible.

12

Azizah

IMPLICATIONS

I arrived at the last word of the last diary entry with a
slack jaw. This was my second rock in the face of the day.
Assimilating the implications was out of the question so
long as these same implications remained beyond my power
to grasp. The best I could do would be to replay a fact or
two. Like: Lizzie was not who she said she was. Like: Jihad
was in for more than he bargained for.

And the rest . . . well, who cared about the rest. That
was quite enough.

Oh. And I felt manipulated.

AH-HALAN WA SA-HALAN

I don't know how long I sat there, or when the diary
papers slipped out of my hand and scattered in the wind. I
just don't know. All I can say is I somehow became aware
of a voice emanating from over my head. I didn't pay attention to what it was saying because I wasn't paying attention
to anything right then. It was just a background of high-
pitched sounds.

Then slowly. Very slowly, I began focusing. First on my
legs, which I could see before my eyes, and then on the

rocks all around and against my back. Finally I focused on the voice. It was calling my name.

I lifted my head towards the sky. Wisps of clouds glowed red-orange in the light of the setting sun. The voice continued calling my name from high and behind. So I stood, turned around and faced the big rock against which I'd propped my back. Then I leaned my head straight back against my shoulders until I saw the outline of a man standing on the edge of the boulder about twelve feet above. I couldn't see more because the sun was directly behind him.

I raised my left hand to shade my eyes. It didn't matter that this didn't help much. I already knew who it was.

"Hello, Dr. Haddi," I said.

"*Ah-halan wa sa-halan.* Welcome, Leo," said the soprano. "You're late."

THE ENTRANCE

"You don't say?" I referenced my watch. "By dingo, you're right. It must have been that jam along the steep incline about halfway up. I was stuck there for hours."

He laughed. "Bravo! Bravo to you, Leo. I like a man with a sense of humor. And after what you've been through! How *do* you do it?"

Dr. Haddi's proximity was having a major effect on raising my state of alertness. Danger is like that.

I should also admit that in addition to the tinge of fear I felt at being in the presence of so evil a man, I also felt a bit of good. I'm not sure I can explain why, except to say that he was a familiar face far from home. I was even flattered that he liked my joke. I decided to take a stab at building up some mutual familiarity.

"You liked that last joke?" I asked. "Well, that's nothing compared to some of the funny things I've heard about you."

Haddi didn't laugh at this one. He just told me he wasn't

surprised I'd heard such "funny" things considering "the company" I kept.

Given what I'd read in the diary, I examined the possibility that Haddi's feelings towards Jihad were as extreme as Jihad's feelings towards him and concluded that getting onto the subject of Jihad while Haddi controlled the high ground was probably a poor idea. I decided instead to see what I could do about improving my strategic position.

I dropped my gaze out of the sun and towards the face of the rock. I said: "Don't you think you should invite me into your camp?"

"Why, of course!" His voice picked up again. "How rude of me! It's just that I'm so excited to have you here that I've completely forgotten my manners. You must forgive me! Please, please come in and enjoy my hospitality. Please, Leo, just step around to the left of this rock and follow the path up . . . That's right, right around there . . ."

I followed his instructions and found myself on a small balcony of land overlooking the Sinai Desert. Haddi himself appeared from around another rock. His arms were outstretched, and his teeth sparkled. He looked exactly as I remembered him from our brief encounter in Cairo. Everything was the same, except now, instead of a galabia, he wore a tuxedo.

"Welcome!" he bubbled as he clasped my right hand between his two. "Welcome to Jabal Amman!"

FIRST REACTION

The texture of his hand was such that had I closed my eyes I would have sworn I was in the grip of a reptile. And though my instinct was to free myself immediately, my brain said this was not the way to react to your host on a mountain in the middle of nowhere. The same brain also counseled that I stand by passively while he shook my arm like a rubber hose for a full sixty seconds.

"You can't imagine how happy we are to have you here. We don't get many visitors, you know. How was your trip? Where are your bags?"

"My bags are lost. And as for my trip, well, you know very well how my trip went, Haddi." This was not the thing to say and I knew it. Yet for some reason I didn't regret it. Maybe it had to do with saying what I meant. Or maybe it had to do with looking down at him.

In any event, now that it was said, I realized that honesty would be the preferred policy with Haddi. This, because he probably already knew everything I could possibly reveal.

Haddi released my hand and looked up with concern. "You're not looking very well, Leo. Not at all." He began shaking his head and making tsking noises with his tongue. Then he raised himself on his toes and reached up to check my eyelids.

"How on earth did this happen? You really should have someone look at these wounds if you don't want to get an infection." He paused briefly then continued when I didn't react. "I can see you're not feeling well. I can see that. You're probably hungry too. Come, take my hand . . ."

"What have you done to Lizzie?" I shook off his grip. "I want to see Lizzie."

If you ask why I asked to see Lizzie after all the revelations contained in the diary, I guess I'd have to say I did it from instinct. She was the one I'd come to rescue. Besides, without her, without this sense that I was doing something right, I would have been left to confront the shocking reality that all my experiences—from Amman, Jordan, to Jabal Amman—were empty and without meaning.

As for this alleged contempt in which she held me, I took a philosophical view. She wasn't the first to feel this way. With luck, she wouldn't be the last.

Haddi was predictably opposed to any meeting between Lizzie and myself. "Now, Leo, calm down. Don't worry, you'll see Lizzie soon enough. I'll take care of everything.

But you must be patient. You've come up to see me and you're my guest now. You would do well to relax and enjoy my hospitality. This is the least you can do. Now come.''

His voice was as soothing as a voice with the tonal range of a prepubescent boy could possibly be. I considered this offer from my girlfriend's keeper. He was giving me the option of playing guest. This was no small gesture, considering that so far as he knew, my only reason for being there was to free Lizzie from his evil grip.

As for why he was doing this—the motives behind his hospitality, well, I really didn't care. I didn't have the strength to. I'd used it all up during my struggle up the face of Amman on an empty stomach and with holes in both my eyelids. Besides, call it what I might, I was still at his complete mercy, and would remain so until I got my health back. For this, I knew, I needed rest and peace.

I decided to accept his offer and follow him.

We stepped by the boulder from around which he'd appeared and began walking down a narrow path. The way continued for about thirty yards until it fed into a large open area surrounded by rocky hills. It was a bowl actually, about a quarter mile around. A number of buildings made from prefabricated materials were set against the rock walls of the perimeter. Large, home-sized tents were interspersed between some of the buildings. The center of the bowl was empty except for a wooden stage and what looked like a well. The entire clearing was reminiscent of some college campus green, except that this one was brown. And there weren't any frisbee players.

In fact, there wasn't anyone.

AZIZAH

I glanced down at Haddi in his formals, then back out at the dustbowl, and once again down at Haddi.

"Slightly overdressed for the desert, aren't we?" I asked.

Haddi looked up with a toothy smile. "It's not often that an honored guest such as yourself arrives, Leo."

I held myself to a polite: "Is that so?"

"Indeed it is."

"So where is everyone?"

"You don't want Lizzie and everyone to see you in that condition, do you? Wouldn't you rather clean up before acquainting yourself with Jabal Amman?"

I didn't have a chance to answer before he brought his hands together for two short, loud claps.

I looked out across the campus towards where he'd clapped and detected a stirring by the entrance of one of the tents. A few moments passed before the beads which defined the doorway were pulled aside to reveal a young woman of olive complexion.

Haddi looked up and gave me a knowing nod as the woman began walking across campus. I nodded back without looking down at him. I couldn't help myself. She had a number of striking qualities. Like, for instance, she was scantily dressed. I mention this outright, though the funny part is, I wouldn't have noticed at all if it hadn't been for one crazy thing. Namely, that as out of place as Haddi looked walking among the rocks in a tuxedo with tails, this woman in her seminude state seemed to fit right in.

Go figure.

As for her clothing as it was, she wore a light, silk vest that barely enclosed the valley between her substantial, yet firm breasts. This caught my eye because it reminded me of the vista of Wadi Firan without the palms. The lower portion of her curvaceous body was clothed in something like pajama bottoms, also of silk, that began at her hips, flared out around the legs, and grew tight again just above her ankles. Her feet were bare.

I caught myself licking my lips as she grew close. Her hair was pulled tight all around her head and collected in a single braid. Intertwined with the braid was a red ribbon. I assumed it was there for more than beauty alone because the braid was standing straight up. That's right, straight up, like a little spear. I figured the ribbon had something to do with that. And if not the ribbon, than at least the silver ring around the braid's base.

The next thing I noticed were her steps, which were shy and modest, and in complete unity with the delicate expression in her almond-shaped, almond-colored eyes.

Then came her lips. Full, rich, and inviting they were. I didn't know what to make of them at first, for their bold appearance flew in direct contrast to the overall mood of her elegant carriage. It was only later, after a second look, that I realized that what I'd mistaken for boldness was just the richness of innocence.

Finally, there was the music. Yes, the music that sang from the tiny bells she wore around her left ankle, and the silver bracelets that adorned her arms. Tingle, tingle, tingle, sang the bells. Jangle, jangle, jangle, answered the bracelets.

Then she was upon us.

"Beautiful, isn't she?" This was Haddi's question to me. I couldn't answer.

"This is Azizah," Haddi began. "Azizah, this is Leo Gold."

I extended my hand to shake hers. She bowed deeply in response. I couldn't help but notice when gravity made her vest fall open.

"Azizah," Haddi continued. "Leo is very tired. Also his eyes have been wounded, you can see that . . ."

Azizah nodded quietly.

"I want you to take care of him. Wash him. Feed him. Rest him. Do whatever he asks, for he is an honored guest."

She bowed again.

"Go with her," he said to me. "I'll see you in the morning."

The phrase "rest him" made me suspicious. I felt caught in a dilemma. I began to worry about appearing too passive. I didn't know whether to go with Azizah or demand of Haddi that he take me to Lizzie without further delay. To play along by saying nothing would expose the fact that I knew he was up to something. Yet speaking up too soon could place me in the awkward position of having to deal with Lizzie before I was mentally or physically able.

"It is late, isn't it?" I asked.

"Yes," he told me sincerely.

"All right," I said. "I'll go with her as long as you take me to see Lizzie in the morning."

"First thing," he assured me.

THE TENT

Azizah led me by the hand to the tent from which she'd originally emerged. Passage through the beads brought me into a world without connection to the one of rock I'd left outside. For inside this world of the tent all was luxury and comfort.

Everything was soft. From the walls and ceilings (it *was* a tent), to the raised floor with its white shag carpet, to the human-sized pillows strewn lazily about, to the padding on the bar, to the siding along the Jacuzzi.

Softest of all was Azizah. That is, the light from the slowly dripping candles along all five walls cast a strangely sensuous shading, a golden hue, all about the room, and it was this hue that accentuated many of my hostess's shadows, rounds, and crevices that had previously gone unheralded.

If anything was to be hard in this room, it would have to belong to me.

"Take off your clothing," said Azizah as she fired a match she used to light some incense. Her voice came from the deepest reaches of her throat. "Come now," she repeated softly (even her voice!). And when I didn't respond: "Or would you like me to undress you?"

That's a quote.

Moreover, she didn't say it with a smirk or any sleazy intonations. Just the opposite. She spoke with sensitivity and interest. With delicacy and gentility, warmth and true caring.

I repeated the phrase in my head. "Or would you like me to undress you?" The woman of gold wanted to know.

I moved my mouth noiselessly.

She tilted her head trying to understand.

"Ub, dub." I pointed to my throat. "Thirsty . . ."

She understood immediately. "Tanqueray and tonic? Perrier? Fresh squeezed juice?"

"Have you got a Bud?"

"No." She shook her head, no Budweiser. Was there something else that might quench my thirst? Her eyes were wide. I could see she didn't want to disappoint me.

"That's all right," I assured her. "I'll take a glass of juice."

She walked over to a pitcher of iced orange juice, poured a glass, and brought it to me.

I drank thirstily.

"Thank you," I said as I wiped my lips with my forearm.

Azizah replied with a slow, deep bow.

THE BATH

I waited for her to straighten up before I removed my clothes and walked up the stairs of the Jacuzzi. An involuntary moan emerged from my lips as I slowly lowered my body into the heated water.

"You're hurt, aren't you?" Azizah spoke through the steam of the bath. Whispered, actually, with those cushioned lips into my hurting ears.

"Yes," I whispered back. "I'm hurt, but you make me feel better."

"I want to," she said as she brushed a soapy sponge across my aching chest.

The conversation trailed off as the bath's soothing comforts began seeping into my bones. Azizah went to work cleansing the previous week's dirt from my body and mind. She poured bath salts into the water and anointed my flesh with oils. She hummed. A low, peaceful hum, it was. From deep in her chest. It sounded like the purring of a contented cat. She went on making this noise for some time. All the while she scrubbed my body with sweet-smelling soaps and let the bubbles fall where they may. Then she whispered: "Close your eyes. Close your eyes so I can cleanse your wounds."

I answered with obedience.

THE TREATMENT

She began the treatment by lubricating my eyelids with a moist, warm pad. Across and back she went, with the delicate touch of an expert.

Next came air. Lilac-scented, heated air that she puffed upon alternating eyelids until the two of them were dry.

She paused here for a few moments while cautioning me not to open my eyes.

I sat quietly until I felt her apply another fluid directly on the points of puncture. This required another extremely precise and delicate pad followed by a gentle sucking from a device she laid over my eyelids. I soon realized that the sucking mechanism and precision pad were both part of the same sophisticated instrument. This part of the treatment continued for a long time. At least five minutes.

I was about to ask how it was going, when Azizah removed the suction and whispered "Shhhhh, just a little longer," and began lapping on another coat of medication with the original pad. This was followed by a second round of puffing and the words "All done."

I opened my eyes into Azizah's radiant face. "That was

wonderful," I said. "Thank you. I'm already starting to feel better. Thank you so much."

Azizah blushed. "Pleasing you pleases me."

A MISSION OF MERCY

I considered what I might do to please her more. Something to show how much I appreciated her stimulating company. Something that said, "Yes, I too sense a feeling, a certain aching deep down, that we could become attached one to another."

I looked into her eyes to see if she understood. She indicated she did by way of dropping her vest to the floor. I gasped at the magnitude of her sensitivity.

"Leo," she begged, "save me . . . I'm on fire." Her nostrils flared. Her head fell back.

FIRE

You may at this point be asking yourself, what of Jihad and Muhammad? Where were they when Leo Gold was about to get his?

I'd be lying if I said I was thinking the same thing. Or that this was the appropriate place to discuss it.

But now that you've asked, I'll tell you: I didn't know then, and I don't know now.

What I did ask myself was: how would Azizah deal with the news that her sexual fire would have to go undoused because Leo's hook and ladder was in the midst of a general strike?

I looked up and found that the news had already leaked. That Azizah saw the problem herself and was about to take steps to solve it. I tried to tell her it was no use, but she wouldn't hear of it. She had experience in these matters, she said.

The first action she took was to climb the stairs of the Jacuzzi, lower herself by my side, and attach her lips to my chest. Most of her attention—basically her tongue—was focused on my right nipple. I closed my eyes to enjoy a sensation that was not unlike that which I'd felt when she'd tended to my eyelids. So similar were they, in fact, that the more I thought about it, the more obvious it became that her mouth and the treatment instrument were one and the same.

If one difference could be found, it was that thought it cured my eyes, it could not cure my size.

"What's wrong?" she asked when she came up for air. "Don't I please you anymore?"

"Of course you do, Azizah. You make me feel wonderful. I guess all the excitement is finally catching up with me. I mean, I've just climbed up a mountain and this is the closest I've come to eating anything all day. I'm sorry, but I just don't think I'll be able to please you until I put some food in my mouth. I'm sorry."

Azizah looked me in the eye, gently caressed my face, and climbed out of the Jacuzzi.

"Forgive me," she said, as she stepped out of her pants. "I should have known." Then she toweled off, donned a robe, and jingle-jangled over to some curtains by the far side of the tent. I strained my head to see what she saw as she drew them apart. All I could glimpse was a small icebox, a microwave, and a velvet pouch from which she drew stainless steel cutlery.

"A microwave?" I asked from my seat in the tub.

"High tech is a big fascination up here."

DINNERTIME

Dinner was served some twenty minutes later on a small portable table covered by a red cloth. There was only one setting. I asked Azizah why this was so.

"This is the way," she said. "You eat, I watch."

There was enough food for Ali Baba and all forty of his thieves. She opened with a rich carrot soup, of which I had two portions. This was followed by a small artichoke heart salad served with a tangy mustard sauce. A second salad of romaine lettuce and miniature tomatoes was also available.

She prepared her main course, a two-inch-thick T-bone steak on a portable electric grill, and served it medium rare, smothered with onions and mushrooms. By its side she placed a baked potato (baked to perfection in the microwave), and Chinese-style stirred vegetables (also prepared in the microwave). Juice remained the drink of choice.

I told her I was too full for dessert, but she served the warm apple pie anyway, along with Turkish coffee.

"You're pleased?" she asked.

It was all I could do to nod.

"I hope it made you feel at home."

"It did. I do. Where did you learn to cook like that?"

"Dr. Haddi teaches me everything."

SPEAKING OF DR. HADDI

The mention of Dr. Haddi's name flashed a warning light over my head. This was the great benefit of the meal. It returned my strength and with it my ability to appreciate the situation's gravity. I looked at Azizah and silently asked myself who this sex kitten really was. Then I asked, though this time out loud and to Azizah: "Speaking of Dr. Haddi, what exactly is your relationship with him?"

"I am one of his wives."

Bingo. Just like that. Without so much as a blink to indicate that she'd paused to consider what effect this might have on the owner of the nipple she'd recently sucked.

So I paused for her. This gave me time under the pretense of playing with the apple pie crumbs on my plate to compare myself with that midget. Why he's not even half the man I am, I thought. Unless, of course, *he* can get it up.

I began considering Haddi in a new light. "He has more than one wife?"

"Yes, many."

"When did you meet him?"

"Just a few weeks before our wedding," she said coyly.

"You mean you had an arranged marriage?"

She nodded. At least this explained how a great-looking girl like Azizah ended up with a sleaze like Haddi.

"How did that happen?"

"He made my father an attractive offer."

"Is that so?"

She nodded again. I recalled Jihad's description of the bedouin marriage customs and the girl's willie, and decided to check my conclusions.

"And may I ask, are you by chance bedouin born?"

"You may," she answered evasively.

"Well, are you? Are you a bedouin?"

"Yes, I am."

"Do all bedouins speak English so well?"

"Not all. But I take classes. Each girl on the mountain must study at least three languages. I speak Arabic, English, French, and Italian."

"That's four."

"That's right."

"And what do you do with these languages? What I mean is, what kind of business are you and the girls involved in?"

Azizah rose and began clearing the table. "Intelligence services," she said.

I checked to see if I'd heard her right. "Intelligence services?"

"Yes," she called over from the sink. "For hire."

"You call what we were doing here intelligence?"

A look of hurt came over her face as she began loading the plates into the dishwasher. "What are you saying?" she asked.

"Nothing. I mean, well . . . are you always so physically close with men other than your husband?"

Azizah turned back to the sink. "My husband told me to make you comfortable."

"How does that make you feel?"

"How I feel is not important."

"Would your willie approve?"

The questions were becoming a little too personal for her. I knew she didn't want to answer. I also figured she had to.

"My father, may he rest in peace, was my original willie. He told me to marry and obey Dr. Haddi. Until I find a new willie, I won't do different."

SPEAKING OF YOU

"But I've said enough," said Azizah in an effort to change the subject. "There are still many mysteries for you to reveal. I don't even know how or why you came up here." She was facing me now.

"You don't know?" I couldn't believe she didn't.

She paused before answering. "No."

Her "no" said "yes." It was just a matter of how much she knew. She definitely wasn't as innocent as she appeared. I figured she'd be reporting the contents of this conversation to Haddi at the earliest opportunity. In fact, I didn't discount the possibility that Azizah's peculiar head spear might even be a transmitting antenna, and that Haddi was listening to our conversation at this moment.

I was further convinced that this whole seduction/meeting was one big setup designed to squeeze me for information. Or at the very least, in the event that all my assumptions about Lizzie were wrong, it was a scene that could be used to discredit me in her eyes. The Lizzie-blackmail angle was also, by the way, the real reason why I refused to make love to Azizah. None of that other stuff, like the broken down fire pump trick, had any basis in reality. I just did it to quell Azizah's suspicions.

The bottom line was, any wife of Haddi's was not to be trusted, regardless of the size of her breasts or the talent of her tongue. Azizah could question me to her heart's content. All she'd learn was what she already knew.

"How did I happen to come up here?" I repeated the question into the ring at the base of her braid. "It all started when Dr. Haddi, your husband, kidnapped my girlfriend."

I paused to judge her reaction. There was none. She didn't even try acting surprised.

"None of the official agencies, neither the police nor the embassies, were willing to handle the matter, so I took up the investigation on my own. I began by retracing our steps and was lucky enough to spot one of the men who helped your husband during the kidnapping. I confronted him and managed to convince him to take me to where Lizzie was being held. That's how I ended up here." I left out any mention of Jihad in the dim hope that Haddi did not yet know of his whereabouts.

Azizah's interest picked up. "Who was that? Who was the man who guided you up Jabal Amman?"

"It's not important." I played Muhammad down. "He was a guide for hire. A mercenary."

MIXED SIGNALS

"I know it's not important, Leo. Just tell me, what was his name?"

That's what came out of her mouth. Her lips, though, said something altogether different. They were thick and red, and posed in a pout. Even her breathing, I noticed, was out of synch with her words, for it was deeper now, and more quickly paced, as if pumped by the rapid rise and fall of her breasts.

Mixed signals wrought mixed interpretations. "Don't say a word," cautioned my brain. "If you can't trust Haddi, you can't trust his wives."

But my groin disagreed. "Let me check her out," it said as evidence of its growing interest in the matter. "I'm a good judge of inner character."

"Look who's back," remarked my brain in a sarcastic tone. "Where were you when we needed you?"

"Don't you have some involuntary responses to attend to?"

It was time to step in. "Now, boys . . ." I was about to say. But Azizah spoke first.

TORTURE

"Tell me," she breathed imploringly as she lay her left hand on my right thigh. "Was he mute?" Her palm slid slowly forward.

I felt the pressure growing. Harder and harder it got not to talk. The ruthless wench, I thought. She's resorting to every last trick in the book. First her fingers, now the treatment machine! I felt myself about to burst. Hold on, I told myself, hold on! Con-trol your-self!

But I couldn't. She had me mastered. "Yes . . . yes . . . yes," moaned the beaten man. "Yesssssss," I said like a punctured balloon. "His name was Muhammad . . . yessssss."

A TRADE

The strike had been broken. Azizah wiped her chin as she fell back into her chair.

"Muhammad," said she soundlessly. "Muhammad," she mouthed again. "Were you alone with him? Did you come up with him alone?"

I answered with a listless nod of the head, yes. I lied, that's true, but that hadn't been my intention. I was just too wiped out to think straight. Such was the effect of her immense powers of persuasion.

"Did he also . . . did you notice, was he wearing a ring on one of his toes?"

I was slowly regaining my presence of mind. She wanted to know if Muhammad wore a ring on his toe. He did, I knew. The question was whether to tell her outright or wait for another round of torture.

Azizah saw my indecision. "It's important, Leo. Was he

wearing a ring on one of his toes?'' Her hand returned to my thigh.

There was danger in this move. ''Show some character,'' cried my brain. ''At least get something in return.''

I waited for a reaction from the relation down south, but there was none.

I removed her hand. ''No more free lunches,'' I said. ''What's so important about the ring?''

''I can't tell you.''

''Then we have nothing to talk about.''

''Don't say that. Of course we do. Maybe I can help you too.''

She was proposing a deal, just like we wanted. Some kind of trade. Now it was just a question of trust. My brain said ''No way.'' My instincts were undecided.

''How can you help me?'' I eyed her skeptically.

''I know many things.''

She looked around like she was checking to see if we were alone. Then she faced me with a conspiratorial look and said, ''Don't worry, nothing goes beyond this tent.''

''What do you know about my girlfriend? Is she here?''

''Will you answer my questions if I tell you?''

''It depends on how good your answers are.''

Azizah appeared to weigh this. It wasn't the best deal, but it was the only one available. ''I trust you,'' she said. ''I'll tell you what I can. What's your girlfriend's name?''

''Her name is Lizzie. Do you know her?''

Azizah shook her head no. ''I don't recognize the name. But I don't know everyone here.''

Very likely, I thought. She wants to make it tough so I'll be satisfied with less. ''Are you sure? I'm nearly certain she's here.''

''Perhaps if you described her.''

''She's a thin, blond British woman.''

Azizah shook her head.

''Well, she's new up here. She was just kidnapped a few

days ago . . ." I suddenly recalled the diary entry. "She sometimes calls herself Miss Sherman. Maybe you know her by that name."

A strong gust of wind shook our tent's outer walls.

"Miss Sherman?" she asked.

I nodded.

"I'm not sure if this is who you mean, but there is an Ellen Sherman here. She resembles your description, but she's not British. You said your girlfriend was British, didn't you?"

"Yes . . . Why? What nationality is this Ellen Sherman?"

"As far as I know, Ellen is American."

HERE'S TO B. F. SKINNER

So be it.

This was my first thought on hearing the news of Lizzie as Ellen Sherman, American. I was pleased with my new attitude. It reflected a growing ability to accept the unexpected. Well, not totally unexpected. This news did, after all, explain why Miss Sherman found me so "contemptible."

I made a silent toast to B. F. Skinner. Here's to conditioning, I said. And to laboratory rats.

THE RING, PLEASE

"Now it's your turn," said Azizah, "to answer my questions."

"A deal's a deal. Would you repeat the question, please?"

"Was Muhammad wearing a ring on one of his toes?"

"Yes, he was, as I recall."

A look of disappointment came over her face.

"He never removed it?"

"Nope." True, I lied, but figured: What the heck, when in Rome!

"Where is Muhammad now?"

'I don't know. He deserted me this morning."

More disappointment. Azizah took it hard. She buried her face in a pillow.

"It's not so bad," I said. "Climbing alone builds character. Looking back, I'm glad I did it. Besides, if you want to know the truth, I never liked the way that guy smelled."

Azizah's face remained engulfed in the pillow. Her back heaved to the beat of muffled sobs.

OVERNIGHT

What a day. First Jihad, then the rock, then the climb, then Haddi, then Lizzie, then Ellen, then America, then Azizah, then Azizah, then Azizah. She was the big question mark. What was her part in all this? Was she just a sensitive girl fallen in with the wrong crowd, or was she some kind of spy living a life of deceit?

I decided to sleep on it.

I waited for Azizah to get herself together before politely asking that she leave the tent so that I might dream in peace. My brain said this was the thing to do if I wanted to evaluate the situation logically. Other, more common instincts disagreed. They counseled tossing "it," and sleeping on her.

So did Azizah.

"Don't make me go," she pleaded. "I want to be with you. Don't make me return to Dr. Haddi before dawn."

Sniffles and hiccups dotted her speech. Salt stains marked her cheeks. She even snuggled like a child when I wrapped her in my arms.

If she's an actress, I thought, then she's even better than Lizzie. I decided to let her stay. It was better this way. It gave me the pretense of control. My only condition was that she sleep on the bed she'd removed from beneath the Jacuzzi, while I curled up on some cushions.

This was a compromise my brain could live with.

13

※

The Academy of Sex

A MORNING ENCOUNTER

The morning air hit me cold in the face as I stepped out of the tent following Azizah's breakfast of microwaved eggs and coffee. I felt rested and strong. Azizah seemed better too. She even rose early to wash my clothes so I'd have something clean to wear.

The campus was as empty as it had been the previous evening. Empty, save Haddi, who stood waiting by the stage in a freshly pressed tux.

"Good morning, Leo! I trust you passed a pleasant evening." Haddi's cheerful front was still in place. I couldn't tell whether this meant he knew I hadn't slept with his wife, or if he assumed I had and he just didn't care.

I decided to probe him. To learn, if I could, the extent of his intelligence sources there in the tent. I also decided to adopt a tough line. This way he wouldn't take me for a patsy.

"Yeah, you can rest easy. Azizah treated me fine. Gave me a bath, whipped up some cooks. Don't worry, Haddi, your wife did good." I winked on "did good."

"That's not what your tone indicates," he replied with a frown. "You don't sound as if you took full advantage of her hospitality. I'm sorry for that. Yet you've no one to blame for that but yourself.'' This was his slip. It meant he knew we hadn't slept together.

An awkward silence fell between us as we both considered the significance of his words. Then Haddi tried to cover himself by continuing on as if he hadn't stopped. ''. . . or else you're just overtired from lack of sleep. That must be it.''

''Yeah, that must be it.'' I encouraged this conclusion while maintaining my pose as rough guy.

''Still, there's no reason for you to speak so gruffly.''

''Really? Are you sure? Then please tell me, what is the proper etiquette for addressing the man who's kidnapped your girlfriend and conked you over the head?''

''If that's it, Leo . . .'' He appeared relieved.

''It is.''

''I completely understand how you feel . . .''

''Do you now?''

''. . . Yes I do. And if you'll just relax and give me a chance, I'll explain everything.''

''What about Lizzie? You promised you'd take me to see her first thing this morning.''

''When you're right, Leo, you're right. That's what I promised you last night and that's what I'll do this morning.''

''Glad to hear it.''

''But I have a suggestion. Why don't you take a few minutes to listen to a brief explanation about life on Jabal Amman before going to see Lizzie? I can assure you that such an explanation will be of immense value later on. Though it's only a suggestion, of course.''

''Let me understand you: this is not an either-or proposition?''

''Ha, ha, ha! Leo, of course not! What kind of people do you think you're dealing with? We're all gentlemen and ladies up here. There's no reason at all for you to be suspicious."

I took this last sentence as a cue to raise my guard. I also decided to take a chance on going with the explanation first and the meeting second, as I figured I'd need to know as much as they'd let me before I confronted Miss Sherman.

"All right," I said. "Explain."

Haddi bowed. "With pleasure."

I walked with him to the side of the campus where a large boulder stood out and apart from the hills and the other stones.

"Please . . ." said Dr. Haddi, and motioned that I ascend the stairs chiseled into the back of the rock. He followed right behind. The top of the boulder was flat and formed a natural perch for looking out on the still-empty campus.

"Well?" I asked.

"You've asked, Mr. Gold, for an explanation, and I've agreed it's your due. Let us begin."

THE GIRLS

"Look before you, Leo, what do you see? An empty clearing? Some stones? A desert mountain peak? Hardly. Take another look. For this place where you stand, it is none of those things. It is more. It is a garden. A garden for growing the most wonderful delights of man. Delights which challenge and bring pleasure to each of the senses, beginning with the sense of sight, and including in equal measures, the senses of hearing and smelling, taste and touch. Yes, my friend, even the sense of touch."

"You see it now, don't you? No? Look again."

He clapped his hands. I sharpened my lookout for some sign of this garden he described. I scanned the peaks of the surrounding hills and checked the facades of each of the buildings and tents along the perimeter of the campus. All was quiet.

I looked to Haddi, who just smiled in return.

I turned back to the campus and noticed some movement off to the side from down a path which entered the campus. It was the same path Haddi and I had taken the previous evening. Only there was a woman there now. And she was dressed, not for mountain climbing, but for a walk down the Champs-Elysées.

She wore heels and a tight black skirt that ran from just above her knees to her tiny waist where it met a sharply cut jacket. The jacket was also black, and fit to the contours of her frame. Its shoulders were padded and its sleeve cuffs laced. I stretched to see her face but I could not for it was hidden beneath a wide brimmed hat.

"An image of beauty," Haddi informed me. "A shadow of all that is feminine."

"Amen," said I, in a new tack designed to avoid further confrontation, at least in front of this delicate form.

"And look over here," continued my guide. "Another example of the ideal woman."

I turned toward where he spoke and saw a white-faced, red-lipped, traditionally dressed Japanese woman. She padded over to where we stood and bowed. Haddi addressed her in what I took for Japanese. He referenced me. She smiled and let out a shy giggle. Haddi continued with a few more words and bowed again. She bowed back before retiring from the scene.

The campus was gradually filling with women. All shapes, all sizes, all colors. They emerged from the buildings and the tents, from the wilderness beyond the campus and the surrounding hills. Their numbers were more than I could count. The garden was in full bloom.

"Behold Uwanda," said Haddi. He pointed to a statuesque black woman at the far end of the campus. "Drink in her beauty, Leo, for it is her perfection. Appreciate her perfection, for it is her beauty.

"And see that one there? She is one of my favorites. Notice how round she is? How juicy?"

He was describing a woman who was in fact, obese, and who paraded this fact in a skimpy cover of see-through veils.

"Not many Westerners understand the beauty of substantial flesh. Do you, Leo?"

"I must admit I'm partial to the narrower model."

"For shame, Leo, for shame! Take a moment now to try and fathom the joys of the ripples of her belly. Their royalty. Their magnificence. Imagine gripping her opulent bottom and mounting between the flesh of her thighs. Imagine falling in, deep within her warm, soft folds . . ."

He looked to see if I shared his appreciation.

"An experience?" I offered.

"More than an experience," Haddi corrected. "A taste of the essence of life itself."

I kept my eyes on this festival of beauty while he spoke. Women were dressed in bodysuits, business suits, bathing suits, and birthday suits (well, at least one). They wore miniskirts and grass skirts, overalls, and saris. Some were veiled and others masked. I saw the height of fashion and the fashion of the street. And not just from Europe alone, but from America too, and Asia and Africa, and Australia and the poles. That's right, the entire world, right there on Haddi's mountain, Jabal Amman.

THE ACADEMY OF SEX

I turned my attention back to Haddi, who sported the admiring look of a parent at the grammar school play.

"Ahhh, Leo, so much beauty in one small spot. Takes your breath away, doesn't it?"

"It certainly does. It's very impressive, Dr. Haddi. *Very* impressive, indeed. These women must be the most highly trained prostitutes in the world."

Haddi's chin turned up in my direction. The look on his

face indicated he hadn't taken my remarks in the complimentary spirit in which they'd been offered. "Where on earth did you get the impression that these women are here for sex?" He was insulted, I could tell.

"Well, I mean, it seems pretty obvious that you've got yourself some sort of high-class prostitution ring here."

"Is that what you think, Leo? You think I'm running some sort of 'academy of sex' up here? Is that what you think?"

I registered a neutral look in the hope that it would nullify my offensive words.

"If so," he continued, "then I suggest you think again because you are very sorely mistaken. These aren't whores, Leo. Not a single one. And they aren't slaves and they aren't prostitutes."

"That doesn't leave many alternatives."

"No, it doesn't!" This was definitely the hottest I'd ever seen Dr. Haddi. No doubt about it, Haddi treated the subject of his girls with the same sensitivity that Jihad treated the subject of his Haddi.

"What you see before you, and I hope you can appreciate it, Mr. Gold, is a collection of the most beautiful women in the world." He was struggling to regain that sense of control he so liked to project. "*The* most beautiful. And I'm not just talking about physical beauty though, as you can see, we appeal to every taste in man. No, the beauty we strive to achieve is that which glows from within. It's a deep inner beauty . . . a certain richness of life often found in fine wines.

"I am speaking too abstractly for you, Leo?"

"I'll raise my hand when I get lost."

"Each one of these women is a perfect physical and intellectual specimen. That is a fact." Haddi was quite proud of his work, that was clear. It was also clear that anyone who questioned the basic perfection personified by his women was also probably the type to question the fact that the sun rose in the east.

"And I'll tell you something about these women . . . *my* women." He made sure my attention didn't wander by poking his index finger into my stomach. "Each (poke) one (poke), in addition to learning the secrets of beauty and health care (poke, poke), also passes through a rigorous course of study that includes classes in science, psychology, philosophy, history, photography, and language (poke, poke, poke, poke . . .)."

I grabbed his hand. "Hey, Haddi, that hurts. You can stop the poking. I'm listening."

"Excuse me," he lowered his hand. "In any event, each student picks an area of specialization after completing the core. The entire course runs one full year and includes up to ten hours of classroom and/or lab time each day, six days a week. Each of our graduates, I'm proud to say, is the realization of the very cream of womanhood. A match of matches for the finest of men."

"You don't say?"

"Indeed I do. I even have the statistics to back my words."

"That won't be necessary."

"Good." He passed a look of relief. "Now I'll show you a couple of examples of the kind of woman who comes through my course."

He searched the campus for a suitable model.

"Take that woman over there. You see her, the one in the leopard skin jumpsuit?"

"Yes."

"She's a specialist in biology."

I tried looking impressed. "Hmmmm." I controlled the impulse to ask if she needed a lab partner.

"And that one there who looks like a samba dancer?" He pointed out a deeply tanned blond in a bikini I could have flossed with. "She plays the organ."

"I wouldn't have guessed." In fact it was obvious. I wondered if she played requests.

"Yes, Leo. You must always seek to see below the surface."

"So I've heard. Thanks for the sound advice."

"You're welcome."

"I also thank you, Dr. Haddi, for straightening me out about the whoring, slaving, and prostitution question." I didn't have to put it that way, of course, but it was Haddi's only sore spot, and I couldn't help scratching. "But that still doesn't answer the main question I've got weighing on my mind. Which is: if they aren't involved in you know what, then what exactly are these women studying for? Is it for self-improvement alone, or are they engaged in the pursuit of some greater good?"

A slow smile came to Haddi's face. It was the closest thing to a genuine smile I'd seen on him yet. "Very good, Leo, very good." He reached up and patted me just below the shoulder. "You're finally catching on. I like it: 'For some greater good.' Yes, my perceptive friend, that's it. You've hit the nail squarely on the head. For some greater good. Yes."

I waited for him to fill in the details which never came. Instead, he said: "Come, let's enjoy the parade a little longer."

A BLAST FROM THE PAST

His abrupt change of subject indicated that he wasn't interested in divulging the nature of the "greater good" for which the girls were being trained. I didn't press him. I wasn't going anywhere, and figured I'd find out sooner or later. Besides, all his talk had distracted me from the real business at hand: the enjoyment of physical culture on display.

So I was pleased when he suggested we continue our observations from atop the boulder. The perspective gave

me a good feeling. One that came from pride that the
parade was just for me. "Girls everywhere," I thought.
"Just for me." I liked the way it sounded.

That's why the sight of the one-eyed man shook me so
deeply. For not only did he stand out like the proverbial
sore thumb, but he brought reminders of a wholly different
and more dangerous reality.

I first spotted him walking near the far side of the campus. Striding actually, with long, purposeful steps, completely oblivious to the girls all around. Just moving
forward until he reached and entered a large red tent.

WHO'S THE BOSS?

I took this as a sign that the carnival was over. Yes, the
one-eyed cab driver from Cairo took care of that when he
turned my attention from the sweet fantasy of these hooker-
shaped intellectuals to the sharp-lined reality of Amman.

"How long have you been following me, Haddi?"

"Excuse me?"

"You heard me! How long have you been watching my
movements?"

"I'm afraid I don't know what you're talking about,
Leo."

"Cut the hogwash." I said it low. Deadpan.

Haddi didn't respond.

"Come on, Haddi. I'm the guest, and you're the host,
remember? 'My wish is your command'? How about coming through with an explanation. How about filling me in
on this Amman crap?"

"You're upset."

"That's right I'm upset. I have a right to be. Now are you
going to tell me, or . . ."

"Or?"

". . . or are you going to tell me." That was about the
only "or" available to me. He knew it and so did I. That, I
figured, was what made him powerful.

"Ask nicely." He was not above rubbing my nose in the fact of his power either.

"Please," I said, bowing to his power. "Please fill me in on this Amman crap." Though I still had my pride.

THE AMMAN CRAP

"All right, the Amman crap. I'll tell you all about it on our way over to Lizzie. Come, let's go."

We both stepped down off the rock and began walking across the center of the campus. The women took our approach as a signal that the show was over and drifted on to new activities. I waved discreetly to a couple of my favorites.

We were about one quarter of the way across when Haddi began talking. "The Amman Corporation, or Amman crap, as you so crudely call it, is a multinational corporation with business dealings spanning six continents. Its products and services are many, and include, in part, a chain of hotels, a fleet of cabs, modeling agencies, and travel services. It even dabbles in import-export, of perfumes mostly, if you can believe it.

"I founded the corporation many years ago as a private postal service for the New York City area. It's a business, I'm proud to say, that still operates today. Our client base began in Harlem and soon spread to places like Washington, D.C., Detroit, Los Angeles, and Miami."

He broke from the story as we neared the edge of the campus. "Please follow me this way." I fell in behind as he cut a path between two tents. This path fed into a trail that climbed up one of the hills which defined the campus border.

Haddi's speed picked up on the incline. "Come now, don't lag," he called back as his tiny legs scooted him forward and down the second side of the hill. I trotted right after until the last signs of the Amman "civilization" were no more. All that remained was a dusty trail, two wadi walls, a tuxedoed black Nubian dwarf, and myself.

We were about fifteen yards down this path when Haddi slowed the pace. He picked up the story when I caught up. "The corporation experienced rapid growth as its products began catching on in the suburbs. New capital brought on new investment opportunities. And the rest? It's enough to say it was a very good time for me . . . for us." His face took on a nostalgic glow.

"It was also during this period that I developed an interest in real estate." He motioned to either side of the trail.

I looked on impassively. There was a limit to how excited I'd get over goat droppings underfoot and the sight of tiny caves plunging into wadi walls.

"And that's all," Haddi concluded. "I'm no longer involved in the corporation's day-to-day operations. I leave that to the professionals. My interest today is in finding the odd project now and again to sink my teeth into." He gestured back towards the campus.

"Now, if you'll please step lively, we'll be with Lizzie in just a few minutes."

I ran to keep up with him. "That's all very interesting, Dr. Haddi," I said. "But it still doesn't tell me why I kept seeing people associated with Amman following me through Egypt. That's what I meant by the 'Amman crap.' "

"What did you mean?"

"I meant that the name Amman kept popping up wherever I went. It began at my hotel and continued from there."

"The name Amman? It's charming, isn't it? Very easy to remember. I'll tell you how I thought of it."

"But . . ."

"No buts about it, Leo. It's my pleasure." His eyes sparkled with insincerity.

"I'm not sure if you're aware of it," he went on, "well

of course you're not. How could you be? Anyway, I was once very much involved in your country's civil rights movement. I helped organize, and worked very closely with, a number of organizations involved in promoting black pride and spiritual reawakening.

"What a time it was! Everything was so small back then in the sixties. So small, and exciting too! I went to marches and gave speeches. I even had the opportunity to meet and work with a number of prominent black leaders including, I'm proud to say, Dr. Martin Luther King, Jr. and Malcolm X.

"I was quite taken with the whole period. The people, the issues, even the slogans. One of these in particular, one of these slogans, had great appeal. I liked it for its simplicity and its force. It stated: 'I am a man.' That's all. 'I am a man.' It was the perfect name for a ghetto-based corporation. So I shortened it to 'a man,' then condensed it to Amman, and changed the pronunciation slightly.

"And that, my friend, is the happy story of Amman . . ."

"Happy for you," I was tempted to add, since he had come no closer to answering my question. It was clear he never would.

"I hope you enjoyed it," he continued with a grin. "It did, at very least, help us pass the time during this little walk to Lizzie's home."

We were standing at the beginning of a narrow path that broke perpendicular to the main trail. The path was short and straight, and came to an end by a door built into the wadi wall.

"After you," said my host.

I walked down the path until I found myself before an old weather-beaten door.

I knocked.

VAGUELY FAMILIAR

No more than fifteen seconds passed before the knob twisted and the door began opening inward. I held my ground until the door was at right angles with the rock wall. I turned back to Haddi for a clue on how to proceed.

"She's inside," he said, and motioned that I step in.

I turned back to the darkened entrance and placed one foot in the threshold. Everything seemed black inside despite the glow of a bare bulb in the distance.

"Go on," said Haddi from behind. "You can only adjust to the light from within."

"Don't rush me," I answered.

"Fine, fine," he said. "Take your time. I'll be right out here."

"You're not coming in?"

"I'm sure you two have much to discuss. I'd just be a third wheel—that is the expression, isn't it? Don't worry about me, Leo. I'll wait for you right here. The fresh air invigorates me."

I turned back to the poorly lit passage and plunged my head inside. The outline of a tunnel began taking form. I decided to step in. I did it because Lizzie was inside. I also did it because I had no real choice. This was where Haddi wanted me.

I was three steps in when the door closed behind me. I sensed something between the door and myself, and spun around to see it. I was straining for a glimpse of what it might be when I heard it say: "Welcome."

The figure of a man emerged from the shadows of the dimly lit corner. He was small and battered and his face was unshaven. His left hand was still on the doorknob.

"Welcome," he repeated.

We each stood our ground. Myself squinting through the lifting darkness. My counterpart staring back through a Cheshire cat grin. I gave him a short bow. I tried to appear as if I were responding to his friendly greeting when in fact

I was straining for a closer look at this vaguely familiar doorman.

"Hello," I said. "I'm here to see Lizzie."

He returned my bow. Very ritualistic it was, and in very good taste.

"Welcome," he said once more. "Welcome to Jabal Amman."

"Thank you," I answered. "Thank you for welcoming me to Jabal Amman. I'm here to see Lizzie." My eyesight had nearly adjusted to the light emanating from the bulb behind my head. It was apparent now that though polite, this fellow was hardly a gentleman. His clothes were old and dirty, and his laceless sneakers were nearly rotted off his feet.

"I'm here to see Lizzie Simms," I said. "Please direct me to her."

The old guy bowed again. "Welcome," he repeated. "Welcome to Jabal Amman. Welcome, welcome, welcome. Happy, happy, happy. Welcome to the happy Jabal Amman."

The airport, I thought. This was the guy who carried our bags at Cairo airport.

"Welcome," he repeated most enthusiastically. "Thank you, welcome, thank you. Welcome to our mountain. *Allah Akbar.* God is great."

MISS SHERMAN, I PRESUME

"Please, welcome. Please, welcome," repeated the doorman/porter as he gestured that I follow him deeper into this stylized cave/apartment.

I could see now as well as I ever would. I noted that in addition to the small entrance alcove in which I'd been welcomed, the apartment (for lack of a better word) seemed to consist of a narrow passageway and another room at the far end. The walls, the floor, and the ceiling were all of bare rock without any kind of decoration. In fact, the entire structure was nothing more than a hole burrowed into the wadi rock lit by a few strategically placed lightbulbs.

We arrived at the room at the end of the tunnel. It was a small, stuffy room, no larger than twelve feet square. I identified it as the bedroom because of a makeshift bed in one of the corners.

A second corner, the one opposite the foot of the bed, was occupied by two pails and a three-foot-high, doorless cupboard for storing a couple of pieces of clothing. The top of the cupboard held what looked like a bar of soap and a few single sheets of ripped, yet neatly stacked newspaper.

The corner diagonally across from the pails was taken up by an old desk and chair. A number of books, some writing paper, and a lamp were ordered on its face. This lamp, the one on the desk, was also the room's single source of light if you didn't count the light which shined in through the passageway.

I nodded to the "welcome" man, who silently bowed before stepping from the room. I was alone. Alone with the thin, blond woman occupying the chair by the desk. She was bent forward reading something. In deep concentration. As if seeking refuge in the dimly lit words of the book lying open before her.

I coughed once to draw her attention.

Nothing. She just turned the page and plowed on.

I coughed again. Again, nothing.

I decided to speak up.

"Excuse me," I said. "Miss Sherman, I presume?"

14

Where Is My Biscuit?

AN EMOTIONAL REUNION

The blond woman raised her head from the book and said: "Wha?"

It was the sound of a woman waking from the dream of a printed page. She followed this sound by straightening her back and turning towards me.

It was Lizzie, all right. Slightly worn. Kind of tired looking. Perhaps even a bit confused in the eyes. But Lizzie nonetheless. I could tell from the way she used the back of her hand to brush the hair from her face.

"Leo?" Her head strained forward to see me through the half light. "Leo? Can it be? Biscuit, is that you?" Biscuit. That's what she'd called me in happier times.

She rose from her seat and approached. Cautiously.

"Leo?" She kept repeating my name like she couldn't believe it was me. "Leo?" Now she was before me. Inches away. Her hands rose to cup my cheeks. "Leo, my love."

A tear welled up and spilled out of her left eye. A second one followed. Then a third. Her right eye joined in. She gripped me tight around the neck and brought her head against my chest. "My God. How did you get here? Oh, I don't care. Just thank you. Oh, thank you!" She was weeping now. Sobbing noises mixed with the sound of tears splashing against the rocky floor.

She fell to her knees and clutched me about the thighs. The sobbing continued. "I can't believe it's you, I just can't believe it's you." She rubbed her head against my knees for emphasis. "I can't . . . I can't . . ." Her words faded into a gentle wheezing.

This was my opportunity. "Funny you should say that," I said. "I can't believe it's you either."

"I know, I know." She was kissing my kneecaps now.

"What I mean is, the game is over, Miss Sherman. The jig, as they say, is up."

"Huh?"

HUH POEM

The following poem was originally written on the back of an envelope during the auditions for a blue jeans commercial. I was on the selection committee. I've inserted it here because it describes what I thought on hearing her last comment.

This poem is about, ending your doubt,
on the proper employment of "huh."
For if others shout when you let it out,
it's a sign of mixed usage with "wha."

As for where you can hear, "wha" used most clear,
call a reader who's glued to the page.
Though the "huh's" use is near, don't try it there,
for it's usually heard on the stage.

Yes "wha" is said, if a book's deeply read,
and a noise shakes the dream from your gut.
But "huh," it is bred, when actors have dread
that their part is about to be cut.

WHERE IS MY BISCUIT?

"Huh?" she repeated from her post at my knees.

"You heard me." Very cold, I was.

"Leo? Leo, what . . . what are you talking about?" She turned up the accent really thick. She wiped her nose. "And what's that? What's happened to your eyelids?"

"Cut the crap, baby!" I barked. "My eyelids are just fine!"

She winced. "Leo? Are you all right?"

"Yeah, I'm all right. No thanks to you."

She rose to her feet. "I don't understand. What do you mean, no thanks to me? I haven't been in a position to help myself, much less anyone else. I've been locked in this room for days. For days! Now, all I can think of is how brilliant it is to see you!"

Brilliant? This was meant to throw me off. Only a limey could use a word like that in a context like this. Yet, *I* wasn't fooled.

"Listen, Miss Sherman," I said into her face. "Or may I call you *Ellen*? I know all about you and what you've been up to. The works. So cut out the dildersquash and come clean."

"I don't understand what you're talking about. What have they done to you?" She searched my eyes. "Where is my Biscuit?"

Her Biscuit? I'd tell her where her Biscuit was! Her Biscuit was somewhere along the rocky slopes of Jabal Amman where he'd disappeared some time yesterday afternoon with his last ounce of faith in mankind and a few well-worn pages from a mislaid diary.

AN INTERRUPTION

Oh, I'd tell her all right, right after I removed the doorman's slovenly face from the space between myself and my adversary. That's right, the little squirt must have come up to check on the commotion. He looked at Lizzie and then at me, then back at Lizzie, and then back at me. And then, sensing the tension, the utter confusion and downright fear that gripped us all, he grabbed at my shirtsleeve and tugged at my arm until I acknowledged him with my eyes. Then he said, asked actually, in the most tentative of voices: "Welcome?"

What insolence, I thought. I'm about to break this case wide open, and he's going around offering greetings. Where did this eunuch (how else could he have gotten the job up here?) get the nerve, the *chutzpah*, to cut into the single most important speech in my—till now—quite insignificant life, with a string of babbling inanities?

"How dare you interrupt my destiny?" I bellowed.

The "welcome" man went crumbling to the floor in a heap of cringing terror. Lizzie went down right after him to see if he was all right, then turned her head back up to me.

"Leo!" she said. "What's come over you?"

I didn't answer. I just turned and walked to the far corner of the room where the sound of that whimpering flea wouldn't reach me.

The two of them remained huddled together on the floor for over ten minutes. This left me time to review the conflicting facts regarding Lizzie/Ellen.

CONFLICTING FACTS

My task was to carefully assess the likelihood that Lizzie would assume a double identity. Sure it was a long shot, but not as long as it had been before discovering that the cab driver worked for Haddi. Besides, hadn't two separate, yet independent sources, Haddi's diary and Azizah's word, each referred to Lizzie as Sherman, with one calling her Miss, and the other calling her Ellen? This was pretty incriminating.

Only the other side of the issue—the one that asked that I believe her story—possessed equally compelling evidence. Like me, for one. I'd been Lizzie's intimate for a number of months. And as one who'd actually witnessed the kidnapping, I was eligible to vouch for her story. Besides, hadn't a friend of mine, Jihad, told me she'd been taken to a harem, and hadn't I later seen this harem myself? Plus, hadn't Lizzie herself just confirmed the kidnapping story?

Darn! I didn't know what to do. I wanted to believe Lizzie because our ties went pretty far back. But I also wanted to believe Azizah because she knew how to make me feel sooooo goooood. On a more objective scale, each of them cried authentically and knew how to deliver a meaningful hug. Yet each of them couldn't be telling the truth.

The dilemma called for extreme measures.

EXTREME MEASURES

I walked up to where Lizzie was petting the "welcome" man's scalp.

"We have to talk." I said.

I waited for her to stand before letting her have it in the biggest, deepest holler I owned. "All right, you!" I boomed. "I'm at the end of my rope. Come out with it already! Who are you, really?"

My voice was hostility itself. The "welcome" man covered his head. Lizzie stared at me in fear. Her back arched. Her lips tightened. She raised her half-clenched fists to waist level. Then she said, hissed, really, in the voice of the queen: "How *dare* you address me in that tone of voice!"

This made me think: "Maybe I've misread her. Perhaps that stare wasn't fear at all." Yet all I could manage to say was: "Huh?"

IT'S LIZZIE

The awkwardness didn't pass. The ball was in my court, and I couldn't return it. I looked down to the "welcome" man for help, but he just sneered back at me. I returned to Lizzie who by now, thank God, was relaxing a little. Her hands, at least, had returned to her sides, and her lips had become unloosed.

"Lizzie?" I asked.

She came into my arms. It was as quick as that. All was forgiven. "I don't know what's come over you, Leo. Did you come here to save or attack me?"

It was Lizzie all right. It had to be. "I'm sorry for yelling, Lizzie. Try to understand. I've had a tough week."

She stepped back to consider this statement at arm's length. "Look around you Leo. I haven't been watching movies in this half-light."

"True," I said. "But you should know that I've had to deal with a lot of weird people who've muddled with my mind like nobody's business. You should know that."

She laughed. "Then consider me. I've spent days searching for ways to pass quality time with this one." She motioned towards the "welcome" man.

I didn't argue her point. I just said: "And I've been led to believe you're not Lizzie Simms, but someone else entirely. Someone named Ellen Sherman."

"Ellen Sherman? Who's she?"

"I don't know. I don't know."

"Well, if you don't know, how should I?"

I was at a loss to respond.

"Leo, I'm your Lizzie. I've been held captive here for who knows how long. There is no Ellen Sherman. There's just you and me. Oh, God! How happy I am that you're here!" Her pale blue eyes twinkled as she took my hand in hers.

The "welcome" man looked up from the floor with a crooked smile. He was deeply touched. I could tell by the way he drooled.

ROOOH

Lizzie released me and walked over to the bed. Her expression was grave. "Leo," she said. "How are we going to get out of this place?"

I thought I detected a hint of a frightened girl in her voice. She was looking to me for direction.

"I'm not sure," I said in as manly a tone as I could. "It wasn't so easy getting up here, you know. But I guess for starters we can get this "welcome" guy as far away from us as we can. He's definitely underfoot." I shook the doorman's arm from the cuff of my pants. "Can you get him back to his post by the door?"

"Of course," she said. Then: *"Roooh!"* It came from deep in her throat. *"Roooh!"* she repeated. Her arm shot out down the corridor.

The "welcome" man walked back to his post.

PRISON LIFE

Lizzie motioned that I sit by her on the bed. "We need to talk," she said.

"I know. I see you've learned Arabic."

"A few essential words. Extended study periods are practically the only benefits of prison."

"Yeah, prison." I gave the place the once over. "This looks pretty bad."

"Bad? It's bloody hell. And to think I used to complain how my apartment back home was so small and dark. Christ, it was a castle next to this. And at least it had windows."

Apartment?

"I guess it makes you appreciate the lights."

"That's true. It's definitely good that they're here. But I'll tell you, Leo, there are at least two power failures a day. And that one's so lazy"—she pointed down the corridor—"he refuses to fetch me a torch."

"So you just stand in the dark?"

"Or sit."

"And . . ."

"And what? What can I do? Talk to myself? Play games in my head?"

"That's an idea," I offered. "The games thing. I read a story once about a prisoner who developed into a chess grandmaster just by playing games over and over in his head."

"That's fine for some, but I can't see myself imagining a soccer game in here. I haven't got a field, much less someone to play against in the dark."

A *soccer field?*

"That's where imagination comes in."

"Imagination's your specialty, Leo. I'm just a practical English lass. I take my imagination from books. Preferably nonfiction."

A NEW REALITY

Her words led me to a new reality. One that weakened my knees.

"Look Lizzie, I suddenly feel weak. Hold my hand."

"Your hand? Certainly." The corners of her lips turned up. "Mr. Gold! Do you intend to seduce me with him right there?" It was clear she wouldn't half mind. I guess she was getting into the spirit of the mountain lifestyle.

"No, I don't intend to seduce you. I'm just tired."

I grew conscious of the bed where we were sitting side by side. It wasn't much of a bed, really. Just a thin mattress on top of a wooden board standing on six bricks. A simple affair.

"I'm just tired," I repeated. "Tired of all the lying. I just want someone to tell me the truth for once. To let me in on what's going on."

"I know what you mean, Biscuit."

I didn't answer.

Then she said: "I love you, Biscuit."

"Please don't say that."

"Why not? It's true." She took my head in her hands and kissed my cheek.

"No, it's not."

"What's wrong, Leo?"

"This is wrong. You're wrong. I'm not sure who you are."

"What are you talking about?" She looked at me critically. "Oh, please, let's not start that again. I thought we were through all that."

"You never loved me before, and you don't love me now."

"That's not true. I don't know what you're talking about. Sometimes you just don't make any sense."

"I don't? Let me try again: What I'm talking about, Lizzie, or Ellen, or whoever you are . . ." I heard my voice rising. "What I'm talking about . . . what I'm asking . . . what I'm fucking begging, is that you level with me once and for all!" Now I was shouting. "Because I am so fed up, it's coming out of my ears! Because, though before I suspected, now I'm sure, that despite that accent, you're not British now, and you never were then!"

"Leo!" She reached out to me.

"Remove your hands," I said toward the desk.

She did as I ordered, then said: "Why don't you look at me when you make these accusations?"

I didn't answer. I didn't even look at her.

HER COUNTERATTACK

"I simply don't understand you, Leo. Something's happened to you. You sound so paranoid. Christ, if anyone's to be paranoid here, it's me. I'm the one who was kidnapped and I'm the one who's been rotting in this cave." She rose and went over to the desk so that she'd be in my line of vision.

"You. You just show up out of nowhere. You come inside, clean and fresh like you've just stepped out of a Jacuzzi, and you start attacking me. How do I know? Maybe you and the guard break bread together at the company picnic. Sure, that's it. And Dr. Haddi's using you to get through to me so that I'll join his harem. That's it, isn't it?''

She moved over to the chair by the desk and sat down. Then she lowered her head in her hands and began to cry. ''I think you should go now. Go back to Dr. Haddi and tell him it didn't work. He hasn't beaten me yet. Tell him I'd rather rot in this cave the rest of my life, than whore around for him! Go on now, tell him. Off with you.'' She lifted one of the books from the desk and threw it at me. I ducked and heard it smack the wall a few inches to the left of my head.

MY ANSWER TO THAT

I stood and clapped three times.

''I'm going,'' I said. ''But not before I tell you what I think.''

Her breathing was heavy. So was mine.

''First of all, I think you're a terrific actress. I'll bet that's what you studied in Haddi's school. Am I right?''

No reaction.

''You don't have to say a word,'' I continued, ''because I'm stepping out of here. Only before I go, I want you to know that I'm on to you. That's right. And while that's not much of a consolation, it's about the best I can do. Sure, I'd rather live with your lie than die with the truth, but given that my future doesn't look too promising anyway, I'm happy that at least some of the truth is out.

''Happy? That's not really what I mean. Maybe relieved is closer? As in: I'm *relieved* that some of the truth is finally out. God, it lightens the feeling on my shoulders. Especially after hearing so many lies for so long.

''You said you loved me,'' I continued. ''Maybe you did. Maybe once, in a distant kind of way. But not anymore. You couldn't love me like you say and yet continue with these horrible lies. Lies . . . Damn, you know something? You know what I just realized? That 'lies' and 'love' are both four-letter words. How about that? Who knows, maybe I've got it all wrong. Maybe you do love me. What a laugh! Just my luck. Damn. If only you hated me. Then maybe I'd hear some truth.

"Well, maybe next life."

I fell silent. The blond woman didn't move or react. She just stared. I got up to leave.

AND THEN SHE SAID

"Wait. Don't go yet." Her voice was suddenly deeper. The British accent was gone. A soft twang from the American Midwest was in its place. "Everything you say is true. Just tell me, please, how did you know?"

HOW I KNEW

That was it? I was right? What do you know? I'd gambled and won. Why, I'd be happy to tell her how I knew. I'd been right, hadn't I?

"What can I say?" I opened modestly. "It was the little things. Like when you talked about trying to imagine a soccer game before. British people don't call it soccer, they call it football. And they play it on a pitch, not a field. Don't you remember how all you talked about in Paris was going to a 'football match'? I certainly do. I didn't even know what you were talking about until we got to the game. As for why you called it soccer now, instead of football, I guess you've been out of character too long."

"And that's it?"

I sensed the British accent slipping back into her voice. I guess she figured that if that was all my evidence, it wouldn't be too hard to bring me back into her confidence.

"And one other thing. Again, a single word, but a significant one."

"Yes?"

"The word was apartment. You compared this place to your apartment. That was the real giveaway, because the English call them flats, not apartments."

I could tell she was disappointed. To be caught on such a small thing by a rank amateur like myself was shameful. She was probably kicking herself for confessing so quickly. If only she'd waited, I could see her mind saying, she could have covered herself with a couple of stock explanations I would certainly have bought. Like, she was only speaking "American" so I might understand. That would have worked. That would have been enough.

Instead she said: "That's a mistake I won't repeat." She didn't sound bitter.

"At least not with me."

TEA

She stood. "Would you like some tea?" she asked.

I eyed her suspiciously. The knowledge that I'd traveled with a stranger all that time was disconcerting. She even *looked* different with an American accent. "What I'd like," I said, "is an explanation."

"I serve my explanations with tea."

"Is that so?" I suddenly felt thirsty. "In that case, I'll take my tea with a teaspoon of sugar, and my explanation straight."

"This will only take a moment." She turned to the table, opened a drawer and removed a metal coil attached to an extension cord. It was a heating element. She plugged it into an outlet and placed the coil into a cup of water. Then she went about preparing the tea.

I used this time to feel self-satisfied for exposing her fraud and to consider my new knowledge.

A PUZZLEMENT

I began with the generally pleasing assessment that more and more pieces were falling into place. If my perspective remained confused, I reasoned, it was only because my station within the puzzle prevented me from seeing the picture as a whole.

I examined my three new pieces:

Piece 1: Haddi was not running a harem as I'd first assumed, but was involved in managing a ring of spies, perhaps for hire. This piece had come from Haddi himself, ("these aren't whores, Leo") and Azizah ("intelligence services" she'd said, "for hire").

Piece 2: All of the members of this spy ring were highly trained women. This piece also from Haddi.

Piece 3: I, myself, had been deceived by one of the members of this ring, a Miss Ellen Sherman. This last piece from the horse's mouth.

The horse returned from her activities and handed me a cup of tea. I took a sip. I could feel the tea moving down my throat and into my stomach. "Tasty," I commented. I savored the heat.

"I'm glad you like it. Now, as you can see, this operation only works for a single cup at a time, so please be patient while I prepare a glass for myself."

It was strange hearing her speak American.

"Take your time," I said. I still wanted to explore the motives behind each of the new puzzle pieces while they were fresh in my mind.

WHY SPY?

Like why, for instance, had Haddi organized a ring of spies? Many theories addressed this question, though none provided a clear answer. One theory, Jihad's, said that a man like Haddi was motivated by a will to evil. This simple answer was not without its appeal, as there was no denying that Dr. Haddi's personality had its quirks. Still, I felt I'd have to know him better before making such a blanket indictment of his character.

A second theory on "why spy" came from Haddi himself. And though he'd been rather cryptic about it at the time, I truly believed there were genuine feelings behind his claim that he did it "all" for "some greater good." Only what was greater than "good"?

Finally, theory three belonged to me alone, and was summarized by the single word: greed. Greed—a controversial motivator associated with both good and evil. I figured Haddi liked money as much as the next person, so why not come to it through renting out spies.

WHY WOMEN?

The second question concerned "why women spys?"

Why not? It was a great idea. Classic even. Who, after all, would ever suspect a member of the "weaker" sex of spying, especially when she'd popped into your life so casually (as Lizzie/Ellen had popped into mine). Besides, it made economic sense (and further justified my greed theory). Women spies could fill that very important segment of the espionage market where information could only be extracted in the horizontal.

Yeah, I gave Haddi credit. The Amman School was a terrific idea that would make him rich.

WHY ME?

Which brought me to the final question of "why me?" Why had Ellen gone to the trouble of disguising herself as Lizzie and attaching herself to me when I knew nothing worth spying over? This just didn't make sense. I was about to explore it further when she addressed me from the table as she stirred her tea.

ELLEN SPEAKS UP

"What are you thinking about so intently?"

"What do you mean?" I asked.

"I mean what's that vacant look in your eyes? I thought you said the tea tasted good?"

"I did. I'm just waiting to hear why you did what you did."

"You were never a good liar, Leo."

"I'm not bad," I said. "Just not in your class."

So ended our period of small talk. What followed was Ellen's rendition of Lizzie's relationship with me, and the subsequent kidnapping. Much of what she said confirmed elements of what I'd already deduced. About that I was proud. About the rest? Well, judge for yourself:

ELLEN'S RECOLLECTIONS

"Listen, Leo," Ellen began. "You should know from the start that there's a limit to what I can reveal about my activities here. You should know that up front."

"Acknowledged."

"That said, I guess the first thing you should be aware of is that the Jabal Amman School is not some sort of women's college, and it's not here to develop debutantes. That's probably obvious. The problem is, I can't state flat out what it actually is. That's something you'll have to deduce yourself. Those are the rules."

"I understand," I said. I took it as confirmation of my assumption that Haddi was running a spy ring.

"Good. Now the next thing you should know is that I didn't happen into that CD shop by chance. Not at all. I went in there because I knew I could find you there each day. I went in there to meet you."

"I understand," I said. I took this as confirmation of my assumption that this woman was a spy. All that remained was to determine why she'd chosen me.

"But why me?" I asked.

"No special reason. I did it as part of a field study training exercise."

"A what?"

"Kind of like a test. For school . . . the Jabal Amman School. Its purpose was to determine if I'd mastered the lingual and cultural skills of a proper Englishwoman. My assignment was to pass myself off as a British citizen to a typical American national. I saw you one day in a fast-food outlet and decided you were typical enough.

"All in all, I think I did quite well, don't you?"

I didn't answer.

She must have read the look on my face. "I'm sorry, Leo. This must be hard on your ego."

"Don't worry about my ego," I said. "Though I think 'quite well' might be overstating your performance somewhat. Let's call it a passing grade."

She didn't argue. "Okay, passing. Anyway, Dr. Haddi thought so too and decided to call the exercise to a close. This occurred while we were in Jordan. You remember when I received a message that my Aunt Heather had phoned?"

"That was the signal?"

"Yes. The signal to return to Egypt immediately. Which is what I did."

"But with me in tow."

"That's right. Although I was supposed to return alone. The problem was, I didn't know how to split up with you."

"What do you mean?"

"I mean I didn't feel right leaving you without an explanation . . ."

"I could do without the sentimental stuff."

"So I did something completely against procedures. I brought you with me. This turned out to be a terrible mistake . . ."

"I'll say."

"You see, I'd been sent abroad to perform a mission, and

now I was returning. A welcoming committee was at the airport to greet me. Yet your presence prohibited contact because it violated Jabal School security procedures.

"So they executed the contingency plan. This called for passing the student, myself, through a series of Amman channels until I arrived in a safe environment."

"By channels," I interrupted, "you mean the porter who carried our bags—the 'welcome' man—and taking me to the Amman Hotel?"

"That's right. I took you to the Amman because it's under Dr. Haddi's control. Then they contacted me while you slept."

"While I slept? But weren't you afraid I'd wake up? I mean, I don't know where the discussions took place, but if they were in the room, I might have heard you, and if they were somewhere else, I might have woken up and gone out to look for you. How did Haddi account for this?"

"The fact is, Dr. Haddi came into the room and interviewed me while you were lying stark naked on the floor. It was quite a scene, I must say."

I thought about the scene.

"There's no need to blush, Leo. No one took advantage of you."

"I wasn't blushing. But how did you keep from waking me?"

"That's the beauty of it. You picked up on it in the perfume shop."

I didn't understand.

"The ventilation system!" she cried. "The ventilation system, that's how they did it. They pumped gas into the room while you slept to ensure that you didn't wake up . . ."

And all the while, I thought, naked on the floor.

"This same ventilation system, by the way, can be found in most properties owned by the Amman Corporation. Even here on the mountain. Dr. Haddi uses it to control different aspects of the environment. Things like temperature and noise level. They can even inject fumes that affect your behavior.''

I was listening closely.

"But that night," she continued, "it was just sleeping gas. The two of us were knocked out at the same time—as we slept. Then I alone was revived by Dr. Haddi and his advisors so we could discuss how best to sever the ties between you and I."

"Why didn't you just pack your bags and leave me a 'Dear Leo' note."

"We considered that. I pushed for it hardest. I wanted the opportunity to say good-bye properly, and this gave me that option. But others disagreed. They saw your presence as a chance to test an elaborate escape mechanism they'd designed around the perfume shop."

"You mean the pink smoke from the Fire of the Gods perfume?"

"That was part of it."

"But didn't you realize I'd go to the police or the embassy?"

"It didn't worry them. The truth is, Leo, there were elements among Dr. Haddi's advisors who wanted to see you disappear permanently. Moreover, it was only because I fought for you back there that they didn't get their way. I did it because I felt I owed you something for involving you in the first place. I daresay, there were times I wondered if I hadn't grown emotionally attached to you."

I let this last comment pass.

"Even Dr. Haddi suspected it. He said it wasn't a very good quality for a woman in my line of work. As you can see, I'm paying for it right now. Why do you think I'm living in this cave?"

"I've got my own problems, Ellen."

"That, you do."

"And that's it?"

"I guess so." She stood and extended her hand. "Congratulations," she said.

"For what?"

"For figuring out I wasn't British."

"Save it," I said, and waved off her hand. "All I discovered was your betrayal. Don't congratulate me for that."

NEVER ANY INTENTION

The time had come to leave the room. I turned to go.

"Good-bye, Leo . . ."

I ignored her.

"There was never any intention to hurt you . . ."

The "welcome" man rose from his squatting position as I neared the door.

"One day, you'll understand . . ."

I pushed the "welcome" man aside.

"I really did care for you . . ."

I turned the doorknob and stepped outside.

15

❖

Another Form of Panic

ANOTHER FORM OF PANIC

I shaded my eyes from the light of day outside Ellen's cave. I looked around for, but could not find Dr. Haddi. He was gone. I decided to wait for him to return. I was too drained to do anything else. I also felt dazed and wasn't sure why. I assumed it was from the elation I felt at learning the truth about her lies, but I didn't rule out the possibility that my shock resulted from the discovery that my worst suspicions were true.

A few stones lay by my feet. I picked one up and threw it hard against the opposite wall of the wadi. It hit with a loud pinging sound and shattered into a handful of pieces. Damn, I thought. Then: "DAMN!" I said it loud.

"Damn!" came an echo thundering back. "Damn, damn, da . . ."

My reproduced voice had a strange and unworldly pitch to it. Like the sound of giving up with a hint of panic thrown in. The realization that giving up was just another form of panic didn't help my mood.

That's also probably why I heard the voice. Jihad's voice. As strong and firm as on the day we met. Familiar. Confident. "Keep your head about you," he said.

I looked up. "What was that? And what about the honor part you mentioned earlier?"

No answer.

Then: "Was that . . . that . . . that . . . tha . . ."

It was all I could do to fight back my tears. Get yourself together I told myself. What are you crying about? Ellen just told you something you always suspected. Now use that information. Come on! Occupy your mind with something useful.

I gave it a shot.

THE QUESTIONS

As I saw it then, the problem was, as always, that I had many more questions than answers. The main one being: Why hadn't Ellen deserted me as I lay knocked out and naked on our hotel room floor? I just couldn't buy her explanation that Haddi needed me to test the "escape mechanism" at the Thousand and One Nights Perfume shop. That just wasn't his way. But what else could it be?

I came up blank and took a step back. I asked myself why she'd attached herself to me in Paris. As part of a training course?

Doubtful, but why else?

More blank.

I was at a dead end. I realized that I needed to examine the situation from a different perspective with a new series of questions.

A NEW SERIES OF QUESTIONS

The series began with: "What of Jihad?" This led to: "What has become of him?" Which yielded: "What's his involvement in all this?" Which begat: "Didn't the diary mention something about Jihad?"

THE SOCRATIC METHOD

Like most subjects of weight the Socratic method falls outside my immediate field of expertise, so you'll excuse me if I quote it incorrectly. About all I can say is it's a system whereby a person asks a series of questions. The purpose of each question is to bring the asker closer and closer to some new essential knowledge. Something like that.

As for how I learned of it, that's not too clear to me either. Maybe I read about it in a book called *Introduction to Pop Philosophy,* or heard it mentioned at a cocktail party. I might even have made it up myself, though this is highly unlikely, since a name like Socratic method never comes to anyone straight out of the blue. So it probably existed before me.

Anyway, I owe a great deal to the Socratic method, for it led me to new realizations based on old knowledge. Or, less succinctly said, without the Socratic method, I would never have thought what I thought when I arrived at the question: "Didn't the diary mention something about Jihad?" in response to a full series of questions which began with: "What of Jihad?"

WHAT I THOUGHT

Of course it had! Of course Haddi's diary mentioned Jihad. It implied that Jihad was being set up! That's what it had said. Why hadn't I realized it then! Haddi was luring Jihad up to Jabal Amman!

And then it struck me. And then everything came into focus—Paris, Lizzie, the perfume shop, Muhammad, Assad, the Amman stuff . . . even my role!

MY PROSPECTS

I was hot! Only two questions remained. One: why did Haddi want Jihad? And two, what did he plan to do with me?

I ignored the first question and headed straight to the second because I realized that understanding what had been wouldn't necessarily save me from what was to be. And wasn't that—saving me—now the point?

As I saw it, Haddi had three options: kill me, corrupt me, or free me. Option one presupposed that I'd been brought to Egypt to perform a specific task and that my current value, now that the deed was done, was significantly less than it had been before. In a word: I was superfluous. The implications: Haddi would kill me, if for no good reason, then a bad one. Though he'd probably tell his friends he'd done it because I knew too much.

Option two had Haddi recruiting me to work for the Amman Corporation. This scenario assumed that Haddi was looking for a few good men, and that I, based on the talent I'd displayed in unmasking Ellen and unraveling the plot, was among their number.

I found this possibility quite soothing, especially in light of option one. Then I considered the wider implications. Like, for instance, the fact that most male employees on Jabal Amman were castrated. Then it didn't seem soothing at all.

Which brought me to option three—freedom. Now *here* was an option with appeal, if little else to justify it.

This was how I occupied my time until Haddi's return. The minutes passed quickly. This was the up side.

The down side was that though my questions and calculations had momentarily wrested me from the onslaught of a vague kind of unease, they'd left me in the end with the knowledge that my prospects here on Jabal Amman were poor at best.

Once again, the specter of panic raised its ugly head.

16

A Serious Problem

SCRATCHING MY SORE SPOT

I was too involved with my thoughts to notice Haddi's return. Yet there he was when I glanced up, his little feet dangling over the edge of the small boulder that served as his chair. I also noticed he wasn't alone.

"Leo!" came Haddi's big welcome when I looked up. "Come on over!"

The truth was, I wasn't feeling very well in my stomach or my head, so it was quite an effort for me to get up and go over there. Yet I did it anyway—went over to Haddi—because revealing my ill feelings might have led the conversation to matters I wasn't up to discussing just then.

Haddi spoke when I was about ten yards away. "I didn't want to disturb you over there. You looked so deep in thought. Anything interesting? Something you'd like to share?"

"No. Nothing worth sharing. Just a daydream." I tried keeping a light tone. I sat down on a nearby rock and crossed my left leg over my right.

"Leo, I have to tell you, I think you handled your meeting with Miss Sherman very well. Very, *very* well." I refrained from asking how he knew. "You displayed excellent tools of analysis, and your final conclusions were without error. An excellent job, I must say, though you'll excuse me if I refrain from offering congratulations. Ha, ha, ha.''

There was no point in taking this last remark personally. It was just his way of getting back at me for scratching his sore spot earlier that morning.

THE SITUATION GETS STICKIER

Haddi paused to judge my reaction to his statement. I didn't know if he expected me to register surprise or laugh along with him at our common joke. I decided to go with my poker face.

Haddi acknowledged my nonacknowledgment by clearing his throat and saying yes. Then he gestured to the one-eyed man standing slightly back and to his left. ''I believe you're already acquainted with Assad.''

''Sure,'' I said. ''Drives for Amman Cabs. Keeps his backseat sticky.''

''What's that? Really? Assad didn't tell me that.'' He let a false look of concern cross his face before moving the conversation on to the real point. ''He seemed more concerned with the damage you did to his cab. Vandalism, he said. Could that be? I told him it couldn't have been you. I told him you're a very responsible person who would never damage anything that didn't belong to you. That's an accurate characterization, isn't it?''

I didn't like this line of questioning. It contained hints that another emotionally stressful meeting was in the offing. So I tried to deflect his accusations with the question: ''What are you talking about?'' Lame, I know, but it was the best I could do on such short notice.

''According to Assad, you and another man hired his cab for a trip to the Pyramids of Giza, and that you broke a window handle during the ride. Is that true? Has he represented the incident correctly?''

''What's going on here, Haddi?'' I asked this as a delaying tactic. I needed time to come up with a good answer. Honest or dishonest—it didn't matter which—so long as it saved my ass.

"Why aren't you answering my questions, Leo?" His voice sank to its lowest reaches. Something akin to high alto. He repeated the original question. Only slower this time, hitting each word like a separate sentence. "Has. He. Represented. The. Incident. Correctly?" He didn't want me missing his meaning.

"No. He. Hasn't," I said using the same studied pattern, only slower, and with more feeling.

"Don't get wise with me, Leo. This is a serious matter. I'm giving you an opportunity to present your version. Why don't you take advantage of it?"

"Who would listen?" I felt this was a legitimate question given Haddi's blatant belligerency. It also kept me in question mode.

A friendly expression appeared on his face. "I would."

It was a lukewarm assurance at best. Still, I decided to give the impression of playing along. "Since I have your assurances . . ." I said through a weak smile. "You see, as I recall, it was a hot day in Cairo, and even hotter in his cab. Opening the window seemed the most logical thing to do. I mean, how else could we inject some fresh Cairo street breezes into an otherwise scalding backseat? So I tried rolling the window down . . ." I was floundering at the end of a story line that couldn't be stretched much further.

". . . and the handle came off in your hand?" Haddi showed his impatience by finishing the story himself.

"Aha! So you heard it before." I chuckled ingratiatingly.

Haddi exchanged a few words in Arabic with the one-eyed man, then turned back to me. "And who was the man sitting with you?"

Here, at last was the point. The one I'd been avoiding for so long. The one, I decided, to avoid a bit longer. "The man was my waiter in the hotel dining room. You know, the Amman Hotel? That's where I met him. I guess that would make him one of your employees. Perhaps you know him." The ball was back in his court.

Haddi's eyes rolled up in his head as if he were concentrating on remembering every last man in his employ. He maintained this pose—a pose that brought me face to face with the whites of his eyes—for a period of time that couldn't have been healthy.

"Now that I think of it," he said when his eyeballs appeared again, "maybe I *can* identify the man who was with you."

I opened my eyes wide like I was surprised.

"But before I do, Leo, I feel I must tell you that I'm afraid the overall situation is much more complicated than you realize." His left eyebrow arched meaningfully.

"Is that a euphemism?" I asked.

"I'm afraid so."

I took this as a bad sign. Not because I didn't realize how complicated things were. Did I ever. But because I understood him to mean that if he was afraid, I should be too.

A SERIOUS PROBLEM

My brain said it would be wise to try calming him. "Why don't you tell me what's bothering you?" I began in what I hoped was a soothing tone. "It sometimes helps to get things off your chest."

Haddi looked me over before turning to the one-eyed man to exchange a secret look.

"All right," he said when he returned to me. "I'll tell you what's bothering me. But I don't want to do it here. Let's go back to the campus. I'll tell you while we walk."

Haddi and I stood (Assad was already up) and started walking down the path from which we'd come an hour earlier. Haddi with his hands behind his back, myself at his side. Assad took up a few steps behind.

"I have a very serious problem, Leo," confided Haddi after we'd traveled a few paces. "And I'm not quite sure how to begin. You see, matters are never as neatly arranged as we would often like. We plan and plan in the hope that circumstances will develop as we desire, but sometimes planning just isn't enough. Do you understand me so far?"

"Let's see. Something to do with the best laid plans of mice and men?" I refrained from referencing his "serious problem" because I wanted to avoid as much as possible the prospect that he'd associate this problem with me.

"A literate summarization. Yes, that's it. To a word. Perhaps we should begin when your involvement in the problem became direct."

"Your problem concerns me?" I tried to disguise my growing panic as a look of surprise.

Haddi stopped in his tracks and looked up at me with a sympathetic expression. "Unfortunately so."

"Oh." It was a sinking "oh." It meant I was sorry too.

Haddi turned to face the path and started walking again. Assad and I resumed our places in formation.

"As I was saying," Haddi continued, "a good place to begin would be when your involvement in the problem became direct. That occurred, I think, when you began acting as a free agent . . ."

"Free agent?" I interjected. "Where did you get that from? I'm not an agent." I wanted my innocence on record.

"Yes, that would be with Miss Sherman's disappearance," continued Haddi as if I hadn't spoken. "Or as you understood it at the time—Lizzie's kidnapping."

"You did a fine job pulling it off. I was completely fooled." I decided to invest in the tactic of buttering him up, as it was growing clearer by the minute that I'd need my friends when things got down to the wire.

"Thank you for the compliment," he said. "I think you're right. We certainly did a fine job pulling it off. That we did. But you have to understand the situation we faced at the time. We, the Jabal Amman School, and myself in particular, were under threat."

He paused for me to react.

"You mean, there was a threat to Amman Corporation's continuing ability to bring the world 'greater good'?" I wanted him to know I was on his side.

Haddi smiled. "Perhaps you're a bit smarter than you look, Mr. Gold."

On his side, yes. Smart, no. These were the qualities, I figured, a man in my position needed to survive. Thus, I immediately set about correcting his misconception by pointing out that the look he mistook for intelligence was actually an illusion created by the unusual lighting on the mountain. I concluded by emphasizing that he had nothing to fear from my mental powers.

"You're too modest, Mr. Gold," he protested.

"No, no," I assured him. "I have tests which prove it."

A MASTER SPY

Haddi looked up with a confused expression that implied he'd lost his train of thought. "I'm sure you do," he said.

"You were about to explain the 'greater good' you and the girls are working towards . . ." I offered. I was trying to steer him away from the matter of the serious problem. I knew I had to, now that my name was being bandied about in connection with it.

The one-eyed man spoke up from behind. His voice sounded gruff. It meant he was against the idea of discussing the greater good.

"You'll have to excuse Assad," said Haddi. "He's the chief of security for the Amman Corporation. He gets nervous any time I say hello to a stranger. It's disturbing sometimes, but I overlook it because it means he's doing his job."

I looked back and scrutinized this master agent more closely. His right eyelid was partially closed over the emptiness of this same eye socket, while the remains of his cheeks sank in over toothless gums I'd had the misfortune of seeing now twice—once in the cab to the Pyramids—and once more now here.

He was ugly, all right, but there was something more. Something else that seemed wrong. For most people who looked as he did would try to compensate by taking better care of the rest of their appearance. Like washing their clothes, or mending the holes in their shirts. But not Assad. He was either too preoccupied with his work to pay attention to these small details, or just resigned to the reality of his hideousness. It was impossible to tell which.

Haddi read my thoughts and jumped in with an explanation. "Doesn't look like much, does he? You're not the first to think so. In fact, I think I felt that way once myself, though today I can't recall when. Perhaps it's because I don't see the physical man anymore. All I see is his good work. Really. That's what I see. A beautiful man. The truth is, I'm glad he looks as he does. It helps him do his job. Think about it. What good intelligence agent would want to draw attention to himself? That's one thing I never understood about James Bond. Too flashy, I thought.

"Not Assad. He doesn't have these problems. If anything, people look away when he comes by. The last thing they suspect him of is spying. I think this is an advantage in his line of work. It's just one more quality that makes him the kind of agent who can unravel and respin a spider's web without breaking the threads."

"It's hard to believe anyone's that good."

My skepticism amused him. "You see over there?" He pointed out a small web stretching across the ancient burrow of some long-dead rodent.

"Yes."

"That's one of Assad's."

ABOUT THE GREATER GOOD

An impressive trick, I was quick to agree, but far from the point I wanted addressed. "You were saying about the greater good."

"Ah yes, about the greater good. Assad has some doubts about the wisdom of sharing this philosophy with you . . . Watch your step here . . ." He pulled off the path and climbed around a small rock which led to another path which fed into the campus. "Assad keeps harping on this security issue of his and I find that now I'm inclined to agree."

"I hope it's nothing that I've said."

"No, not at all. Standard security concerns. Nothing more."

"But Dr. Haddi, you promised." Begging like that was undignified, I knew, but I had the feeling that my safety was assured so long as the conversation centered on something other than the serious problem.

Haddi scratched at his chin as if considering my appeal. "You know something, Leo, you may have something there. A promise is a promise, and I always represent myself as a man of my word, at least to strangers. Let me speak with Assad again, to see if I can convince him of the justice involved in keeping one's promise. Let me do that, and I'll get back to you."

"If that's the best you can do."

"It's the very best. You see I'm sure Assad is still very concerned about the serious problem I mentioned earlier. I know I am. It just wouldn't be right to speak casually without resolving this matter first. Don't you agree?"

Haddi came to a stop. We were standing by the entrance of a red tent. The same red tent I'd seen Assad enter earlier that morning while the girls were displaying their goods on campus.

"I couldn't agree with you more," I said, though I couldn't remember what exactly it was he'd said. I was too busy examining the thick wooden beads which defined the tent's doorway.

"Perhaps you'd like to step into this tent while Assad and I consult. It shouldn't take us long to resolve the matter."

He pulled the beads to the side so that I could step in. I passed a quick look around the campus. It was empty again, except for the three of us and a toga-clad man who had just come up to meet us from around the tent's other side. The man was holding a spear.

Assad and the man took up in conversation. I gave Haddi a questioning look. He explained that the spearman, Faisel, was there to look after me while the two of them—Haddi and Assad—consulted. I thanked him and told him there was no need to bother Faisel, that I could entertain myself. But Haddi insisted.

Faisel and Assad ended their consultation and Haddi motioned me into the tent with an after-you kind of look, though it was clear I'd be heading a one-man line. I gave Haddi a nod, stooped slightly, and stepped inside. "At least," I consoled myself, "you kept him off the topic of the serious problem."

DÉJÀ VU

The inside of the tent was dark, though not in the way of Ellen's cave, which was cold and airless, but in a softer way. A way that told me the veil of darkness would lift as soon as my eyes adjusted to the sunless environment.

It didn't take long. Different aspects of the room were quick to take shape. The first thing I noticed was the predominance of red. In the cushions lying all about, in the curtains which defined three walls, in the carpet, and even in the folds of the clothed ceiling. It was a room with a familiar feel. Like a déjà vu.

Only it wasn't déjà vu. It was worse. Worse because I actually *had* been here before. In Cairo. In the Thousand

and One Nights Perfume shop. It was the Red Room. To a T.

I marveled at my discovery as I approached the mirrored wall with its shelves of perfume bottles behind glass. All was ordered and in place. There were even spaces I noticed for two of the bottles I'd taken from the original room. As for the third bottle, the one I'd left in my stolen pack, it was standing back in place.

I decided to ponder this point from a sitting position. I walked to the opposite side of the room, careful to sidestep the table on which my tea had once sat, and approached a cluster of pillows. One of them was higher than the rest, a characteristic which made it the closest thing to a chair in the room. I turned and lowered myself.

What happened next was not what I expected. What I expected was to sink into the cushioned fabric of an over-stuffed pillow. What happened instead was that my rump hit a hard sloping surface. "Very strange," I thought as I slid off the pillow and onto the carpet. It meant that the pillow was covering some hard object—hiding it from view. I rubbed my backside and I removed the pillow to reveal what lay beneath. There I saw, to my great shock, what looked from behind to be a curled-up lump of human flesh.

TOGA PARTY

I ran for the exit. The approximate distance, something I judged to be twelve feet, didn't take long to cover. My right arm arrived at the flexible doorway and swept the beads aside.

Outside. Freedom. It came fast and hard and mixed with the sound of tumbling bodies. Mine and the guard's. He rose first and placed his spear between the two of us. The sharp end pointing at me.

I maintained my position on the ground. "There's a body in there! There's a body in there!" I made frantic gestures towards the tent's inner sanctum. "Go! Go! See for your-self."

He didn't budge. Didn't even change his expression or take his eyes off me. Maybe he thought this was some kind of trick. I looked around for Haddi, but he was gone. I even searched for Assad as I was sure he'd be interested as head of security. But he was gone too.

"Go in there!" I repeated. "Or better yet, get Dr. Haddi!" The guard didn't move. "Haddi! You know him. Your boss! Dr. Haddi!" I raised my hand a couple of feet off the ground in an approximation of Haddi's measure. "Haddi! Dr. Haddi!"

More blankness, only this time, accompanied by a slight swinging of the spear. A kind of gesturing, or pointing towards the tent's entrance. His meaning was clear.

"Oh no, you don't." I protested. "I'm not going in there. Do you understand English? Not me! Not in there. Dead body. I don't go." I emphasized these words with a broad series of pantomimes which included vigorous head shaking and the waving of hands before my face. I even mimed the body, but only for a moment, because the guard mistook my seat cushions as a target for the point of his spear.

"Ouch! What do you think you're doing?"

"Grrrr!" growled the toga-clad guard. The spear pressed forward menacingly.

I stood to face him. I figured my best chance was on my feet. The guard realized this too, and quickly lodged the spearhead in the small gully where my neck reached my chest. I could move back through the door, or die. This was the choice. I chose life.

THE BODY

Back in the tent it took my eyes some time to adjust to the light. This didn't bother me one bit. Better in darkness, I thought, than in the light with what lies before you.

Only the inevitable was soon upon me. And the body, I

could see, was still there, curled in the fetal position, facing the red curtain along the opposite wall.

I wondered if it was dead.

I kind of hoped yes. I was afraid it might hurt me.

Then I changed my mind. That is, I didn't want it dead. I wanted it alive. Have compassion, I thought. Someone may be watching. Set an example he can follow.

I approached the body. I could see from up close that it wasn't yet dead. That is, its back seemed to inflate and deflate on a regular basis. I crept closer until I heard the sound of gurgling. It was the sound of troubled breathing, as if there was a lot of blockage in the nose or the mouth, or from wherever the air was entering.

"Hey. Hey, you." I whispered, as if I might be disturbing it. "Hey, you, are you okay?"

There was no response. I assumed this meant it was unconscious.

I went up and tapped it on the shoulder. Still, nothing. So I gripped it, the shoulder that is, and I pulled it towards me. Only it didn't move. So I added a second hand, and doubled my effort until the body began making a slow turn. I kept pulling. The body's legs extended as the flat of the back approached the floor. I could see the face now, what was left of it. Everything was swollen: the forehead, the cheeks, the mouth, the eyes. Everything. And blood was everywhere.

I jumped back in disgust. I could see now for sure that it was a man, or what was left of one. A dark fluid oozed down through a gap in his lips. It was the same gap through which he was forced to draw air now that his nostrils were sealed with clotted blood.

I was struck by the incongruity of it all. Not the incongruity of the body in the room, I'd seen enough strange things of late to get over that. But the incongruity of the brutality that had been brought upon the body, with the well-cut design of the victim's clothes. Not that they were glamorous, mind you. In fact they were dirty and stained with their owner's blood. But they were nice clothes. High quality. The loafers were Italian made.

I stepped up to inspect the victim's face. Blood, as I said, was everywhere, and this made identification difficult. I bent and ripped his shirt, and used the rag to wipe the mask of red away. It gave me the better look I knew I needed.

"Jihad?" I was tentative. I didn't want the answer to be yes. "Jihad, is that you? Can you hear me?"

I brought my ear up to his mouth to catch any sound he might make. He was basically silent aside from some gurgling.

"Jihad, it's me."

His head moved.

"Jihad, Jihad. What have they done to you!"

Now his mouth began moving. Not much. But there was movement and I could tell he was trying to speak.

"I'm here," I said as I took his hand and leaned my ear close to his lips. "It's all right. I'm with you now."

He moved his lips some more.

"What was that? Repeat it. I couldn't catch it all."

My right ear was touching his lips.

"Ghrlghb," he said. Then: "Enflswhb."

I clutched his hand tight. "I know, Jihad. I know. Don't worry. It'll be all right."

It wasn't easy understanding him. He was tired and speaking came with difficulty. Still, I knew what he meant. He'd called my name.

"Lion," he'd said. Followed by: "We've got a serious problem."

17

Uuud Auwwwgns

TENDING WOUNDS

I tried to take Jihad's mind off his troubles by offering encouraging remarks. These included lies about his good looks and comments like "conserve your strength, you'll feel better." It didn't matter that the ruckus from his breathing made it hard to hear my words. Saying them was therapeutic enough. It gave me the sense of doing good in the face of a condition I couldn't repair.

Which is not to say I didn't do what I could to clean him up and make him comfortable. The truth is, I wasn't bored a minute, what with all the dirt and blood. I began by propping his head on a pillow and scraping some of the blood from his nostrils so that he could breathe more easily. Then I went about tending his wounds. This proved more difficult than anticipated because shredded curtain just didn't do the job that a bandage might.

I stepped out of the tent and mimed the idea of supplies and water to Faisel, who left without argument and returned a few minutes later with everything I'd requested and more. This didn't surprise me one bit as it was obvious now that Haddi had sent me into the tent for the express purpose of finding and caring for Jihad. What was unexpected, though, was that in addition to tape, real bandages, disinfectant, and water, Faisel brought with him a stack of freshly made tuna fish sandwiches.

I busied myself with Jihad's visible wounds. Most of these displayed themselves about the head in shades of purple. Like his eyelids, for example, which were also swollen closed. I was tempted to employ the surgical technique I'd developed along the mountain slope, but decided, in the absence of a ready stone, to give Mother Nature first shot. This was the attitude I took as well with his cracked lips and newly flattened nose. It struck me that Jihad's unique facial composition was not unlike Muhammad's, and asked myself, in passing, if these two men could not have had their alterations performed in the same shop.

The invisible wounds were harder to tend for obvious reasons. I assumed they were centered in the chest and stomach areas, but didn't even pretend to know what I might do to help them heal, so I didn't do anything.

That left the final task of checking to see if his you-know-what was still-all-there. It was.

This was good news. I ate a sandwich. Tuna, as I said, prepared with mayonnaise and onion, on white bread with lettuce and tomato. I liked the way it tasted and had another. Then I set the last two aside for Jihad for when he came around.

I stepped out of the tent once more around sunset. I was struck by how fast the day had passed. It occurred to me to share this observation with Faisel, but reconsidered after picking up some noticeably cooler vibrations from his direction. I can't say I held him responsible for his new attitude, though. He was, after all, a corporate man, and as such could not be expected to think for himself. He had his orders concerning me, and these didn't include doing anything beyond fetching what had already been fetched, and forcing me back into the tent. That was that. My one complaint—pain, really—was that he performed the second task with a little too much enthusiasm.

OVERNIGHT

The comforts of the cushions were never more welcome. Sleep came quickly.

UUUD AUWWWGNG

I woke in the morning feeling rested and fresh. Jihad was already up, though hardly about. I could see that the swelling about his face had gone down somewhat. This allowed him to smile when he saw me rise. Or more precisely, it meant he could reveal his mildly deformed gums through the gap which widened when the edges of his mouth stretched upwards. I took his efforts as a very positive sign.

"Good morning!" I chirped. Sounding cheery was also part of my comprehensive therapy for returning him to his former self.

"Uuud auwwwgng," he answered.

The inelasticity of his mouth was giving him trouble. So was the sparsity of teeth and the size of his tongue. The effect muffled his voice, and, as a consequence, made him difficult to understand. I asked him to repeat himself.

"Uuud auwwwgng," he said with no less effort than before.

"Good morning?" I confirmed.

He nodded and cringed. I admired his determination in overcoming the pain.

"Do you want water?" I asked.

Again he nodded, though this time just once, and in a much more compact motion.

I lifted his head in my palm and brought the water container to his lips. Much of the liquid couldn't make it in through the narrow opening that had once been his mouth, and passed out instead, down his chin and neck. About half the container's contents were on the ground before there came the grunt that said he was sated.

I laid his head back and told him to rest. Rest would cure his ills.

"Wo!" His tone was a mixture of nasal/mumble. *"Ust awk."*

"What?"

"Ust awk!"

"Must talk? We have to talk?"

"Uh."

"I agree," I agreed. "But watch what you say. The tent flaps have ears."

THE CONVERSATION

The conversation proceeded slowly, mostly because I couldn't understand without hearing things twice, but also because we spoke in lowered voices so as not to be overheard. Our little chat began with my personal rendition of everything that had happened since Jihad left me unconscious two mornings before. He said he was sorry (*"ahwwie"*) for what he'd done, and I accepted his apology. I told him I understood now why he'd done it, and that my only regret was that I hadn't taken his advice and left the mountain when the chance had been there.

I also told him about Haddi's diary. I said the diary mentioned that he—Jihad—was heading into a trap. Jihad nodded at this like he knew, then waited without further comment for me to continue.

And I did, rounding off my report with a full appraisal of what I thought Haddi was up to. I told him I'd seen Lizzie, and that she wasn't Lizzie, but Ellen. I emphasized the importance of all the Amman types we'd seen with the words "I told you so." Then I described all the people I'd met and seen since reaching the top of the mountain, including Azizah and Assad. I said I thought they were all involved in a spies for hire scheme.

Jihad flinched at the mention of Assad's name. He said I'd done good work, but that he was tired now and needed rest. We'd continue this conversation, he said, later. *"Eeed eeep,"* he said.

I agreed. He definitely needed sleep.

BREAKFAST

Faisel entered the tent a few minutes after Jihad dozed off. He held in his hand a tray filled with breakfast goodies. Bread, fruit, juice, cheese . . . that sort of thing. I asked if he'd worked through the night without break. He didn't answer.

Jihad got up six hours later. The rest did him well. A lot of the swelling in the jaw and around the eyes had gone down. It was a more human look.

Sitting up unassisted and eating preground food were also now possible. Speaking came easier too. "Give food," he ordered. I gave him some mashed banana and showed him the tuna fish.

The patient's hearty appetite kept his mouth continuously busy. This restricted the conversation to comments from me alone. Comments like: "It's good to see you Jihad," and, "I'm glad you're alive."

DEEP SHIT

Jihad's first real sentence came just after wiping the last crumbs of tuna fish from his mouth. He said: "We're in some deep shit, Lion. You and me both."

"Shhhh," I cautioned him. "Haddi hears everything we say."

"That's all right. Haddi knows it too."

Though he was still having trouble pronouncing some words, it was evident that the cumulative effect of the food and the rest was to sharpen his mental powers. This pleased me no end, for it meant that some of the more recent mysteries surrounding our activities would soon be straightened out. I took to questioning him immediately, for there was no way of knowing how long his newfound strength would hold out.

"How did you get up here, Jihad?" I began. "How did they catch you and what have you learned?" I whispered very low and directly into his ear. I indicated that he should answer me in the same manner. This he did. That is, he brought his lips to the tip of my earlobe and spoke in the most breathless of voices.

His answers were as short and direct as the questions themselves. "By foot," he said. "With ease, and not much."

"What do you mean by that?"

"I mean, dear Lion, exactly what I say. There's not much I can add to what you've already revealed."

I pulled my ear back from his lips to give him my "come on" look. I held this pose for a good seven seconds before resuming my previous position.

"Really," he whispered. Then he lowered his voice even further and said: "About all I can add is that Haddi's also heavily involved in the drug trade."

I took this news with studied calm. "What? Drugs! Are you kidding?"

"Shhhh. Relax," he urged. "Yes, drugs, that's what I said. And, no, I'm not kidding."

"Drugs?" A menacing word, I noted, especially when whispered. "How did you learn that?"

"From the bedouins of Firan when I met with their leaders. I didn't want to tell you at the time. Haddi pays them to smuggle his product—poppy and opium mostly—down from Lebanon through Sinai and into the Egyptian mainland. Connections there handle the refining and shipment. The smuggling business, by the way, is also why the bedouins opposed our climb. They didn't want us interfering with their main source of income."

It occurred to me that the bedouins we'd walked in on,

the ones whose truck we'd smashed, might also be from Firan. I asked if this was so.

"Good question," observed Jihad. "I asked the bedouins of Firan the same one though much more discreetly. It turns out that the two bedouins we surprised were independents—not from Firan—operating beyond their territorial boundaries. That's why they were so nervous when we walked in. They thought we'd report their activities to Firan."

"And did you?"

"Certainly. It was our ticket up the mountain."

I smiled at this.

"But why does Haddi do it?" I asked. "The drugs, I mean. I thought the spy ring was his main concern."

"It most likely is. The drug operation is probably a subsidiary born out of need. Don't forget that this mountain is in the heart of bedouin territory and that Haddi needs these people's support—at least tacitly—for his protection. Employing the bedouins buys this support. Besides, the drug operation probably provides Haddi with a steady flow of money for meeting day-to-day expenses. Money that offsets the seasonal swings in the spy market."

"So it's like rent money?" I ventured.

"In a manner of speaking."

An impressive analysis, I thought to myself. One that reminded me of the Jihad of old. The Jihad I'd known before all that crazy ranting and neurotic stick dragging took up in Sinai. I attributed this return to lucidity to one of two possibilities: A) that looking for Haddi had the same effect on Jihad's emotional state that flying through a hurricane would have on a plane, and that finding Haddi was like entering that storm's eye; or that B) Haddi's pummelings had finally knocked some sense into Jihad.

Yes, I was very impressed by Jihad's analysis of Haddi's operation. I even prompted him for more with the question: "But why use the bedouins for smuggling?"

To which he answered: "Why not? It comes as naturally to bedouins as paranoia to Jews."

This brought to mind a third theory on Jihad's mental transition: that C) he was an unpredictable anti-Semitic bastard who probably also talked about me behind my back.

I decided to move the questioning down another, less sensitive line.

"Look, Jihad," I whispered. "I've got to know. Why has Haddi lured you up here? What don't I know about you and Haddi?"

Jihad seemed to reflect a moment before answering this one. His eyes were focused on something over my right shoulder and behind my back. Finally, he said: "I really can't answer you, Lion." Then he gestured towards the door. "Perhaps you should ask him yourself."

COMPANY

I swung around to see the object of his reference. Dr. Haddi was standing a few feet away, just inside the tent's entrance. His tuxedo looked fresh. To his left and slightly behind stood Assad. Lastly, farthest back, that is, and to Assad's left, stood Faisel—spear in hand.

"Pssst, pssst, pssst. Whisper, whisper, whisper. What's the big secret, girls?"

Jihad stood. The strain on his face revealed what a struggle this was. It suggested that his physical revival lagged well behind that of his intellect.

This, I soon learned, was a misinformed suggestion. For when he took to antagonizing our captor with the words: "What's with the squeaky voice Haddi? Cat got your balls?" I realized that the dynamics of his recovery were not at all as I had assumed. That in fact, they were just the opposite.

An embarrassing stillness descended on the tent as each in attendance considered the image of his words.

"Jesus Christ, Jihad," I mumbled. "Shut up."

"Ees tameah leh-sahebuck," commanded Haddi.

Jihad sneered. *"Inti ma bit-khawif-nish."*

A shouting match ensued. Raised voices, harsh expressions, shaking fists. Words flew fast. Faisel raised his spear. Assad blinked his eye.

I didn't understand a word until Haddi switched languages and said: "You'll watch your mouth, Jihad, if you know what's good for you." His voice cracked on the second rendition of you. I took this, and the way the veins of his neck strained against his shirt collar, as a sign of Haddi's continued excitement.

Jihad, by contrast, gave the impression of inward calm. At least on the surface. I figured that this had a lot to do with his recent beating and the way it impeded his ability to move. In any event, he stood motionless, breathing heavily for sure, and making the most of what expressions he could muster.

"Perhaps we should continue this little discussion in English so Mr. Gold can understand what's happening," suggested Haddi.

"Leave him out of this, Haddi. The entire matter's between you and me."

"Is it now? I don't think so, Jihad. Here's where we disagree. I think Mr. Gold is very much involved. He's here, isn't he?"

The stream of conversation that had formerly spun around my head was now directed at it. All eyes—all seven of them—rested on me. Jihad projected disgust, while Haddi smiled. Assad looked sinister, and Faisel, like he could use some action.

I decided to speak up. "Don't worry about me, Jihad." Then to Haddi: "Tell me what this is all about."

GETTING ORGANIZED

"I warned you before and I'm warning you now, Lion, stay out of this. For your own good."

"Oos-kut!" shouted Haddi.

"I've come all this way, Jihad," I said. "Now I have to know."

"Lion . . ."

Just then, Haddi snapped his fingers, an act which brought Faisel forward with his spear extended. The point came against Jihad's throat in just the way it had come against mine. His skin bent under the pressure.

"Now if we can have a some order here . . ." Haddi waited for quiet. "Mr. Gold wants to know."

I looked to Jihad. His eyes were locked on Faisel's. They threatened. Faisel didn't back down.

Haddi called my name and motioned for me to sit.

"First take that man off Jihad," I ordered in a voice much braver than I felt.

"Jihad's a troublemaker."

"Let Jihad sit, Dr. Haddi. He won't cause trouble. Then we can talk like men."

"Like men, you say? Does that include Faisel?" Haddi laughed at his own joke. Then he said: "Say 'please.' "

"Please," I repeated without hesitation, like my old, natural self.

"Very well, we'll all sit."

Haddi snapped his fingers. Faisel released Jihad's throat from the pressure of the spear. He even took a step back, though the spear remained extended. Jihad lowered himself onto a cushion. I followed. Then came Haddi. Assad and Faisel remained standing.

HADDI'S CHARGE

"Life is complicated, Mr. Gold, isn't it?"

I nodded.

"Yes. For me too." He gestured to his guards. "Even for Assad and Faisel."

Then he turned towards Jihad. "And especially for Jihad."

Jihad didn't react. Haddi continued.

"For you see, my men discovered Jihad prowling around the grounds the other day. Trespassing. That's right, we caught him trespassing on Jabal Amman. Since then we've had a number of long and thorough discussions, during which Jihad has admitted, among other things, to torturing one of my assistants. Imagine! He's a very devilish man, this Jihad . . ."

I looked to Jihad whose face remained without expression.

"I also learned," continued Haddi, "that Jihad's actually a private detective hired by you, Mr. Gold, to find a woman named Lizzie. A woman who, I assured him, was not to be found on this mountain.

"Now ordinarily I would say he'd made an honest mistake—a wrong turn, as it were—and ask him to leave as quietly as he'd arrived. Ordinarily I would do just that, Mr. Gold, if only these were ordinary times.

"But alas, they are not. These are times when every man must take care to protect his life and property so that the greedy and the dishonest do not try to take what is not theirs. These are times when the rule of law and just punishment must prevail if civilization is to endure. These are times, frankly, when those who elect to break the law, must also stand before it and be judged." Haddi's voice dipped for emphasis.

"What's your point, Haddi?" This was Jihad. He said it deadpan.

Haddi stood. "The point?" His voice shook with emotion. "The point is that you've committed crimes, Jihad. Serious crimes. Crimes like torture . . . like trespassing . . . like spying! Crimes for which you must pay with your life."

Faisel raised his spear.

I was about to whisper, "Jihad, did you hear that?" but his response indicated he had.

"You're going to kill me right here? Right now?" He lifted his arms slightly, as if in surrender. It was a painful effort.

"No," Haddi laughed. "What do think, we follow the law of the jungle? Don't worry, there'll be a trial. A fair one. Bedouin style. With Sheik Shebob as judge."

Jihad's face went pale. On trial for fraud in the court of Sheik Shebob! Jihad's knees must have weakened with the news. Mine certainly did.

"A trial?" asked Jihad. His voice was strong and calm. I couldn't imagine how he made it so.

"That's right," said the soprano. "To take place tomorrow morning on the . . ."

"You're a bastard, Haddi."

A silence not unlike the one which fell right after Jihad's "cat got your balls" remark enveloped the room again. Everyone was shocked, I could tell, because the words had come from me. I shared their wonder.

Jihad winked at me through a swollen lid. Haddi looked off guard. "What was that?" he asked.

I used the moments between my admittedly impulsive remark and Haddi's rhetorical question to compose an appropriate response. "What I meant was," I began tentatively, "I feel there are reasonable grounds for doubting that Jihad will receive a fair trial on this mountain."

"That's what you said? That's not what I thought I heard. Wasn't your original phrasing more concise?"

"Might have been," I offered. "But the point is, the deck seems stacked against Jihad. I, for one, have never heard of Sheik Shebob, and I can't help but wonder if he isn't an Amman employee."

Haddi brought his right hand index finger to his lips and began to tap. It was a false gesture meant to convey thought.

"Lion," Jihad said, "don't you see yet? It doesn't matter what the charge is, the outcome is predetermined . . ."

"Silence!" bellowed Haddi. Then, when all was quiet: "Thank you. Your rudeness, Jihad, shocks me. Mr. Gold asked a question, and I'm going to see that he gets an answer." The speaker rested here to impart without words the magnanimity of this gesture.

"You see, Leo," he said when his breath was full again, "I wouldn't be honest if I didn't confide that I find your lack of faith most insulting. After all, if you can't trust me . . . ?"

Again, a pause. This time to play fill in the blank. I imagined many possible responses. Most affirmed his last four words.

"As for your question about Sheik Shebob, he's an eminent bedouin legal authority. His experience is as vast as his judgment's respected. Ask any bedouin. Better yet, you'll see for yourself."

"I know," I said, "at Jihad's trial."

"That's right. First at Jihad's trial. And then . . ." Yet another pregnant pause. Wasn't he aware that overrepetition was dulling his intended effect? Did he need to be told that the art of conversation was less like masturbation, and more like making love? That it was not a solitary pursuit performed for selfish pleasure, but a shared experience based on meeting mutual needs?

Probably, yes, though it wasn't for me to say. So I simply cooled my heels and waited for Haddi's voice to return. And it did, eventually, with it the words: ". . . at your own."

So stupendous was this news that I found myself struck deaf. I asked him to repeat.

"I said," he said, "you're about to witness bedouin justice as executed by Sheik Shebob. In fact, you're going to witness it twice. Once at Jihad's trial and once at your own."

"That's what I thought you said," I said as I discovered that I wasn't really deaf, only a man who wanted to be.

"On what charges?" This was Jihad's voice. Strong, secure, challenging.

"On the charge of aiding and abetting a wanted criminal. On the charge of sleeping with a married woman . . ."

"I didn't sleep with her!" I yelled.

". . . and, finally, on the charge of spying on Jabal Amman. Yes, these are the charges to be addressed at your trial. Prepare your defense! Court will convene first thing tomorrow morning. Sentence will be pronounced immediately after."

INTO THE DARKNESS

I was thinking how ominous this last phrase sounded when a sudden surge of activity took up all around. A few more toga-clad henchmen entered the tent.

Haddi explained their presence. "These men will escort you to your quarters for the night. They will also bring you to court in the morning."

One of them extended his hand to help me rise.

"What should we do, Jihad?" I whispered.

"I don't see that we have much choice." He spoke in conversational tones. Very calmly.

I took the offered hand and stood. Jihad ignored the one before him and rose under his own power. Haddi and Assad were already through the beaded gateway. Faisel stood back against one of the curtained walls. His spear was primed. He made a motion for the tent to be cleared. Jihad began limping forward. He grimaced, then fell.

"Jihad!" I bent down to where he rested on all fours.

"I'm sorry, Lion," he said, looking over at me.

"Sorry? About what?"

"For letting you get into this mess. For leading you up here . . ."

It was shocking to hear this from Jihad. He appeared to be blaming himself for my actions. "Don't talk that way,

Jihad," I whispered. "You have nothing to apologize for. You've done fine. After all, you did warn me to stay away. You said I should watch out, because Haddi was a dangerous man and that I'd be best served by keeping my distance."

"I said that?" His spirit seemed revived.

"You did."

He glanced around the tent. "Then I guess all I'm sorry about is that the facts seem to bear me out."

Indeed they did. Though why hadn't I listened to him the first time? What kept me from recognizing then what I saw so clearly now? That the air on this mountain was thick with evil.

One of the guards lifted Jihad to his feet. Faisel grunted for me to rise too. Jihad shuffled through the beads with assistance from a guard at his arm. A second one came up and took mine too. We passed outside and turned to the right. Jihad was no longer in front. I looked over my shoulder to catch a glimpse of him being dragged off in the opposite direction. "Jiha . . ." I began to call, but a slap cut me off.

"Where are you dragging me?" I demanded to know. The guard was silent. I understood this as a sign that like Muhammad, he too had had his tongue cut out.

The campus perimeter was soon behind. Mountain peaks sprouted all around. The pace quickened. Two more togamen appeared up ahead standing by a large boulder that seemed to be stuck into the wall of a hill. The two of them moved to the same side of the boulder and began to push as we grew near. It looked as if they would fail at first when the rock held its place in spite of their strain. But then it moved, accompanied by a large creaking sound. And then it rolled one-half rotation until it landed on its second side with an earthshaking thud. We were very close to these men now. And I could see there was a hole in the place where the stone had once stood.

"What is this?" I asked my guide indignantly.

He answered by throwing me in.

18

See No Evil

SEE NO EVIL

Darkness fell as the boulder was rolled back into place. I sat quietly for a few minutes in the hope that my eyes would adjust to the absence of light. They didn't. There was nothing to adjust to. The cave was blackness itself.

I felt myself drifting as if in space though I knew I wasn't. I reached out to touch something, to gain a sense of anchor. Only there was nothing nearby on which to latch my fingers or press my palms. Nothing but space.

The need to end my isolation grew stronger. I called out in search of an echo. "Ahhhhhhhh!" Again, nothing. Just the sound of my voice swallowed in vacuum.

Even the smell of the cave was blank. That is, its smell had no smell.

An hour passed. Maybe two. I occupied my time peering down into an endless abyss of invisible silence. Very disheartened, I was. Near despair. As if the revelations and the coming trial weren't enough!

A lump rose to the crest of my throat and my spine went chill. I took heart at having sensed something.

TOM

"You doin' She-bab t'mara?" A low, raspy voice came out of the void.

"Huh? What? Who's there?"

No answer. My eyes peered into the empty. My ears strained and my arms waved. I began sniffing in different directions. Nothing. I rejected thoughts that I'd imagined the voice and doubled my efforts to track down its source. I closed my eyes (they weren't doing me much good anyway) and tried to relax. I let the pace of my breathing slow and my body loosen. My arms fell slack. My head dipped. I waited. Patiently. Quietly.

I sensed someone breathing. The sound was faint but perceivable. Was it me? No, it was someone else. He was breathing through his mouth about ten feet to my left. Yes, a he, I could tell.

"Who's there?" I called out. "Speak up." An unsuppressible trembling crept into my voice. I was beginning to regret finding the sound.

"Hee, hee, hee, hee."

Yes, I definitely regretted it. Oh my God, I thought, please let me be imagining this.

"You doin' She-bab t'mara?" It was back. This time from some unknown distance to my right.

"Yeah," I whispered, just as my bladder let loose.

"Too bad," came the answer. "You jus' lost 'trol o' yoself, didn' chu?"

"What? Lost myself? What do you mean?" I couldn't figure out how it knew I'd wet my pants.

"Listen. This place ain' good fo' much, but what it do do is make you senstive in deh ears an' deh nose."

"That's something to look forward to," I said absently as I shifted in my dampness.

"I wouldn' say."

The voice had the same gravelly texture of Louis Armstrong's. I found the familiarity reassuring.

"Who are you, anyway?" I asked. "What do you know about Sheik Shebob?"

"Mo den I'd like. Met 'im unce. Didn' like 'im den. Cause 'im I'm heeya. Das 'nough."

"Who are you?" I repeated.

"'Oo was I? Ma name was Toms Jefsn Washin' Linkn' X."

"Thomas Jefferson Washington Lincoln what? I didn't catch your last name."

"X. You know, like deh las' letta' o' deh alph-bet?"

"Your last name is X? Thomas Jefferson Washington Lincoln X?"

"Das right. But ma friends call meh Tom."

"And your friends call you Tom?"

"Yup."

"Glad to meet you." I meant it. "My name is Leonard Gold. But my friends call me Leo." It occurred to me that Tom might already know who I was. That he might be a Haddi henchman in disguise. But I discarded the idea. Call it instinct. Call it loneliness.

"Names don' mean much in heeya. Either I's talkin' t'you or I's talkn' myself. Neither way, don' make no diffrnce."

I saw his point.

BROTHER SLAVES

"Ju boy?" he said after a time.

"Am I a boy?" I tested my voice. "I'm certainly not a girl. But if you're asking if I'm an adult, then yes, I think so . . . . I mean I vote," I added as an afterthought.

"Didn' ax if you boy, I ax't if you ju boy."

"Am I a Jew boy?" Was he a racist? Wasn't everyone equal in the dark? "I've been called worse."

"I could tell you's Joosh 'cause yo name."

It was an observation, I realized, not a racist threat. I reevaluated my earlier conclusion.

"Gold? You think the name 'Gold' sounds Jewish? I actually changed it from Goldshlager."

"Wha'?"

"Goldshlager was my original name."

"Befo' yous was slave, right?"

"What do you mean?"

"Joos was slaves once, right?"

"Once upon a time . . ."

"Jus' like deh black man."

"That's right."

"An' Gold's yo' slave name."

"What do you mean?"

"I mean, the black man los' his name when he came to 'merica as slave. Slave owners wanted t'take 'way deh black man's 'denty, so dey took 'way his Afkin name and gave him a slave name 'sted. My slave name's Toms Jefsn Washin' Linkin'. This ain't no black man's name. This soun' like Afkin name t'you?"

"No."

"Das right. 'cause it ain't. My las' name's 'X.' I gave myself this name to reminds myself that I gots an Afkin name and 'denty that's been stole.'

"What I wants t'know," he continued, "is if they tried t'take 'way yo 'denty too by givin' you a slave name. What I wants t'know is if Gold's yo slave name."

I didn't know what to say. "Not exactly . . ." I began. "Well, sort of . . . well, I mean I . . . I chose . . ."

"I knew it," he cut in. "I knew it. We'z both gots stolen 'denties. Like dat we'z bruhz." I could hear him smiling. "Nice t'meet you, bruh-tha."

DEH NOIZ

Brothers? I didn't really understand what he was talking about, but I wasn't about to reject an offer of friendship from the only other person in my world. "Nice to meet you," I said, and extended my hand to shake his. He'd sounded like he was right near me, but I couldn't reach him. "Keep talking," I said, "I want to shake your hand. I'm holding mine out."

"Don' waste yo time. I cain' magin never findin' yo hand." There was a sudden change in his tone. It was like I'd brought greetings from a reality he'd been trying to forget.

"No. I want to. I really want to." I lunged forward into the darkness towards the voice. "What are you, a ghost?" I was face forward lying on the floor.

"She-it," his sound was behind me now. "I sho 'ope not." I shifted around to face it. "Donja be tryin' t'find me. Id no use. I tried wit deh last fella."

"Last fellow? Someone was here before me? What happened to him?"

"Don' know. Jus know 'e ain' 'ere no mo. Thin 'e did She-bab. Didn' come back. Maybe they put 'im in deh noiz."

"What?"

"Deh noiz. Deh noiz."

"The noise?"

"Yup."

"What's the noise?"

"Don' know for sure. I think ids where deh sound's so big ya can't 'ear nuthin'. Not even yoselfs think."

"Kind of like in here, except the blackness is in your ears?"

"Das rite, if ya thin' a it dat way."

"Sounds horrible."

"I don' know. Id be a nice change fo me."

DREAM VS REALITY I

It wasn't a confidence-building remark. I decided to let the conversation fall off so I could figure out how things worked in here. Like the funny way time seemed to move in The Dark. This was really strange. For while it never passed quickly and it never dragged, it always seemed to do both. The combination brought disorientation. Nausea was common too.

Tom asked what I was thinking about.

"I'm trying to understand this place."

"Cain' un'stand this place. Ain't nothin' t'understand."

"That's what I'm learning. Like how do you know then it's time to go to sleep?"

"When I'z tahd."

"No. What I mean is, how do you know when it's day and when it's night?"

"Cain' know."

"You can't know? That's terrible."

"Des worse."

"There's worse than that?"

"Das raht. Like not knowin' deh diffrnce 'tween when you's sleepin' and when you's up."

"I don't understand."

"Like for all I knows, Iz 'sleep right now, and you's jus' a dream."

DREAM OR REALITY 1?

I discovered what he meant some indeterminable amount of time later when I found myself standing by a stone wall facing a group of people arranged in a semicircle. Many had familiar faces, though none of them were friendly. Haddi, Muhammad, Ellen, Assad, the "welcome" man, the old couple from the train, Faisel, Sheikh Shebob (an old guy with a white beard in long flowing robes), and many others I didn't recognize. Azizah and Jihad were the only two missing. I wondered why.

My trial was coming to an end. Haddi rose, announced I was guilty and told me to approach the rock wall for sentencing. Three medium-sized stones sat at the base of the rock. Below each of these stones, I was informed, lay an envelope. Each envelope contained a description of a different punishment. I was free to select any one of the stones.

I went over to and lifted the rock labeled "1." I picked up the envelope.

"Bring it to me," ordered Haddi.

I did as he said. He opened it and read: "Castration."

My first reaction to this news was to unconsciously deny its relation to me. How similar their interests, Jihad and Haddi, I thought. That was all.

Then I heard applause and Haddi offer: "Congratulations!"

I sensed an atmosphere of encompassing false warmth. I was nearly taken in when reality dawned. Struck, actually, as a swift pain about three inches below my belt. This brought with it a sudden need to protest. To say things like "I gave my bit years ago," and "Once is enough!" But when I moved my mouth, nothing came out.

The applause died down.

Haddi spoke again. "Your fate is to suffer castration, a punishment that includes safe passage off this mountain."

Safe passage? What a cruel twist, I thought, for what good would I be down below, if I hadn't on down, my below?

Haddi recognized my unspoken doubts. "Now I realize you may not be entirely pleased with this choice, so here's what I'm going to do: I'm going to give you a chance to trade the sentence you're holding now, for an opportunity to choose one of the two remaining sentences hidden beneath rocks two and three. This is the deal. The only catch is that you can't get your current sentence back once it's been traded away."

Something told me that rocks two and three were no better than one, but I felt I owed some allegiance to the little fella who'd given me so much pleasure over the years.

The crowd began calling out. I heard some shout: "Take two," while others cried: "Three's for you!" Only one guy said "Don't trade," but he was sharpening a knife at the time.

"I'll trade," I said, pleased that my voice was back.

Cheers.

I walked forward and picked up rock number two. I brought the envelope that lay underneath to Haddi. He opened it and removed a piece of paper.

"Sorry, Leo," he said after looking up. "The word here is 'death.' Looks like you picked a zonker."

Death?

"Listen, Dr. Haddi, I'd like to trade for number three." I rushed up to the last rock.

"I'm sorry," he repeated. "No more deals." He was trying, I could tell, to sound compassionate, yet for all his efforts, the words came out with all the sensitivity of a grocery clerk's apology for bruised tomatoes.

"But, Dr. Haddi. I don't want to die. I don't want to die!"

"Who does? Sor-reee. Next contestant, please!"

ON TOM

I repeated this experience to Tom, who said it proved his earlier point about The Dark: that waking into the darkness was like entering into a dream, and that falling asleep into a dream was like waking into reality.

I responded by saying we should talk about something else. I suggested he describe how he landed here.

" 'Ere or *'ere,*" he asked obliquely.

"Here," I prompted.

I heard Tom clear his throat. He began: "It was durin' da mid sixties, I was in New York . . ."

I sat and listened to this voice through the black for what seemed like an extended period (I'd long since given up trying to estimate time in terms of hours and minutes). Tom described how his path to the darkness began with his search for spirituality and his association with a religious group known as the Nation of Islam. It was through this group, he informed me, that he met Malcolm X, and later changed his name to "X."

His membership in the Nation lasted about a year, and ended when Tom found that he couldn't maintain the group's strict moral code. "Deh ladies," he explained. "I was weak fo' deh ladies."

It was at about the same time that he met Dr. Haddi, who was also living in New York then, running a small-time prostitution ring. He told Tom he needed some help.

"What kind?" I asked.

"Wit' deh ladies o' course."

"Of course. So how did you finally end up here?"

"How I ended 'ere? Well, 'tinued workin' fo' Haddi through deh years in New York. D' opration grew. Spread t' drugs. Times was good, bu' dey got dangrous. Haddi decided it was time t'leave. To return t'Egypt, and he ax't me t'come with 'em."

"I see."

"I was 'ere three months fo' Haddi 'cused me o' stealin'."

"Stealing? You stole from Haddi?"

"Din' matter if I dids 'o didin'. Jus' 'cusin's 'nough 'round 'ere. Dey gaves meh a trial, and Sheik She-bab foun' meh guilty. Told meh I'd have t'live de rest o' m'life in deh dark."

LET THERE BE LIGHT

The story ended with stifled weeping. It was Tom trying to keep his pain from me. I gave him his privacy.

I was somewhat stunned myself. I'd never been in a place where the absence of innocence was so widespread. And it wasn't just that no one was innocent, not Jihad, not Haddi, not Tom, not even myself, but that everyone was guilty. It was a damn depressing thought, I thought, and it made me want to cry too. That's why I was lucky Tom spoke when he did. The two of us bawling would have been quite a sight even in The Dark.

"Speak up, boy. Tell meh what chu thinkin' 'bout. Don' be so quiet. You gots t' speak t'me. Your voice i' deh only light I gots."

Speak? What was there to say? I answered with the first thing to come to mind.

"Tom," I said. "I'm scared. I'm scared of The Dark."

I guess my own weakness brought out the strength in Tom, who managed to say between sniffles: "Ain' nuthin' be scaid a Lo [Leo], 'cause ain't nothin' worse'n deh dark. Dis i' deh worst."

This wasn't exactly what I had in mind when I'd appealed for his support. But he did, after all, have his own problems. I tried to be understanding. I also tried to imagine how he kept his mind together within this insanity.

"Don't you ever wish you were dead?" I asked.

"Dea'? No. I wiz I was alive."

DREAM OR REALITY II?

It was sometime during this gloomy reminder of our predicament that Tom faded out.

"Tom?" I called out. "Tom, are you there?"

An eerie silence enveloped the cave.

"Tom?"

I knew he was there because I heard him breathing.

"Answer me, Tom. This isn't funny anymore."

I sensed someone near.

"Tom! Why don't you speak?"

"Tom's asleep." A deep voice. A woman's voice.

"Azizah?"

"Yes, Leo. It's me."

It was. I could tell by the scent of her skin as it caressed my nose and filled my brain like an intoxicating drug.

"Azizah, how did you get in here?"

"That's not important, Leo."

"Maybe not to you. But it is to me."

"No, it's not. Not even to you."

"No?" I asked with rising suspicion. "Then what is important?"

"Us."

"Us? You've got to be kidding."

"I'm not."

This was something she could only have said in The Dark because it freed her from having to keep a straight face. The time had come to clarify a few things. "Azizah, first of all you're married to my biggest enemy in the world, and second of all, how can I trust you because of first of all?"

"You have to. I can't live without you."

"Can't live without me? Are you for real?" (A legitimate question, I felt, given the circumstances). "Because if you are, then you've got a big problem, which is mainly, but not exclusively, that I'm going on trial tomorrow, and that I may not be around afterwards."

"Really? A trial?" she asked, pretending like this was the first she'd heard of it. "Then let's just say, I *can* live without you, I just *don't want to*."

I appreciated her honesty though I realized I preferred the original phrasing.

She sensed my disappointment. "You asked," she said.

"Let's be frank, Azizah, shall we? We both know that Haddi's listening to this conversation, so why don't you get to the point."

No response.

"Azizah?"

I sensed the humidity around me rising. My heart sank.

"Oy," I groaned. "Don't start crying. Why are you crying?"

"It's that tone of voice. Why did you talk to me in that tone of voice?" Sniffle, sniffle.

"Look, don't listen to me. I'm disoriented in here. I don't know what I'm saying. What do you want to know?

I'll tell you anything you want to hear. Just don't cry," I pleaded.

"Okay," she said blowing her nose. "If you're really sorry."

"I am. I swear it."

"I'll believe you *this time*."

"Do," I encouraged her. "You won't regret it."

"Now about your question," she said. "You have nothing to worry about. Haddi's not listening."

"I don't? He's not? How do you know?"

"No. No. You see Dr. Haddi keeps The Dark free of any unnatural furnishings—listening devices included—in order to maintain the character of the place. He says they pollute the perfect blackness."

"I see," I said. Then, in an effort to move the conversation along: "Surely you didn't just come here to discuss interior design. What is it I can do for you?" (I intentionally avoided the more crass, and potentially misunderstood, "What do you want from my poor life?").

"I want you to do me a favor tomorrow."

"Anything."

"I want you to kill Dr. Haddi."

"WHAT?"

"Shhhhh."

Had I heard her correctly? Had she said *favor* or what? Since when did one commit murder as a favor? More to the point, wasn't her request just a wee bit beyond the borders of obligation as defined by our current relationship? Well, wasn't it? It seemed to me, yes.

"What," I repeated, though this time in a whisper, "are you talking about?"

"I want to be with you. Always. This will only be possible if you kill Dr. Haddi."

"Shhhhh! There you go again. Look, I'm in enough trouble already. You want to make it worse? Anyway, even if I was in a position to kill him, I wouldn't know how to do it.

I could even get killed myself (God, forbid). Besides, isn't murder a job for your willie—your guardian?"

"I already told you, my father is dead. He was my willie."

"Just because your father's dead doesn't mean you don't have a willie."

"What do you mean by that?"

Good question, I thought. Damned if I knew. Damned if I cared, for that matter, if it had nothing to do with removing my name from the list of guns for hire. But I figured it did (have something to do . . . et cetera, et cetera). Because my answer could obfuscate the issue and cloud things. And both of these, according to me, were justifiable ploys if they steered the candidate search away from me.

"I mean," I said, "just because your father's dead doesn't mean you don't have a willie."

"You just said that."

"Ehhhh . . . right! What I meant was . . . ah . . . the role of willie can be fulfilled by another close family member. Someone like . . . ah . . . your brother, for example."

Azizah gasped. "How did you know I had a brother?"

THANK YOU, GOD

Brother? She actually had a brother? I didn't know that. Thank you, God.

I knew a gift horse when I saw one. That's why I decided to tell her how I figured out she had a brother. To tell her everything there was to tell and to spell it out in vivid, glorious, Technicolor detail. All of it. Everything. Everything, that is, but the truth. That's right, I'd skimp on the truth. And why not? The truth was too common for a woman like Azizah. She deserved better.

Thus began my silent search for a story which described how I'd learned of Azizah's brother's existence. It was a tough assignment, complicated by the fact that I was starting from scratch. This meant I'd have to take my leisure (as it was) and collect my thoughts. But in the meantime, as I bought time, I declared, "It was easy," and proceeded to elaborate on my lie.

MY LIE

"I figured it out by analyzing a number of seemingly insignificant, extremely subtle clues," I began tentatively. "Of which, the first was the ring on Muhammad's toe. You made a big deal about the ring. You said it was important and wanted to know if Muhammad had given it to anyone. When I told you no, you were upset."

I sniffed at the air for a reaction. I needed to learn if my bluff had taken. This would give me an idea of how to continue.

Unfortunately, my nose was stuffed.

"So . . . ah . . . so . . . your story happened to fit . . . ah . . . well with another story I'd heard not long ago," I said, making it up as I went along.

"And what was that?"

"And what was that . . . what was that?" I searched frantically through my memory for some known story structure that might act as frame for my own composition.

I found one.

"Once upon a time," I began, "a small boy's father, who happened also to be bedouin, decided to up and leave Cairo and return to Sinai. The city life, it seemed, was not for him. Neither, for that matter, were a wife and son.

"But the mother refused to accept reality—as women tend to do—and pursued her man into the desert. However, before she left, she told her son that after she found the father and settled him down, she'd send back a sign that it was time for the boy to follow. That sign would be a ring. A ring!" I repeated excitedly as I realized I'd found, albeit, quite by chance, common ground between Azizah's concern for the ring on Muhammad's toe and my own story line. "A ring, that had been in her family for many, many generations.

"Only the sign never came." I said sounding as sorrowful as befit the tale. "That's right, day after day, the boy sat by the mailbox waiting for the ring which never came. Then one morning, about nine months after she'd left, the postman brought word that the mother had died. During childbirth, he said," I imagined. "Just after bearing a beautiful, healthy, baby girl.

"Sound like a familiar story?"

Say yes, I prayed.

"It sounds pretty familiar."

That was close enough for me. It meant that while still in the dark, I was on the right track. I plunged ahead, drunk with hope.

"The girl grew up alone with her dad—her willie—who refused to send for his son because the responsibility of raising one child was already too much. And they lived together a happy life, until the dawn of the day a man named Dr. Haddi appeared and proposed an exchange marriage.

"The father was flattered. So was the girl. A doctor!

"They struck a deal and made the exchange. It didn't matter to the father that the terms of agreement were weighed in Dr. Haddi's favor. That was unimportant, he said. It was the joy that made the difference, and the girl's future happiness."

"Wait a moment," Azizah interrupted. "It was too a fair exchange."

"That's not what I heard," I taunted. Then, in an effort to take the onus of making up tales off my back: "Why don't you tell your side. Prove to me it was fair."

She thought this over a moment before taking up my challenge. "All right then, I will. The first thing you should know is that my father regretted the exchange as soon as my marriage was consummated. You see, I told him about

Dr. Haddi forcing me to prostitute myself, and I told him about all the other perverse and degrading things that occurred on Jabal Amman.

"I told him I wanted a divorce, and he agreed it was the thing to do. He went to Dr. Haddi and told that scoundrel to let me go. My father made this demand as was his right as my willie. He even returned the bride he'd received in exchange. But Dr. Haddi just laughed in his face. In his face! Do you understand? Never before had a husband defied the wish of a willie.

"My father took the matter to the village elders who told him their hands were tied. They explained that the village couldn't afford to oppose the man whose whims directed the local economy."

"What did your father do?"

"What could he do? He decided to face Dr. Haddi alone. He knew it would be tough, but his honor was at stake.

"The end came quickly. Dr. Haddi captured my father prowling around the mountain looking for me. They beat him and threw him in The Noise. Then they took him out and beat him again.

"They brought me to see my father as he lay near death. His strength was spent. His manhood, I assumed, detached. It was then, with his dying breath, that my father first told me the story of the ring and my brother. He said that he and my mother had once had a son, but they'd put him in an orphanage when they decided to move back to Sinai. They chose not to take him along because he was young, and the trip would have been too difficult. You understand?"

I said I did.

"Yet they didn't intend to leave the boy behind. They promised to send for him after they'd established themselves. To send back my mother's ruby ring as a signal that it was all right for the boy to come out.

"But when my mother died—as I was born—my father

realized he wouldn't be able to care for us both. So he held onto the ring."

"He never sought out the boy?"

"I don't think so. I think he was too ashamed. Though I have reason to believe he kept in touch with the organization which raised him."

"Why do you say that?"

"I remember while I was growing up, letters from an agency for orphaned children would arrive periodically. I asked my father about this once, but he said it was nothing, so I let the matter drop. I didn't think of it again until the night of his death when I realized there might be a connection between my brother and this agency. So I immediately rushed back to my father's house to search for these papers. Only when I arrived, I found that the place had been ransacked. Destroyed."

Azizah fell silent.

"And your father only told you about this brother as he was dying?"

"Yes, that's right. I couldn't believe it. 'Tell me his name!' I begged. 'Father, please!' But he was too far gone. It was all he could do to thrust the ring into my hand and will me, with his eyes, to find my new willie and have him save the family honor."

"Through a blood feud?" I asked ominously.

"Yes. A blood feud."

"So you gave the ring to Muhammad when you learned he'd be in Cairo, in the hope that your long-lost brother would see it and follow him back up? Is that it?"

"That's right."

"Well if that's so, there's just one more thing—more or less—I don't understand. How did you know you could trust Muhammad? That you could depend on him to show the ring around? I mean he was, after all, sent down on other business."

"Each of the women has a eunuch who acts as her servant. Muhammad was mine. He'd been working with me for about a month when Dr. Haddi announced he was sending Muhammad to Cairo. We'd established a very strong relationship by then and I felt I could trust him. Besides, I never told him the significance of the ring.''

''You kept from him something as important as a search for your brother?''

''I didn't want to burden him with the pressure.''

I questioned this tactic through my silence.

''Listen,'' she explained, ''Muhammad was a good worker. He always did his job, but he was not an initiator. In most cases he was controlled—manipulated—by someone else . . .''

''Like Assad?'' I asked.

''Exactly. To get him into the right place at the right time.''

''Like when I spotted him at the Pyramids . . .''

''What was that?''

''So let me get this straight. The matters of you sending the ring down to find your brother, and the one involving Haddi's attempt to get Jihad up to Jabal Amman, were completely unrelated.''

''Who?''

''And in fact, their only common elements were the use of Muhammad as lure. Also true?''

''I don't understand. Who's this Jihad?''

''Jihad? Jihad's a guy who helped me get up here. He's also going on trial tomorrow. But what's really incredible is that it was all just a coincidence.'' Then, parenthetically: ''I mean the chances of such a thing happening are so incredibly small as to not be worth considering, you know? I mean, well, you had no idea when you slipped that ring onto Muhammad's toe that your brother and Jihad, were one and the same, right? I mean, you and Jihad, sister and brother? Well, golly! I mean, well, who would have thought?

"You know what I mean? Azizah? Azizah? . . ." sniff, sniff, sniff . . . "Azizah are you there?"

FINAL THOUGHTS

Now I was really alone. Alone with my thoughts. I decided to review what I'd just learned. It helped ward off loneliness.

My first conclusion was that aside from the benefits of the company I'd shared with Tom, and the happy news of Azizah's love, I wasn't one who occupied a very enviable position. On the contrary. I recognized that I was, as Jihad so aptly phrased it, in very deep shit. And I couldn't, no matter how much I tried, think of any right-minded man or woman who'd freely change places with me.

Really.

For the way I saw it, all the pleasures of life in The Dark weren't worth diddly-squat, if, in the final analysis, they had the weapons (which I knew they had) and they aimed to use them on me (which I felt sure they did) in the morning (which, I continuously worried, it nearly was).

19

✥

Oom, bah, wah, wah

OOM, BAH, WAH, WAH

My time in The Dark came to an end when the boulder rolled away from the entrance. Blinding daylight shot down into the cave. How ironic, I thought, as I shielded my eyes.

Two men clad in white togas took my arms and led me out into the fresh mountain air. The sight of the sun slicing through the western horizon told me it was evening. The implication was that the trial had been pushed back from the morning. I was neither surprised nor disappointed by the delay, just reminded I was still in Egypt.

My escorts held up a black galabia and indicated that I put it on. "Over my clothes?" I asked.

They pretended like they didn't understand English.

I put it on over my clothes. It had a loose, comfortable fit, though the sleeves were a little short.

The sun had set by the time we reached the campus periphery. I sensed a festive atmosphere amidst the large group of people gathered around the stage in the middle of the clearing. The sound of drums took up in the distance as my escorts guided me onto a torch-lit pathway leading to the torch-lit stage. *Boom . . . boom . . . boom.* One *"boom"* each second for three seconds followed by a one-second rest. It was a pattern.

Boom . . . boom . . . boom . . . rest. *Boom . . . boom . . . boom . . .* rest. I noticed that my escorts and I had taken, unconsciously, to walking in step with the beat. The ceremony had begun.

There was another threesome about ten steps in front of us. Two toga-men supporting what looked like a black-robed puppet in their midst. It was Jihad. He didn't look well from the back. His head wiggled just a little too freely and he stumbled a lot.

I also noticed, as we approached, that most of the audience was made up of monks. Or what looked like monks. For as we began to pass I was able to see that the faces within the generous hoods of the ground-length, formless, deep brown robes, belonged to women. The women of Jabal Amman.

The crowd crushed to the borders of the path as we approached the staircase leading to the stage. Jihad stumbled once on the third step. His escorts lifted him the rest of the way. I mounted without help while my guides stood by at the ready.

The stage had undergone a number of changes since the previous day. Most apparent were the walls that now stood around three sides. Walls of wood hung with intricate tapestries.

Also of note was the table which now stood in the middle of the stage. On its face sat a pitcher, a glass, and a small black box. The pitcher was filled with some clear liquid.

To the table's left (from the perspective of the crowd on the ground) were three rows of chairs. These chairs faced the table and were occupied with what I took to be dignitaries.

Three more seats stood along the back wall of the stage a few feet behind the table. Haddi sat in the rightmost chair. He wore a white ceremonial robe. Assad stood to Haddi's right. And to Assad's right stood Faisel. Faisel held a spear in either hand.

I looked for but could not find anyone looking remotely sheik-like. Shebob had yet to arrive.

Seats had been reserved for us next to Haddi. Jihad was placed in the one in the middle, while I sat myself down on the end.

The audience—both onstage and off—was much easier to see from this angle. A few familiar faces sprinkled the dignitary section. Like Ellen's. I spotted her sitting in the back row. Her gaze was focused straight ahead, into the back of the person before her. To her left sat the "welcome" man. He appeared as cheerful as ever. He even waved and mouthed *the* word when he caught my eye.

Muhammad!

Muhammad was there too, standing behind the dignitaries among a group of monks and toga-men. In fact he was wearing a toga himself. A white one with a matching turban. He looked good. Very local. We acknowledged each other as soon as our eyes connected. He waved his hand once from his waist, while I gave a short nod in return. The whole encounter passed very quietly. I stifled a smile. It felt good, somehow, to know that my old friend Muhammad was there.

Muhammad turned his attention to the monk on his left. He bent to hear what the monk had to say, then rose once again to face me. The monk looked my way too. I tried peering into the hood to see who it was, but a shadow blocked my vision. The monk understood my efforts and turned her head slightly so the flickering light from one of the torches could illuminate her face. It was Azizah. Did she wink at me? It seemed that she had, just before her face fell back into shadow.

I nodded to her like I'd nodded to Muhammad. Quietly. Discreetly.

I turned to Jihad for the first time since taking my seat

(about fifteen seconds had passed in all). I noticed that his face was freshly beaten and that his eyes looked dimly focused. He'd been drugged.

"Jihad," I said as I took his arm in mine. "Jihad, it's Lion. Can you hear me?"

"Lion?" he asked weakly.

"Yes, it's Lion. I'm here. I'm right by your side."

"Lion . . . this is the end."

"No, Jihad, don't say that! It's not the end. Gather your strength. You've a trial before you."

"Trial?" His speech was slow and slurred. "Trial . . ."

"Yes, Jihad. Very soon. As soon as Sheik Shebob arrives."

I became aware that the drummers had taken up another beat. Four staccato *boom*s in rapid succession. A marching beat.

The crowd on the ground—the monks and the toga-men—began chanting to the beat. *"Oom, bah, wah, wah. Doom, bah, dah, tah. Ah, bah, wah, lah."* They repeated it over and over, like a mantra.

"This trial's fixed . . ." said Jihad with effort.

". . . *Oom, bah, wah, wah* . . ."

"Jihad!" I interrupted. "You're innocent. Don't talk like that."

". . . *Doom, bah, dah, tah* . . ."

"It's fixed . . ." he repeated and shook his head.

". . . *Ah, bah, wah, lah* . . ."

I could see my friend needed some boosting. "Listen, Jihad. I have some good news. It's about your parents. You see when your mother came to Sinai . . ."

A loud cry went up from one of the toga-men: *"Allah Akbar!"*

The drumming stopped. Voices fell silent. I figured Sheik Shebob was about to appear.

THE PLEA

Two henchmen stepped up from behind and lifted Jihad by the arms. Jihad made a remark in Arabic without drawing a response.

Haddi stood too and marched up to the table. His steps were short and quick. Very business-like.

"We will conduct our affairs here today in English," he began in his squeaky tone, "so all the defendants will understand the trial proceedings." He turned and acknowledged me with a warm expression.

Where is the sheik? I thought.

Haddi addressed Jihad. "You've been charged, Jihad, with perpetrating the crime of torture—of torturing a helpless peasant. You are also being charged with illegal trespass on Jabal Amman, as well as spying. How plead you?"

All eyes turned to the two toga-men and the tottering figure between them. "Have your men unhand me, Haddi." Jihad's voice was weak but steady. The drug he'd been given was strong, but so was his determination to withstand its effects.

Haddi paused meaningfully before signaling for Jihad's release. The toga-men obeyed. Jihad's legs wobbled as he fought to find his balance.

The campus hushed as Jihad's figure struggled for strength. A sharp wind ripped across the stage. Torches fluttered. The crowd bundled as one against the sudden cold. Jihad nearly blew away, yet in the end he held his ground. More or less.

"The prisoner will enter a plea," repeated Haddi.

Jihad's eyes met his accuser's. "You know how I plead, Haddi. I'm innocent."

Haddi gave a disdaining look. "Let the record show that the accused pleads not guilty."

Assad took out a pen and made a note.

"The accused has entered his plea," called Haddi to the assembly. "He claims innocence. Others contest this. As is our custom, we bring the matter before Sheik Shebob! He will arbitrate. He shall judge!''

The crowd reacted with the chant. *"Oom, bah, wah, wah. Doom, bah, dah, tah . . ."*

THE RINGS

Haddi reached for the small black box on the table. He opened the lid and removed two rings. The first was silver and quite simple, while the second glistened of gold and held a ruby. He took this second ring—the one that had once belonged to Azizah's mother before it passed from Azizah's father to Azizah, to Muhammad, to Jihad—and placed it now with a glance towards Azizah, on his own right-hand thumb.

Then, referring to the simpler ring, the one of silver, he said: "This is the ring of Sheik Shebob." He held it aloft for all to see. "This ring holds the great man's spirit. It has served the cause of Allah and justice for over seven generations. We ask it today to serve us again. . . ."

"*. . . Doom, bah, dah, tah . . .*"

A ring? Sheik Shebob was a *ring?* My hopes for a fair trial dimmed.

I LEAPT TO MY FEET FOR JUSTICE

"Just one minute, Haddi. What's going on here? How can a ring appear in place of the Sheik himself? Where's the main man?"

Haddi never answered. Someone from the audience called out instead: "Sit down! You're disrupting the trial!"

I searched the area by the stage for the person who'd spoken. "What do you mean, disrupting the trial? This isn't a trial. It's a kangaroo court!"

A chorus of boos and whistles took up in the crowd. There were calls of "Sit down!" and "You'll get yours!" Someone even spoke ill of my mother.

Haddi raised his hands to quiet the rabble.

"They're right, you know, Leo. There's no need to interrupt. You'll get your chance to speak at your own trial. Let's see . . ." He looked over a piece of paper he'd removed from his pocket. ". . . your trial's scheduled for . . . for right after Jihad's. Don't worry, you won't have to wait long."

I looked from Haddi to Jihad. My friend still struggled to remain on his feet.

"But I want to speak," I insisted. "I want to speak since Jihad can't."

"That's nonsense, Leo. Of course Jihad can speak. You heard him make his plea. If anything, he's having some problems standing. You can see that, can't you? It's forcing him to waste precious energy he'll need for the trial. Settle yourself. Then we can move along."

Jihad seemed oblivious to the whole discussion.

Two guards stepped towards me in a threatening manner.

"Keep 'em away from me, Haddi. Let me have my say. I want to have my say before the trial."

Haddi made noises of exasperation. The goons kept coming.

I made a final appeal: *"Please."*

The magic word! The henchmen stopped in their tracks. Haddi smiled. "Leo, your appeals have touched my heart. I'm giving you five minutes to state whatever it is you want to state. After that, it's *show time.*"

An interesting choice of words I thought, then checked my watch.

"Five minutes is plenty, Haddi. Because all I have to say is: I'm onto you, Jack. I've got your number."

"Jack?" he squeaked. "Onto me?" His face screwed up as if he had no idea what I was talking about.

"Yeah, onto you," I said pointing at him. "Like a rabbi onto a cheeseburger in a kosher deli."

Haddi seemed undisturbed. "That's quite an image for a man with just four minutes to get to the point."

I took his word on the time. "The point is, Haddi, this is nothing but a show trial. You've got it in for Jihad. You want him dead."

Haddi frowned. Jihad drew his pulped face into an expression of studied cynicism.

"A very presumptive remark on your part, Leo. Tell me, do you base it on anything substantive?"

"I base it on a couple of things. Like the fact that he's already half dead, for one. I doubt you would have rearranged his face like that if you wanted him alive."

Haddi smirked. "If I look skeptical, Leo, it's because I am. I don't think your argument's won any converts."

Indeed, the audience was silent. My one comfort was their continuing attention.

"I'm not trying to convert anyone," I fibbed. "I know the truth."

"Perhaps. Now you say you base your theory on a couple of things. Would it be impolite to ask what that second *thing* might be?"

"No, Haddi, not at all. The second thing . . . my second proof that you want Jihad dead, is the fact that you can't possibly let him live."

"Can't let him live? Oh, ho, ho! This *is* getting interesting. Three minutes to go. Continue, please."

I glanced over to Jihad. He looked interested too.

"That's right. Because if you don't kill Jihad now, he'll kill you as soon as he gets the chance."

A check with the dignitary section revealed, if not edge-of-the-seat tension, then at least heightened alertness.

"That might be," reasoned Haddi. "Any man who'd come all the way up here to trespass might also be capable of murder."

"That wasn't what I meant, Haddi. And by the way, he didn't climb all the way up Jabal Amman to trespass. But that's besides the point. The point is, Jihad thinks he came up here to find Lizzie for me. What he still doesn't realize is that you lured him up here for purposes which have nothing to do with anything he's heard until now.''

Haddi raised his right eyebrow in a show of skepticism. ''What are you talking about, Leo? What do mean *lure*?''

''I mean, Dr. Haddi, that you've had your eye on Jihad for quite a while. And you've been biding your time for just the right moment to do him in—in just the right fashion. So you had Lizzie—your Ellen—check us into the Amman Hotel. A hotel whose main feature is that it is located right next door to Jihad's detective agency. That's why you purchased it, isn't it? So that your man the receptionist could put Jihad in touch with me as soon as Lizzie disappeared.

''From there it was simple. First you had Assad take us where we wanted to go, and then you had Muhammad set up so he'd be captured and divulge your whereabouts.

''You even sent assorted spies to monitor our progress. Spies like the Binsbergs, the old couple from Brooklyn we saw at the Pyramids and met on the train. Only I doubt now they're really from Brooklyn.

''It was a great plan. Everything would seem innocent. Jihad wouldn't suspect a thing.

''It was also very complicated, a fact that meant it had to have been planned well before my arrival in Egypt.''

I turned to the dignitary section.

''Which further meant, *Ellen,* that you lied yesterday when you told me you brought me to Egypt because you didn't know how to say good-bye. Because the truth is I was brought into Egypt all the way from a Parisian record store for the express purpose of acting as an unknowing participant in this plot to capture Jihad!''

Ellen rose. She looked upset. ''But Leo. There was never any intention to hurt you . . .''

''Enough, please. You already gave me that line in your cave.''

She looked for a minute as if she were stunned, then she sat back down without another word.

Haddi spoke up. "This is all very interesting, Mr. Gold, perhaps even thrilling, but with just two and a half minutes remaining, I suggest you dispense with the theatrics and get to the point."

"I'm about to, but I hope you're not counting that woman's interruption against my time."

Haddi didn't answer.

"The point, Dr. Haddi, and it's the same one I was trying to make before you asked me to describe how you lured Jihad up here, is that you want him dead because he has a long-lost sister among your women. A sister who, until this moment, he never knew existed."

I paused to let assembled monks and toga-men consider this shocking revelation. This they did, though in silence. The single real sign of interest came from Jihad, who picked up his head and turned toward me.

"That's right, everybody!" I exclaimed. "And when do you think Haddi learned about this relationship?"

Another pause. Another deathly silence.

"I'll tell you when. He learned about it when he eavesdropped on Azizah's father's deathbed confession that Azizah had a brother."

The audience stirred. Finally.

"What are you talking about, Gold? What brother . . . ?"

"I'm talking about the boy Jihad's father left behind when he returned to the desert. The same boy whose mother died while giving birth to Azizah nine months after trailing her husband into the desert. The same boy who never received the ring Azizah's dying father placed in her hand—the ring you're now wearing!

"But the real significant part," I said with emphasis. "The part that scared you silly, was the realization that Jihad became Azizah's willie after their father died. So you went back to the old man's house right after killing him to look for some clue that would help you find this new willie.

And you did—in the letters and records from the orphanage where Jihad grew up.''

The crowd gasped. Azizah shrieked.

Two toga-men jumped up and dragged her from the stage. Muhammad followed them off. Another two henchmen stepped up and seized Jihad, who still looked slightly confused.

"I haven't finished, Haddi," I called out over the commotion. "I still have one and a half minutes!"

"Indeed you do," said Haddi in a tone that indicated he wasn't as shaken as the others. "Only I must tell you that I don't see the relevance of Jihad's role as willie. Why should this be a motive for me to want him dead?"

Up to this point I'd been dabbling in the realm of facts and conjecture. Now was the time for conclusions. I cleared my throat. "I figure, and you probably did too, that once Jihad learned he was Azizah's willie he'd be determined to free her from this sordid marriage. That would have been enough to make you feel threatened."

"Nonsense. The law states that a willie can pull his woman from a marriage anytime he wants. The husband is powerless to object."

"Hmmmmm." He was right about that. I'd learned the same thing earlier. Darn. I felt a moment of confusion. Where had I gone wrong? "You'd have set her free?" I wanted to make sure I understood.

"Not twenty-four hours after hearing the word from her willie."

I reviewed the facts. Time was working against me. I asked the following question: "Then how come you didn't free her when her father asked you to? He was her willie."

"I think we've spent enough time on this matter, Leo," said Haddi curtly. He held up his watch. "Your five minutes are up."

"Wait a minute, Haddi. Answer my question. Why did you kill Azizah's father when he ordered you to free her?"

"Enough of this nonsense, I say. It's time to get on with the trial."

Then it struck me. The real key.

"I've got it!" I declared. "You feared Jihad because he wouldn't have given you the chance to deceive him. He would have killed you right off as revenge for all the degrading things you brought on his sister.

"Isn't that right, Jihad?"

I thought I detected a nod.

"I order you to be quiet!" hollered Haddi.

"But that's only half the story. Because even if Jihad had never become Azizah's willie, he would have had to take revenge on you for killing his father. That's right, because your savage act created a blood feud. Jihad would have had to kill you to preserve the family honor."

"Nonsense!"

"It's not nonsense," I said. "It's a tragedy. It's a tragedy because Jihad would have had to kill you for murdering his father—a man who deserted him as a child!"

A cry of shock went up in the crowd. One of the monk women dabbed her eyes.

Haddi looked unhappy too, though not for the same reason. I congratulated myself for figuring it out. I was about to take in Jihad's reaction when two lugs came up from behind to keep me from swiveling my head. "Haddi, you scoundrel!" A palm clamped down on my mouth.

I heard Jihad speak: "Sister? Blood feu . . . ?" until he too was cut short.

THE TRIAL

Haddi addressed the crowd in Arabic before switching to English. "Enough. Enough!" He shouted. "It's time for the trial! Come to order."

The audience on the stage returned to their senses. Those on the ground quieted themselves. My revelation had had its moment, and the moment had passed. For all the greatness of my deductions, the size of my disappointment was even greater.

Haddi was back in control. "Thank you all for your co-operation. Let us begin . . ."

A few from the crowd cheered: "Hooray for order!" Faisel signaled his support by tapping the stage twice with the base of his spears.

"Only, since Mr. Gold has shown such a strong interest in our legal culture, we've decided to hold his trial before Jihad's."

"Wrmghrph?" I asked from beneath my gag of flesh.

"Yes, *we*," explained Haddi. "But first we'll explain the trial procedures for the court of Sheik Shebob. It's quite simple, really. It begins when this glass is filled with well-drawn water . . ."

Haddi picked up the pitcher as he spoke and poured a portion of its contents into the glass. He replaced the pitcher.

"Next we place Shebob's ring, and with it the old Sheik's spirit, into the glass of water." Haddi did as he said and watched as the ring fell like a stone to the bottom. "The wisdom of Sheik Shebob has entered the water."

The campus crowd cheered.

A momentary lapse by my handlers allowed me to catch a glimpse of Jihad. He too strained within the grip of his captors. His face was stiff and his eyes intense. Beads of perspiration stood out on his forehead as he focused his energy on the proceedings. I imagined I looked much the same.

"The accused—you, Leo—will take this glass and drink continuously until all of the water has been drained and only the ring remains. Succeed, and you'll be judged innocent of all crimes with which you stand accused. You'll be free to leave the mountain."

Haddi inspected my face to see if I understood. It seemed

simple enough. "Nod," he said, "if you have any questions."

I nodded.

A gesture by Haddi brought the hand away from my mouth just long enough for me to say: "You're a lousy skunk, Haddi."

"I repeat, Mr. Gold, all you have to do is drain the water from the glass."

What's the catch? I thought as the midget headed back to his seat.

"Just one more thing . . ." Haddi stopped in his tracks, turned and offered an absent gesture toward the glass on the table. "Fail . . ." his voice rose an octave, ". . . gag, delay, or leave a single drop along the edge of the glass, and it will be taken as a sign from Allah, with Sheik Shebob as his messenger, that Jihad is guilty as accused. Is that clear?"

"*Jdkweljp?*"

"That's right. You heard me. Your failure to drain the glass will be taken as a sign that Jihad is guilty." He paused to let this sink in before continuing. "You should also know that the penalty for guilt is death. But don't feel under any pressure. Ha, ha, ha."

Jihad began a violent struggle against his captors. A tumult took up all around. Five more goons came up to subdue him. Blows were struck. Jihad fell beneath a pile of men.

"There's no need to look over there, Leo. Jihad's all right."

The commotion quieted down. The human hill above Jihad stopped shaking. One by one, the men of the assault team got up. The last one lifted Jihad by the collar. My friend was still conscious, that I could see, though hardly all right.

Haddi cleared his throat before continuing as if nothing had happened. "And as a special consideration on my part,

Leo, so you'll have something to concentrate on during the trial, and to avoid any delays later on, I'd like to ask these kind gentlemen"—he referenced Jihad's guards—"to please position Jihad by the wall."

This was the far wall. The one opposite the dignitary section. The guards dragged Jihad to the wall's approximate center and secured him with a rope. The rope was then knotted to a large metal ring attached to the wall.

The guards stepped back. Jihad struggled without moving.

"One more thing, Leo. Punishment will be carried out immediately."

The guards released me. "No appeals?"

"Not in the court of Sheik Shebob."

Members of the audience took up a new chant. It was low and more monotonous than the previous one. They sang: *"E-ma, Ah-ba, E-ma, Ah-ba . . ."*

Haddi gestured for me to pick up the glass and drink.

I held my ground. "Why should I play your game, Haddi?"

"As you yourself said, I'm an honorable man. Succeed, and you both go free."

I thought this over. In fact, I'd never called him an honorable man and I doubted his pledge to let us go. But what choice did I have?

I looked over to Jihad, whose eyes seemed suddenly bright. He called out to me, "Don't worry, Lion. Relax. There is no spirit of Sheik Shebob. It doesn't exist. This is just a psychological game. Haddi's trying to make you nervous. He's counting on weak nerves to make you fail."

A toga-man stepped up and laid his fist into Jihad's stomach.

Another guard pushed me toward the table. Someone placed the glass in my hand. Water reached up to its rim.

"E-ma, Ah-ba, E-ma, Ah-ba . . ."

"There's nothing to fear, Lion," came Jihad's voice

weakly from beneath the din. "It's easy . . ." Another fist pounded into his abdomen.

My hand shook violently. Water splashed out in all directions. Easy? Is that what he'd said?

"No fair cheating, Leo," said Haddi. He took hold of my wrist and refilled what had spilled from the glass.

I turned to answer but couldn't. My tongue was stuck to the roof of my mouth. I tried swallowing. No luck there either.

I looked across to Jihad. His head hung forward. The whites of his eyes were red. He winked. He winked! Just like Azizah, he'd winked!

"Come now, Leo," Haddi prodded. "Drink up."

"E-ma, Ah-ba . . ."

I was frozen.

"Faisel!" Haddi called. The guard brought the point of one of his spears in touch with Jihad's forehead.

"Mr. Gold," said Haddi calmly. "Either you drink now or your friend dies without a trial."

I found Jihad's face again. "Do it," he mouthed. "Just do it."

My eyes passed over to Haddi. "Do it now!" he said. I scanned the dignitary section, where a couple of girls were leading that insane chant. I turned back to Jihad and raised the trembling glass in a toast.

I closed my eyes as the glass broke the seal of my lips. The water began seeping into my mouth. Slowly. I swallowed. More water. Another swallow. Slowly. I tipped the glass a bit. A slight scratching sound told me the ring was sliding along the bottom of the glass.

"E-ma . . ."

The water cooled my throat. I began gulping.

"Ah-ba . . ."

Slow down, slow down I thought. Not too fast. Easy . . . easy. Keep the flow steady.

The ring, I could sense, was already midway along the

stem of the glass. I sipped more water. I had a rhythm. Sip, seal lips, swallow. Sip, seal lips, swallow. I tried not to think about Jihad standing up against the wall with the spear against his head. Sip, seal lips, swallow. Sip, Seal lips, swallow.

"E-ma . . . Ah-ba . . ."

The ring lay against my lips. I took another sip. The last remaining gulp of water entered my mouth. I brought my lips together.

There was a problem! I couldn't close my mouth. The ring was in the way. My rhythm!

"E-ma . . ."

I inhaled through my mouth instead of my nose. I swallowed. Water rushed down my windpipe. I began coughing. The ring fell to the ground. I doubled over. I reached out for the table to steady myself.

THE DEATH PENALTY

The chanting ceased. Silence.

"You have failed the test of Sheik Shebob, Mr. Gold. It is the will of Allah. This is certification of your guilt. Jihad's too. The penalty for your crimes is death."

Though this shouldn't have surprised me, I admit that it did. "But, but . . . Haddi!"

"Silence!"

But there wasn't silence. Jihad called out from his point along the wall. "Lion," he cried. "Lion!" He was calling me.

"Jihad!" I stepped towards him. Two henchmen grabbed me.

I heard Haddi say: "It is time to bring this to an end." He walked over to Faisel, took one of the guard's spears and turned to address the audience. "The word of Allah has come down through Sheik Shebob. He has spoken. Prepare yourself, Jihad, to meet the Master of Eternity. May Allah have mercy on your corrupted soul!"

Someone began pounding the drum again. Haddi fixed his grip around the base of the spear then moved back toward center stage. He stopped and positioned himself. He raised the elongated needle over his head to the full extent of his arms. The sparkling point preceded his nose by at least five feet.

"Boom, boom, boom, boom . . ."

"Lion!" Jihad called. "Lion, I need you."

But I couldn't move. The goons were holding me too tight.

Haddi took aim and began moving towards Jihad. His teeth flashed in a steely grit before his mouth slowly opened. *"Allah Akbar!"* He was charging forward across the stage. *"Allah Akbar!"*

"BOOM! BOOM! BOOM! BOOM! . . ."

Jihad looked out in horror as the point approached his head. He struggled lamely.

"Lion!!" he yelled. "Liiiiiiioonnnnnnnnn!!!"

"Jihad!!!" I answered. My face was wet with tears.

"Liiiiiiioooooonnnnnn!" he kept repeating it. "Liiiiiiooooooooonnnnnnn! Liiiiiii . . ." Until the wall against which he'd been tied fell backwards toward the ground. Haddi went next. Over the edge of the stage, that is.

THE FIGHT

Screams of confusion took up all around.

A group of people ran over and stooped where Jihad lay tied. Haddi was somewhere on the ground hidden from view beneath the horizon of the stage. I struggled in vain against the men who held me.

The people around Jihad stood up. One of them, I could tell from his forehead, was Muhammad. This meant that the monk by his side was Azizah. Muhammad reached down and helped Jihad to his feet. Toga-men were closing fast from every side. Muhammad punched one in the face. The man fell like a stone. The other toga-men halted.

"Run!" I cried. "Save yourselves!" Someone hit me then covered my mouth.

Jihad and Muhammad stood shoulder to shoulder. Two other men guarded the rear. Azizah held the space in the middle. Jihad picked up an abandoned spear and began swinging it back and forth. The mob held its ground. The five of them backed up slowly. Jihad kept swinging. Muhammad's fists were high. Azizah and the others checked the flanks for approaching attacks.

The crowd around them grew larger.

I bit the hand that held my mouth. "Run!" I yelled.

Jihad rushed forward with the spear in the lead. The crowd parted. Azizah came next, then Muhammad. The two others brought up the rear with threatening gestures.

They were through this small gap and running towards the darkness by the edge of the campus when a high volume, high-pitched scream came up from beneath the edge of the stage. It was Haddi.

I heard the words: "You can't get away from me. I'm bigger than all of you!" Then I saw a spear shoot out as if launched from below ground. The missile flew long and low before falling to the earth on a path that took it directly through Jihad's back.

Azizah shrieked before collapsing next to her skewered brother.

"Ackhi!" she moaned. "My brother!"

A pack of toga-men was nearly upon them.

Muhammad bent for Azizah. He took her by the waist with one hand as he struck the first toga-man to arrive with the other. The man crashed to the ground. Another toga-man stepped up. And another. And another. Muhammad handled them all, though with greater and greater difficulty. They'd begun hitting back when Muhammad saw he had no choice but to turn with Azizah beneath his arm and run.

Azizah flapped within his grip. "My brother!" she cried. "My brother!"

I watched in shock as they disappeared into the shadows.

I turned back to where Jihad had fallen. A group of togamen were just then pulling the spear that had pierced him from his back. It was clear that Jihad was dead. I could tell by the way his arms scraped limply along the ground as they dragged him away.

Though I felt sick, I controlled myself—I kept my head about me—because I knew if I didn't I wouldn't survive.

MY TURN

I fought within the clasp of my keepers as Haddi trudged up the steps to the stage. The white of his robe was marked with dirt and his face was scratched and bruised. He was panting. His eyes declared my time had come. He approached under the escort of two oversized guards. Their height was accentuated by the fact that Haddi's head barely reached their thighs. He signaled for my release.

"Justice is done, Mr. Gold, one way or another." His voice cracked on the word "another."

"You call that justice?"

"I did it myself."

What a strange thing to say, I thought, though I said: "Well, I guess that means you'll be letting me go shortly." Even though I figured it didn't.

Haddi shook his head. "Still making jokes, I see. Don't worry, that too, will soon come to a halt." His voice was cold. He meant business and I was expendable inventory.

"Listen, Haddi, I can't help it if I make jokes at serious moments. It's just a defense mechanism. I'm scared shitless and I want out. Let me go and I won't tell a soul. I have no reason to. My needs and yours are completely separate and nonintersecting. I'm a tourist in Egypt, here to enjoy the wonders of the Pyramids and a brief ride on the Nile. Your business, what you do, what you've done, your dreams, and such, these are of no interest to me whatsoever. Let me go and I'll return to my little world and forget this small unfortunate incident.''

"Sheik Shebob has found you guilty," Haddi sneered. "Besides, don't you feel a responsibility for Jihad's honor? And what of Azizah? Haven't you fallen in love with her?"

"Jihad's dead. I can't help him now . . . And Azizah? No. No! Azizah's your wife. Nothing would ever happen between us. . . ." I felt distracted. I wanted him to wipe the blood from his lips. "You see, even if I did fall in love with her, nothing would happen, you see, because the thing between you and me is much more important than the thing between she and I. Do you understand? I'm no threat to you."

A look of disgust crossed his face and he spit.

"You sniveling pig! Have you no honor? Don't you believe in anything?" He muttered a few words to the guards, who once again stepped up and took me forcefully by the arms.

Someone took hold of the drum which had fallen during the hullabaloo and picked up the beat again.

"Dr. Haddi! Please! I beg you. This is not my reality. This can't be happening to me. I'm an ordinary person caught in extraordinary circumstances. I don't belong. Killing me would serve no purpose because I don't exist anyway."

Haddi barked another command. The lugs began dragging me towards the back wall where I imagined I'd be speared.

"BOOM, BOOM, BOOM, BOOM . . ."

"Dr. Haddi! I want to live! I want to live!"

Haddi moved to the side to let us pass. The guards stopped for a moment to face and receive a final word from their master. They continued holding me by the armpits, though more loosely than before. I whimpered silently and thought of my approaching end. I saw the spear winging towards my head. I saw blood, my own, spilling harshly onto the ground.

It was a horrible image and it made me jerk and lift myself in the arms of my captors. This, in turn, sent my right foot flying up into the crevice between Dr. Haddi's legs. The force of my stroke brought Haddi himself into the air. His face registered shock as his eyes bulged and his face color changed from brown, to blue, to white. My foot was still between his legs as he hit and crumbled to the ground.

I found myself momentarily released as the guards stooped to help him. I used this opportunity to disengage my foot from Haddi's groin and step out onto center stage.

Unfortunately, my plan of escape was just as developed as my plan of attack, and I had no idea what to do next. So I did what came naturally. I jumped to the ground and charged through the crowd of screaming monk women. Then I ran and ran and ran. I ran as fast as I could. To no place in particular. Just away.

CAPTURED

Looking back, it would have been wiser to run somewhere, because in the end, I arrived nowhere. Or, more accurately, I arrived nowhere where I should have been. For Assad was soon upon me. And he didn't come alone.

I gave up without resistance. His spear-toting friends convinced me that this was the thing to do. Then they took me gruffly by the collar and pulled till my feet began trailing in the dust. Fear moved me to incoherence. I began babbling. Repeated requests for assistance went unheeded.

The campus was dark by the time we returned. Everyone was gone. Two or three torches remained smoldering. We approached the well I'd once noticed standing in the center of the campus opposite the stage. They lifted me onto the small platform hanging where there would have been a pail had this actually been a well. But this wasn't a well, as I was soon to find out. It was something much worse. It was The Noise.

HEAR NO EVIL

Assad's assistants turned a crank that sent me descending. A low humming noise like the whistle one hears when blowing across the opening of a soda bottle became audible. First it sounded like it was coming from below. Then, as I fell deeper, I imagined it was coming from above. Finally, as I neared the bottom, I concluded that it was emanating from everywhere, spinning off the rounded walls, and careening back on me.

It grew louder and louder, shrieking and wailing like sirens of death. Like a million howling hounds. Like as many sticks of chalk, scratching and screeching, down and about endless rows of blackboards.

Collected pain cells from my frontal lobe fused together in a tight ball and shot themselves hard against the back of my skull. The ball shattered, breaking up into scores of tiny metal hooks. Each hook embedded itself in a soft spot along the fabric of my brain and began moving, some faster, some slower, as strategically stationed reel handlers wound it all home. Some ripped southwards through the neck and down the canal of the spine. Others sought exit through the ears but found that the unusually heavy traffic forced them into torturous circling patterns.

I raised my hands to my head in an effort to contain the explosion that sent me rolling off the edge of the plank. I was vaguely aware of waiting to hit bottom, then vaguely aware that I'd long since arrived. I watched through squinting eyes as they raised the tray back up.

I wanted to scream: "Don't leave without me!," but all I could manage was: "*Ahhhhhhhh!*" It was just as I'd hollered in The Dark. Only this time, instead of being absorbed, the noise was reflected back. And when it reflected it multiplied, and when it multiplied it grew, and when it grew it multiplied. So when I heard my voice again, it was my voice times ten thousand. And then ten thousand more, until my bones began shaking and my mind started breaking.

My instincts issued orders to escape. Any way, in any direction. I somehow stood and charged towards a wall, only to be tripped up along the way by a small mound. I looked back and saw the tortured grimace of a rotted skull.

I struggled to my feet and continued my charge into the rock. I hit it hard and began clawing with my nails until The Noise forced me down.

I rose again and repeated my charge and claw. Again and again. Hand over hand. Hand, over hand, as the Mormon Tabernacle Choir sought out, found and hit high C within the newly cleared areas of my brain. Hand over hand away from The Noise. Away . . . away . . . away . . . away . . .

20

❧

The Unknown

WINE

I woke amid cushions with the taste of wine on my tongue.

"Drink," came Azizah's voice.

A cool, smooth surface pressed onto my lower lip. I opened my lids. Before me lay the stem of a silver goblet cradled in the pads of Azizah's fingers.

"Not too fast," she cautioned. "Slowly . . . slowly."

I drank as she suggested while my eyes took in the drama of her new, simpler presentation. Gone was the exotic monk suit. In its place she wore a plain white, loose-fitting galabia. Most of her bracelets and bells were also away, as was her braided horn. Set free like this, her dark, thick mane ran like wild flowers over her delicate shoulders and shapely form.

"Is this heaven?"

Azizah chuckled softly. "No, Leo, you're in a secret cave not far from the campus."

"But The Noise? . . . What about The Noise? That's the last I remember."

"Assad placed you there to die."

I took a closer look at her. Her eyes were red. She'd been

crying. She was also more beautiful than I'd ever seen her before.

"Yes, I know," I said. "But what happened? How did I survive The Noise? How did I get here?"

"Muhammad saved you." She moved aside so I could see, smoking a cigarette in the glow of a torch near the cave's opposite wall, the happy face of my savior, Muhammad.

He waved.

I waved back.

"Jabal Amman is crisscrossed with secret tunnels," she explained. "Muhammad took one to The Noise where he found your body shaking violently on the ground."

I shook once again as I recalled what that had been like.

"Don't worry," she said as she began stroking my forehead. "It's over now. Here, drink. The wine will calm your body." She raised the goblet and I sipped till I had my fill. Then I asked what time it was.

"It's about eleven at night. You've been out of The Noise for over an hour. You were in for fifteen minutes."

"Fifteen minutes? That's all?"

"That's plenty, don't you think? It's said that a man can't survive in The Noise for more than twenty-five minutes . . ."

I motioned for more wine.

". . . but you're exceptionally strong," she added. "I think you would have lasted thirty."

I brought the wine to my lips.

OF JIHAD

I turned to her a little bit later. "Jihad's dead, isn't he."

She blinked her eyes in affirmation.

I extended my arms to hold her—so she might hold me—and we could share our common sorrow. She rested her head against my shoulder. Her cheeks were dry, her tears spent.

I asked her later if she'd been able to say anything to Jihad before he died.

"Just a little," she said softly. "And then only through the wall. He'd already been fastened to the hook and the trial was about to begin. I wanted him to know he wasn't alone. I whispered through a crack that I was his sister and that I was there to save him. I even asked him to send you a signal. I wanted you to know that everything was going to be all right."

"That must have been when he winked at me!"

Azizah's eyes went wide. "He winked? Why, that's a mannerism he must have picked up from my . . . from *our* father. Our father used to wink at everyone . . ." Her voice faded as her head dropped.

"You did all you could," I said in a consoling voice. "You almost saved him."

LATER, STILL

Later, still, after I'd quenched my thirst with more wine I asked: "What exactly happened back there at the trial?"

"Do you mean before or after Muhammad and I left the stage?"

I nodded.

Azizah moved closer to check my eyes. "Are you all right, Leo? Perhaps you shouldn't drink so much."

She took the wine goblet from my hand.

"I'm fine," I reported. "Just a little light-headed."

"Yes, I can see that. Here, eat this while I describe what happened." She placed a slice of cheese in my hand. "First of all, I didn't learn that my brother was on the mountain until you broke the news."

I said I'd figured as much when she left The Dark so abruptly. She apologized if she'd been rude, then explained that she'd run off to devise a plan for Jihad's escape. Her accomplices, Muhammad and the two toga-men I'd seen dragging her from the stage, were waiting for her back in this cave.

"You mean all that screaming was prearranged?"

"Yes," she admitted. "We did it to allay any suspicions as we left the stage. An accompanying diversion, something we'd prepared earlier, was abandoned when we saw that your revelations about Jihad were serving the same purpose. Once backstage, we prepared the side wall for lowering."

I smiled at this and reached out for some fruit. A collection of papers sat to the side of the bowl. They were dirty and crumpled and looked rather familiar.

Azizah saw the question in my eyes and explained: "From Dr. Haddi's diary."

"But how? Why?"

She shook her head. "I'm not sure. Muhammad brought them back. About all I could get from him was that he'd taken them from Dr. Haddi's tent the other night."

"From Haddi's tent?" I asked.

"Yes. And then, if I understood him correctly, I think he placed them outside the camp, on the ground."

"That's what he said?"

"He didn't exactly *say it,*" Azizah explained. "The problem is, I can't imagine why he did it."

I looked over to Muhammad, who was watching us closely. Then I turned to Azizah. "I can explain it. But first tell Muhammad thanks for the warning. Next time I'll take it."

MORE MYSTERIES

"And that's another thing," I added after thanking Muhammad personally and releasing my hand from his warm, firm grip. "Why in the world did he ever become a eunuch?"

"He didn't know what he was getting into."

"I'll say."

"What I meant was, he took the job because he needed money to help his family—a very poor clan living in northern Sinai. Assad performed the castration and tongue severing—the *cosmetic surgery* as it's known around here—himself, though Muhammad was kept in the dark about the true nature of the procedure he was about to undergo. All they told him is it would be *cosmetic . . .*"

I thought back to the reference to cosmetic *something* that had been ripped from the diary.

"Muhammad only learned he'd undergone the real thing after it was too late. By that time his only remaining option was to make the best of it by continuing to work and sending his earnings back home."

What a good son, I thought. Then: "Speaking of puzzlements, I still have a question about Haddi's tactics."

"Yes?"

"I know this may be difficult for you to answer, but I'd like to know why Haddi needed to lure Jihad up here. Why didn't he deal with him down in Cairo?"

Azizah spent some time considering this before speaking. "I can only guess myself, Leo, but I think it had to do with Haddi's vanity, and his need to dishonor me. He wanted to do away with Jihad before my eyes in order to dash any last hope I might have had of ever regaining my freedom. That's what Haddi meant when he put the family ring on his finger. He wanted me to know I was his forever—that my willie was dead."

AND ME

I had by now finished the last of the fruit and was anxious to know our plans. "And what now?" I asked. "Aren't Haddi's men looking for you?"

"They are, yes. I expect they'll arrive soon. Only we don't plan on being here when they do. The other two confederates descended the mountain about an hour ago. We three are the only ones left."

She accompanied the words "we three" with a gesture towards Muhammad, who was leaning up against the opposite wall. He paid us no mind. His attention was occupied with cigarette rolling.

"It's good to hear you've got everything under control," I said. "For my information, though, what's the escape plan?"

"That shouldn't worry you now. Just know there are plans. Our first concern is your strength. Here, have another sip . . ." She offered up another goblet. "You know you caused quite a disturbance this evening."

"That speech was unplanned."

"I meant what you did, not what you said."

I didn't understand.

"You know, when you attacked Dr. Haddi. That was very brave."

"You saw me high step into Haddi's groin? How could that be? You'd already left the campus."

"We weren't going to leave you behind, Leo." Her palm came up to my cheek. "We were in the shadows near the stage when you brought matters under control."

"Under control? Funny, the idea was to take things out of control. Especially Haddi's."

"You were very effective."

"Did you hear what I said to him just before I kicked him?"

"No. You were whimpering too softly. All we saw was your escape. Very impressive. Quite glamorous."

"Yes, well . . . I was exceptionally stressed. Besides, he left me no choice."

"Dr. Haddi has yet to recover."

"How do you mean?"

"He had to be carried from court . . . I think you injured him. He's in his tent now, resting."

I felt a bolt of satisfaction on hearing this. It confirmed a new hypothesis I'd been working on about the joys of pain and revenge. I called my theory "the cycle of violence."

A FAMILY AGAIN

Azizah refilled the goblet. "I never knew my brother. What was he like?" She brought the wine to her lips while her eyes remained on me.

"What was he like? The Jihad I knew was a brave man. A strong, sensitive man. A man who stood for things he believed in . . ." I let my voice trail off.

"That's it?"

"More or less." In fact I saw no value in exploring Jihad's second side.

"How do you think he felt when he learned he had a sister?" She bit down on her bottom lip, then let it slip out, shaking.

"I have no way of knowing, of course. I can only speak for myself. I guess he would have felt great respect . . . and pride . . . and love."

Azizah touched my arm. Her eyelids fluttered against some internal pressure. "Thank you. That was very kind."

"I meant it. The proof is that when he found the ring on Muhammad's toe, he spared no effort to find where it had come from. To seek its source—his family."

A pained and tentative look came over her face. Then: "Oh, Leo!" as she threw herself to my shoulder and began spraying tears of mingled joy and sadness.

MY NICKNAME

Azizah gathered herself together about five minutes later when she rose to address Muhammad in Arabic. She must have said something like: "Would you please excuse us?" because no sooner had she spoken than Muhammad picked up a candle, bowed to us both, and began walking off towards a far corner of the cave.

"I see that your injuries are nearly healed."

"My vision is better than ever . . ." I reached up to touch the two tiny scabs on my eyelids. "Thanks to you."

"It brought me pleasure."

"Me too." Our eyes met and held. "Once again, thank you."

Azizah glanced down. "Why did Jihad call you Lion?"

"I don't know. It was just a nickname."

"Come now. Didn't it have something to do with your character?" Her head rose again. Her lips, I noticed, were moister than before. Redder too.

"That's what Jihad once said. But I kind of doubt it."

"I don't think you give yourself enough credit. You certainly behaved like a lion at the trial."

"What you saw was a cornered lion." I wanted to stick as close to the facts as possible.

"I don't agree." Her voice sounded hoarse. "I think you behaved like the king of the jungle."

"Let's not swell the truth," I said as I noticed two darkened points rising beneath her galabia.

"All right, if not the king of the jungle"—a glazed look took up in her eyes just before they rolled up and into her head—"then the king of Azizah."

"Azizah?"

Next I knew, the soft cushions of her lips were on mine.

"Lion," she breathed during a brief pause for air, "Lion, my lion . . ."

She was near swooning, I could tell, as her body felt limp in my arms. Yet she continued. Yet *we* continued. For there seemed no other way to keep things from spinning completely out of control. And though I didn't do anything preventative, I do recall thinking: "How distorted her breathing . . . can it possibly be healthy when a face is so flushed?"

But Azizah had something else in mind. "Lion," she moaned, as she ripped the neck of her galabia, "I'm seriously overheated."

I wanted to answer: "Yes, I can tell from the way you're perspiring," but when the remains of her garment fell stripped to the ground, and what ornaments there were jangled away, I thought to myself "What had you thought?" then I thought: "Why bother with thought?"

Azizah stood before me now, as God had intended, naked of all but her hair. I offered thanks and a blessing to the womb that bore her.

She prostrated herself and gripped at my ankles: "My lion, my master, my eye of my soul: take this gift I offer you now, for it is all I have. My lips, they are yours. My tongue, it is too. My breasts and my belly, take them as well. For they are my offering to you, my love, my all, and my everything, my heart and my soul."

It was an offer I couldn't refuse.

THE UNKNOWN

I want to say right here, for the record, that I'd known more than a few women before Azizah. The point is, until Azizah, I never realized that knowing a woman was not the same as loving one. And that the two—loving and knowing—were in fact incompatible, one with the other.

That's right. Azizah took me far beyond the realm of any of my past experiences and made me reevaluate what before I'd called having sex with, or making love to, or gaining knowledge of (my own characterization, thank you) another. For she showed me that love was infinite and could not be known. And that she herself was unknowable.

Naturally this made me feel a little uncomfortable at first. But I soon found, once I adjusted to the ride, that the benefits of exploring the unknown far outweighed the security of the known.

And, anyway, I didn't enter the unknown immediately. It was a gradual process. Step by step. So when I finally looked around and noticed I didn't know where I was . . . well, I couldn't have cared less.

But I'm getting ahead of myself. For in fact we began with the basics.

THE FIRST STAGE

The first thing I did was do with my clothes what she had done with hers, until I too appeared as I'd been born.

Then one of us said: "Kiss me, please, my sweet. Hold me in your arms. I need your love to fill my heart."

And we became as one.

So began our game of rolling and kissing and moaning and splashing that continued until her body went loose as she breathed: "Lion . . ."

And I answered: "Yes, love?"

And she whispered: "Again, my darling. I beg you."

And I obeyed. First slowly. Then more rapidly. Until her head started flaying back and forth, and her throat took to emitting low guttural sounds from deep within.

This was how it went until the noises grew stronger and began sounding remotely animal-like. And if that wasn't strange enough, I also noticed that she wasn't alone in these calls to the wild, but that I was right with her, singing in tune.

So when she cooed like a dove, I cooed too. And when she brayed like a donkey, so did I. And on and on, through dogs and wolves, with panting and howling, to cats and birds with purrs and craws. The entire animal kingdom. First she, then me, until we called out as one.

Finally she asked me: "Where is your den, Lion? Where do you live?"

And I replied: "I am home."

THE SECOND STAGE

We cleansed each other's bodies with varied scents and oils. She rubbed me until my skin glowed, and I did the same for her. All the while I appreciated anew: how perfect her shape, how tantalizing her fragrance.

I looked into her almond eyes and heard their call. We embraced and rubbed cheeks and drew the fire hot. Then we were ready and I found her.

She began chanting once again in a low voice. This time, however, she left the zoo stuff outside. "Red, red, red, red . . ." She seemed transformed, far away in this land of red. The chanting continued: "Red, red, red, red . . ."

I grew concerned and was about to ask what she meant when I became aware of my vision growing blurred. I felt spurred to move on her faster, and I did. And as I raced, so did her chanting. "Red, red, red, red . . ." I began seeing red.

I shook my head. I looked below. Azizah was red! I looked about. The walls of the cave were red! My skin too! The cushions! Everything. *RED, RED, RED* . . .

We rode together hard, yet smooth. As two separate parts of one complete unit. And though the color stayed with us always as long as she chanted, its accompaniment ceased—melted, in fact—when her mouth lost its voice.

Only after we changed positions, with Azizah mounting on top, did the chanting take up again. Though this time, instead of red, the color was violet. "Violet . . . violet . . . violet . . ." She groaned as she rocked and moved, lifted and fell. "Violet, violet, violet . . ." until just as before, the color violet clouded my vision and filled my sight.

Then she called "Amber!" and we shifted and found amber. Then "Turquoise!" and we made turquoise. Then yellow, then hazel, then brown, and then green.

Soon every movement or shift on her part or mine drew another color. Rust, orange, scarlet, white . . . anything, everything. I called the colors and she responded. Then we called them together and mixed and matched, until that night we loved the spectrum.

We'd been going for longer than I knew when she asked: "What is your color?"

And I replied: "You are my rainbow."

AN INTERLUDE

We rested and drank and ate some more. We adjusted ourselves on fresh cushions and sprinkled each other with rose petals and water. Words of love passed back and forth.

"No one's ever told me that." She blushed.

"That's because no one's ever not known you the way I haven't."

She blushed again.

THE THIRD STAGE

"Do you think," I asked later, "any of our noise disturbs Muhammad?"

My question surprised her. "Muhammad? Don't worry about disturbing Muhammad. He doesn't understand a word of English. But if it will make you feel any better, we can do it this time quietly."

"But I'm not ready," I said.

"But you will be," she promised, then took me with her hand, and did what she did, until what happened, happened.

"How valiant he looks," she declared.

"And happy too. Let's celebrate."

The party began with a festive bath that continued until not a pore on her body was ignorant of my tongue.

Then Azizah said: *"Ya Allah.* Let me put him in myself."

Thus he was hers.

Our movement together began as I slipped into her depths while her jaws spread wide and her lips stretched heavenwards. I felt myself sinking further and further into a warm, moist, silent abyss until I was completely consumed and enveloped.

Azizah sensed my concern over losing control. "I've got you," she murmured.

Her face held dots of perspiration. "I have youuuuu." Her eyelids fluttered as she bit down on her lip and drew a spot of blood for me to kiss.

Her arms floated up in the air before cascading down along the sides of my body. I was securely within her now. And I feared not, though her movement was like a rippling sea and I was like a small boat lost in her currents.

"I'll guide you home," she said.

I made an unintelligible noise.

"Where is my willie?" she asked.

"He . . . is . . . in . . . you."

We continued the journey wrapped in each other's arms, spinning and hurling through a whirlpool of love.

Then she questioned: "How is my willie?"

And I answered: "He is strong."

We were almost there. All was black and peaceful and warm. Just Azizah and me, united as one, flying towards the unknown.

And I heard her whisper: "Who is my willie?"

And I answered: "The Lion."

AFTER LOVING AZIZAH

Azizah and I were floating now, somewhere in the deep unknown. A refilled wine goblet passed between us. How beautiful, she is, I thought. How good our prospects for deeper unknowledge if we can just get off this mountain.

"I understand the escape plan now," I said after we'd cooled down. "A willie's gotta do what a willie's gotta do. Haddi must die by my hand."

We got up. Azizah slipped a fresh galabia over her head and had a new one for me as well. We went over to the second side of the cave where a single torch cast flickering light over a few well-stuffed cushions.

Muhammad stepped out of the darkness. The three of us gathered together.

"Follow Muhammad," said Azizah. "He'll take you to a

small clearing near Haddi's tent. You'll find your target inside resting alone. How you get in is up to you. Just remember: two guards are posted outside and the camp is on high alert."

Muhammad reached into his toga and drew out a long, glistening hunting knife.

"You'll need it," she said.

The weapon passed from Muhammad to me. I examined its sparkling form in the light of the fire. The silver blade was freshly polished and razor sharp. Its face was broad, flat, and heavy. I passed my finger over the tip of the weapon. A bubble of blood oozed out from the spot where I'd sensed contact.

MY DEED

Muhammad took a torch in his hand. The four of us, my guide, myself, my shadow and his, moved off through the tunnel in silence. Five minutes passed before we reached a dead end. Muhammad pointed to a ladder. I climbed.

A bush over my head marked the hole's covering. I struggled out and found cover behind a nearby boulder. Haddi's large round tent stood about fifteen feet away. The outline of a guard was visible near the side farthest from me. He held a glowing cigarette and a narrow spear. He was talking to someone beyond my field of vision.

I put the knife in my mouth and slithered over to the tent without being seen. The cloth by the base was secure. I took the knife and sliced upwards. I crawled inside.

A small lantern lit Haddi's sleeping face. I crept up. My prey's breathing was steady and quiet. His expression, undisturbed.

My knife was raised to do the deed when his eyes suddenly popped open. He smiled at me and acknowledged the oversized knife in my hand. He was alert and unafraid. "Leo! What a surprise. Welcome."

"Keep your voice down, Haddi. Don't make any sudden moves."

He reduced his voice to a whisper. "I take it you're here to learn about 'the greater good.'"

I brought the edge of the knife to his throat. "That's right," I said. "And for this." I reached over and slipped the ring from his finger. It came without difficulty, as did the appearance of a thin red line where his skin began unzipping under pressure from the chilled steel.

Haddi's lips turned up in a smile. "You can't kill me, Leo," he said. "I'm bigger than you."

"Is that so?" I asked. Then I thought: How softly it slices under my touch. Just like butter.

21

A Beginning

LATER THAT NIGHT

I wasn't the only one busy that night. Muhammad saw to it that Assad tasted the same bitter medicine he'd forced on all the mute eunuchs. A slight disturbance ensued when Faisel appeared on the scene along with some of his partners, but Muhammad took care of them too, just before setting their tents alight.

The three of us, Muhammad, Azizah, and I, regrouped a little later by the entrance to The Dark, where we pushed as one until the boulder rolled aside. Tom felt his way out unassisted. I stepped in to see how things worked in there. I learned that the trick of The Dark was based on acoustics. Slanted floors, curving walls, and a domed ceiling created an environment where a whisper could carry a mile. It meant that two men standing plains apart could converse as if side by side. As for the mystery of Azizah's appearance, secret tunnels did the trick.

The flames of the camp were still visible above when the four of us reached the foot of Amman just as the sun came up in the east.

A BEGINNING

We stuck together all the way back to Cairo, where we split up the fortune we'd found in Haddi's tent. Then we celebrated for a few days before Muhammad returned to his village and Tom caught a plane back to the States.

Both of them report doing well. Tom, as a well-known friend to "deh ladies," and Muhammad, as his village's rich yet kindly benefactor.

As for me, I've used the last twelve months here in Cairo to write about what I've taken to calling "The Cairo Conspiracy." It began as a project to help me understand why I behaved as I did throughout the whole thing, and it's served that purpose well. One of my main conclusions is that I didn't always behave as a genius might. Like when I refused Jihad's advice against climbing Jabal Amman. Doing the right thing then would have saved me from a lot of difficulties. Of course, it would also have caused me to miss doing the smartest thing I ever did: which was finding Azizah and making her mine. So perhaps I'm almost a genius after all.

And speaking of Azizah, so far as our relationship goes, things have never been better. About our only arguments involve the romance novels she enjoys reading so much. You know the type: glittering wealth, exotic locations, fantastic beauty, melodrama, sex, greed, riches, blah, blah, blah, and all that stuff. She can't get enough of it.

"But Azizah," I explain, "there's no need for such books when life with me is a romance novel. Besides, we've got our own blah, blah."

Her answer is that I don't understand. And you know what? Perhaps I don't. Anyway, I don't let it come between us. I wouldn't dare. Not when so much of our love remains unknown.

AMMAN LIVES

About the only loose end was Ellen. I used to wonder what became of her—if she'd reassumed her identity as Lizzie, or what?

Yet as with all things, even my wondering came to an end. It happened one evening just last week. Azizah and I were drifting down the Nile in a rented *felucca* as the day's last light set the water shimmering. Salam, our infant son whom we named after Jihad (and whose name means "peace" in Arabic), lay quietly in her arms. I was reaching out to take the boy when I noticed a striking picture in the newspaper Azizah had brought aboard the boat and placed down by her side.

It was a photograph of a bejeweled woman in a black evening gown entering a stretch limousine on the arm of an elegant, dark-skinned gentleman in a white tuxedo. The caption described them as: "X——, the famous Greek shipping tycoon, leaving the gala opening of Broadway's latest hit show in the company of an unidentified companion."

I scrutinized the woman. Her hair was short cropped and black. Her gown, it appeared, of silk. It was Ellen. I remarked to myself how well she seemed to be doing for herself and how much she'd changed in the course of a year.

In fact, the truth is I don't think I would have identified her if it hadn't been for one thing. One person, actually. The man in the back of the picture who held her door. I assumed he was her driver from the hat he wore on his head. And though he was a bit out of focus, I recognized at once that dumb grin he'd seen fit to stretch from ear to ear. It was the same grin he'd flash whenever he was about to say "Welcome."